NORTHERN SEAS, HARDY SAILORS

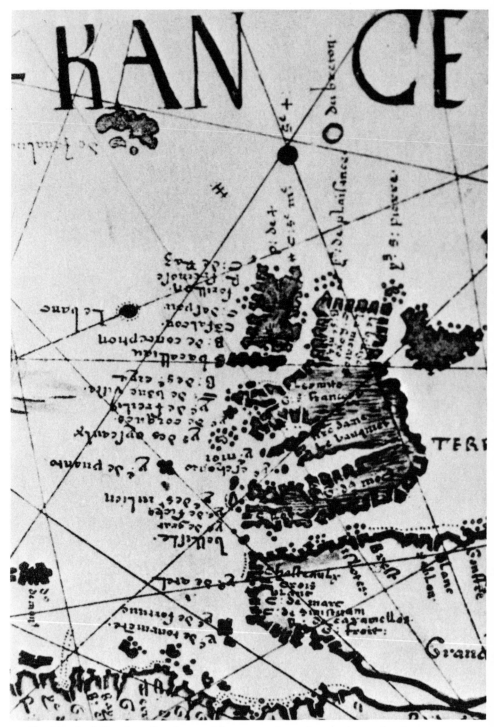

The island of Newfoundland resembles an equilateral triangle, each side measuring about three hundred miles.

NORTHERN SEAS HARDY SAILORS

by George Whiteley

W·W·NORTON & COMPANY

NEW YORK   LONDON

The text of this book is composed in Gael, with display type
set in Palatino. Composition by Com Com. Manufacturing by
The Murray Printing Company.

Library of Congress Cataloging in Publication Data
Whiteley, George.
Northern seas, hardy sailors.

1. Seafaring life—Newfoundland.   2. Newfound-
land—Social life and customs.   3. Newfoundland—
Description and travel.   4. Nova Scotia—Description
and travel.   5. Whiteley, George.   I. Title.
F1122.W4 7   1982   917.18′044   82–2244
AACR2

W. W. Norton & Company, Inc. 500 Fifth Avenue, New York,
N.Y. 10110
W. W. Norton & Company Ltd. 37 Great Russell Street,
London WC1B 3NU
ISBN 0-393-03270-1
1 2 3 4 5 6 7 8 9 0

This book is dedicated to Charlotte, my wife,
and to the memory of my mother and father.

Contents

Maps and Charts

Introduction

George Whiteley, a marine biologist on a cruise around Newfoundland in his able ketch *Neptune,* revisits scenes of his youth and early professional life.

Incidents winnowed from the narratives of his remarkable father, Skipper George, and from many others, are retold; stories of the old days, some from more recent times, stories of danger and of fortitude, all stories of the sea.

To those of us fortunate enough to have known the author's father, this book will be a particular joy, bringing back memories of many occasions at sea or on land when we listened spellbound to that ancient mariner!

Recollections of the author's early days on Labrador describe a way of life that no longer exists. There are also interesting incidental ideas about the history, geology, bird life, and the folklore of Newfoundland. The resourcefulness, almost unbelievable endurance, and the humanity of the Newfoundland outport fishermen are well illustrated by the rescue of sailors from two United States Naval vessels wrecked on the bleak south coast during the last war.

To any who have sailed these northern coasts, this book will bring back many agreeable memories; to those who have not yet done so, it will provide an incentive to gain at firsthand an insight into the spirit and character of the seamen of these rugged shores.

Paul and Carol Sheldon

Princeton, New Jersey

Acknowledgments

I am glad to have the opportunity afforded by this book to express my gratitude to all those who have shared with me certain events in their lives. To friends who crewed on *Seal* or *Neptune*, especially Bill Maclay, George Campbell, and Will Hamann; to Spaulding Dunbar, for his interest in *Neptune*'s design, to Joe Conboy and his crew who built my sturdy ketch in Urbanna, Virginia, and to Mrs. Robbie Robertson of the Newfoundland Historical Society, for her assistance, I offer many thanks.

I am also indebted to Henry I. Strauss for the vivid description of the wreck of U.S.S. *Pollux*, to Dr. Edward Belt of Amherst College, for geological information, and most of all to Thomas C. Ettinger, Jr. without whose friendship and encouragement I would not have persevered with the collection.

Special thanks go to Dr. Paul and Carol Sheldon, who wrote the Introduction. As joint recipients of the Cruising Club's Blue Water Medal for their northern voyages, the Sheldon's knowledge of Newfoundland and Labrador probably exceeds my own.

I would also like to thank Cruising World for permission to reprint certain portions of this book which originally appeared in that magazine. *The European Discovery of America: The Northern Voyages*, by S. E. Morison (Oxford Univ. Press. 1971) and *The History of Newfoundland*, by D. W. Prowse (Macmillan and Co., London 1895) are good sources for those who may wish to know more about Newfoundland or the northern seas.

Lastly, for the counsel given me by Eric Swenson of W.W. Norton, I am profoundly grateful.

NORTHERN SEAS,
HARDY SAILORS

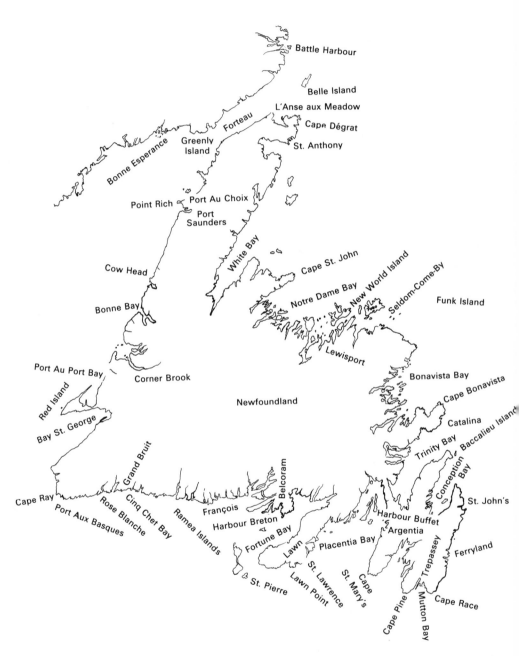

The island of Newfoundland.

1

Return to Newfoundland

Off watch for an hour, I was lying on the cushioned bench along the side of the main cabin table completely dressed in foul-weather gear, rubber boots, mittens, and sou'wester, when I must have fallen asleep. A hand touched my shoulder and I sat up, startled. In a low voice, hushed to avoid disturbing the blanket-covered body asleep in the adjacent bunk, Will said, "Come on deck, skipper. . . . RDF bearings are puzzling. . . . It's about three o'clock now . . . a black dreary night . . . fog thick as mud . . . wind has not let up."

We were crossing Cabot Strait in late June, 1977, aboard my forty-two-foot ketch *Neptune.* We had left home port, Friendship, Maine, the week before to cruise in the western Atlantic as far as Newfoundland and Labrador. Having spent youthful years in northern seas, I looked forward to seeing familiar places, perhaps for the last time, as my seventieth birthday was imminent.

Sheets of spray blew over *Neptune* as she rose and fell, rolling from side to side, pushed by the force of surging seas, but in the partial shelter of the deckhouse the man at the wheel and the lookout were dry and secure. This solid structure, consisting of a glass windshield in front of the wheel station and safety-glass windows on right and left sides, first attracted me to architect Spaulding Dunbar's design. The small deckhouse reduced the boat's ability to sail to windward, but on our present course, under sail and power, *Neptune* was making fair progress despite intermittent plunges into gaping chasms as the hull fell off crests of ferocious combers. To feel the warmth of a dry wool shirt on one's back when water is flying about on a rough night is a genuine luxury.

I took the wheel from our navigator, George Campbell, who

Early mapmakers, circa 1550, drew the New Found Land as a group of separate islands. The triangular shape was established during the next century, although the outline of some sections was still distorted. Such places as Cape Razo (Cape Race), Bonavista, Baccalieu, Belle Island in the Strait of Belle Isle appear on the oldest maps, indicating their importance to explorers and fishermen.

smoothed out the large chart of Cabot Strait and the south coast of Newfoundland. A wide shelf to the left of the wheel provided a spacious chart table, another useful idea of Dunbar's, an experienced offshore sailor as well as naval architect.

"What do you say, George! A dirty night, eh!" I inclined my head in the direction of the electric wipers sluicing layers of seawater off the windscreen. Lights on the compass and instrument panel glowed red to help maintain our night vision, not that much could be seen forward of the mainmast, except for an occasional flash of white in the darkness as a rogue wave erupted and broke with a hissing roar. I looked around at my two companions as we swayed like slowing spintops in order to keep our balance on the unsteady deck. "At any rate," I said, "this is better than being soaked to the skin . . . freezing in an open cockpit." Vigorous nods indicated an affirmative response.

George was so muffled by several folds of thick wool scarf inside parka and oil clothes, I could scarcely see his cherubic face and twinkling eyes in the dim light from the compass.

"We are still on the 066 degree course," George said. "The log registers about ninety miles on that course."

"Here is the problem," Will broke in. "RDF bearing on Channel Head indicates we are far to the west of where we should be. I can't pick up any signal from St. Paul Island in order to get a fix."

Will turned the aerial of the radio direction finder around and back several times searching for a more accurate null. George plotted various radio bearings on the chart that Will called out. After a while, Will became extremely anxious: "If this bearing on Channel Head is correct, and the null seems to come in consistently, we are heading for the rocks at Cape Ray. That really scares me!" He pulled vigorously at his reddish beard.

"When George works out a heading, we will change course," I said.

Soon we were steering 080 degrees. Will continued to swing the RDF aerial. Later, he said, "I would like to have 110 degrees." Course was changed again.

The three of us had been on watch for many hours and were short on sleep. While I puzzled over the various decisions we had made,

Neptune in the Bras d'Or Lake near Baddeck. (George Thomas)

Neptune's cheerful main cabin is made of cypress, finished bright with white enamel on bulkheads; bunks and cabin table are teak. Stove runs on bottled gas. Cold Spot frig. is belted to engine and has two large holding plates.

Neptune labored on the new course. The heading was now close to the wind. Mainsail was luffing quite a bit. The engine was giving the boat most of the push. To keep on course in the head sea required all my attention but, after ninety minutes or so, bits and pieces of intelligence gradually began to reassemble into a coherent pattern.

"It seems to me," I said finally . . . "this present heading is nonsense. Our last dead reckoning position, the one we had a couple of hours ago, before we changed course the first time, could not possibly have been fifty degrees off the mark. The radio bearing must be, for some reason, quite inaccurate. We certainly were not pushed westward by wind or current to the extent the radio bearing indicated. Let's work out a new course based on the last dead reckoning position. Allow for the easterly error over the bottom that we probably have made."

Our predicament presented a good example of the trap weary mariners set for themselves. Too much dependence can be placed on instruments when critical faculties are dulled by loss of sleep.

Darkness slowly gave way to dawn. As the longer wavelengths of light diffused through the fog and the sky at zenith reflected a rosy glow, I realized again the relief primitive man must have felt, when night, with all its unseen dangers and terrors, was replaced by the warming rays of the sun.

After *Neptune* had progressed for some time on the new course George established, Channel Head's radio-bearing began, for some reason, to make more navigational sense. As the sun rose invisibly behind the mist, the wind softened, the sea flattened, and the fog thinned gradually. Our invaluable depth recorder began to show that the ocean bottom was slowly coming upward . . . since the instrument could not record depth of water over six hundred feet, we had obviously crossed the one-hundred-fathom contour. Looking for a clue to our position, George scanned the chart, carefully following the wiggles of this well-marked isobath. The great depths of the St. Lawrence River canyon were now behind us.

There was still no sign of land but fog was visibly lifting its white shroud. We persuaded ourselves that the circle of vision was increasing. By the log, our distance run indicated land was not far away. Although all eyes carefully searched a wide arc of the horizon, a line of high land suddenly appeared, as if by magic, dead ahead. At one moment there was sky only, a curtain of cloud descending to the ocean; then, seemingly in an instant, a high escarpment, bluish gray in the morning light. Land was probably seven or eight miles distant, but there was no mistaking the rugged hills for a cloud bank. During past voyages, I have often felt confident that land was in sight, only to have mountains fade and disappear into amorphous clouds on the horizon. But this time we were not deceived.

As *Neptune* sailed toward the coast, what appeared to be a treeless island with a fringe of gray and brown mosses on its rocky slopes loomed against the distant mainland. By checking with binoculars, the land was definitely observed to be an island. Patches of snow lay in the deeper gullies. To port, a string of black-looking ledges extended seaward, encircled with foam. The configuration of hills far to the left suggested that a promontory there marked the mouth of a bay; this topographical feature, together with the position of the island, left no doubt that *Neptune*'s location was abreast of Cinq Cerf Bay. (French fishermen, long ago, probably killed five stags there.) We were twenty miles east of our planned landfall having made insufficient westward correction to compensate for the miles we had gone in the wrong direction during the night. We had changed course to the eastward misled by the confusing radio-bearings. Effect of wind, sea, and tidal current may also have contributed to error. Now, Rose Blanche, La Poile Bay, and the village of Grand Bruit, which I had visited in 1951 and had hoped to see again, lay quite a

Grand Bruit is typical of small fishing villages on the south coast.

South coast near Cape LaHune. From the sea, most of Newfoundland's coast appears to be a high escarpment of granite or metamorphic rock. This majestic barrier resists the assault of grinding ice in winter and pounding surf the rest of the year. At the extreme right a glacier has worn a sloping valley.

Looking north toward Grand Bruit. Village and harbor lie directly north of the island in foreground. A bird's-eye view reveals the indented coastline. Air Photo Division, Canadian Government.

distance to the west. To push westward, and then, later, sail east again would take too much out of the six weeks I had allotted for the cruise. Moreover, there was to be a crew change in ten days at St. John's. Unfortunately, we would lose George Campbell and his son Stewart, also my grandson, Henry Woodward and Steven Webster, grandson of the late Leslie Webster, M.D., with whom I had cruised on Labrador fifty years ago. So, reluctantly, *Neptune*'s bow was pointed toward Ramea Island, lying over the eastern horizon.

But I kept looking intently at the landscape, my eyes straying from the high sunlit ancient hills of the coast to the outlying kelp-fringed ledges. Once more I had returned to Newfoundland—to my birthplace—after many years of absence.

2

~~~~~~~~~~~~~~~~~~~

Early Days on Labrador

I was fortunate in my choice of grandparents. My mother was a Canning, the Newfoundland branch of an English family that had, for generations, produced soldiers, sailors, and statesmen, even a prime minister, and, in 1858, the first viceroy of India. Grandfather Canning's brother, my great uncle, a surveyor and artist, had joined an expedition exploring the Great Western Plains and the Colorado Plateau and was killed and scalped by Indians on the North Platte in the early 1840s. Clearly the Cannings were not stay-at-homes. But my paternal grandparents had greater direct influence on my upbringing.

At the beginning of the nineteenth century, shoals of mackerel supported an extensive fishery in the waters of southern Labrador and the Strait of Belle Isle at the northern tip of Newfoundland. Schooners from as far away as Massachusetts were sailed north to engage in this business. Many of these vessels hailed from Newburyport. Grandfather William Henry Whiteley came to southern Labrador on one of these fishing vessels in 1850. At sixteen he was interested in learning about the business of fishing. He had been a printer's apprentice at the *Traveller,* a Boston newspaper. This was well before the first transatlantic cable. One of his duties was to meet the Cunard steamers upon their arrival at East Boston. The ship's captain would have a bundle of English newspapers to give him with the latest dispatches from Britain and the Continent for the *Traveller.*

The challenge of an outdoor life on Labrador must have forcefully appealed to the young man for by 1855 he had settled on an island called Bonne Esperance with the intention of carrying on a marine

For about a century, from 1780, schooners from Massachusetts and New Hampshire harbors but chiefly from Newburyport visited southern Labrador to fish for mackerel.

products business. He was twenty-one years old and had strong entrepreneurial instincts. In his diary he wrote: "I regard myself as a frontiersman." His father, who had migrated from England to Boston in the 1830s to join a brother in a manufacturing venture, had been murdered in a payroll robbery while crossing the Charles River Bridge. The young son evidently decided to seek his fortune in a less hazardous region.

In 1858 William Whiteley fell heir to a property in England and while arranging his affairs there met and married a distant relative, Louisa Thompson. After a winter spent in Newburyport, the young man brought his bride to Labrador, taking passage on a fishing schooner. The contrast between life in London and the isolation of her new home must have appalled the young lady, but she had a forgiving yet resolute disposition. The husband, whom she teasingly called "Bossy"—a term of endearment used by all his family during his lifetime—vowed he would build her the largest and most com-

Louisa Thompson Whiteley, the author's paternal grandmother. Married in London, February 1859, came to Labrador in June of that year. Ten of her twelve children lived to adulthood.

fortable home on the coast, which eventually he did. Twelve children were born to this couple. My father, George Carpenter Whiteley, was the tenth, in 1874. William Henry died in 1903. Louisa outlived him by eight years, dying on her seventy-seventh birthday.

The family lived on the island of Bonne Esperance, one of many islands forming an archipelago at the mouth of Eskimo River (now called St. Paul's River). At the mouth of this river, some ten miles from Bonne Esperance, a winter settlement had grown to a dozen houses grouped around a small church and a one-room school. Since most of the offshore islands were uninhabited, widely scattered families looked to winter as a time for sociability. Before bays froze in late November, households located furthest away gathered at the river mouth. The Whiteley family followed this pattern at first but when the large winterized home was built chose to remain there. Since the moss- and lichen-covered islands lacked trees, firewood for all cooking and heating had to be cut in winter and the following spring rafted to summer homes after ice cleared from the frozen bays. The river valley also provided a trail into the wooded interior, a source of game to supply fresh food as well as fur-bearing animals, whose pelts were traded, producing a valuable income.

A clergyman who traveled the coast by dog-team during winter

The Whiteley family in 1881, the year they first decided to spend the winter in Newfoundland. W. H. W., Jr, her eldest son, stands behind his mother. George Whiteley is sitting in front of his father.

sometimes visited the river settlement; to attend a church service was always a special occasion for my grandmother. An Easter Sunday excursion to the settlement is a recollection from the store of memories of his island boyhood that my father shared with me.

After a long, snowy winter, the April morning is clear and sunny, warm enough for outdoor work without fear of frostbite. Following breakfast, George and his younger brother, Fred, attend to their chores: dragging stove-size pieces on a toboggan from the big woodpile to the kitchen wood box. They also stack birch logs in the porch adjacent to the large room that in winter serves as both dining and living room. This twenty-foot square, low-ceilinged room is heated by a black four-by-two-foot double-decker cast-iron stove. The lower deck forms the firebox which holds three or four stout logs, each three feet in length. The upper compartment, fitted with two doors, serves as a warming oven or for baking purposes. The ample radiating surface of the stove sends warm air currents upstairs—the only source of heat for the second-story bedrooms. The big stove is an efficient source of cheerful warmth but going continuously, day and night, it burns a quantity of wood. To maintain a supply of dry logs

The Whiteley house on Bonne Esperance Island, built in 1869, became a center of hospitality for visitors to southern Labrador.

is a duty the two boys are glad to undertake. After they make several trips to the woodshed with the toboggan and roll each other in the snow a few times, they are told to get ready for church going.

Usually the family has a simple ceremony at home led by the mother or the father, but for Easter they are going "up the river." Since the children have not seen anyone their own age for many months, they look forward to the journey by dog-team with pleasant anticipation, sharpened by the prospect of a splendid Easter dinner on their return. A few days ago, the older brothers had shot a dozen black ducks, the first of the season, and the young lads had helped pluck the birds.

For the journey to church, two dog-teams are to be used. Israel Griffin, a Labrador man in the employ of the family, will drive the big team. All the boys help Israel harness the ten dogs, straighten the traces, and set their mother's coachbox firmly on the big komatik. Father, mother, and their three sisters will ride with Israel. Their mother gives last minute instructions to Rhoda, a local girl to whom she is teaching the rudiments of cooking. My grandmother tries to impress Rhoda with the importance of being sure that dinner will be ready by the time the family returns. Rhoda's namesake, a damsel mentioned in Chapter 12 of the Acts, refused to let the apostle Peter

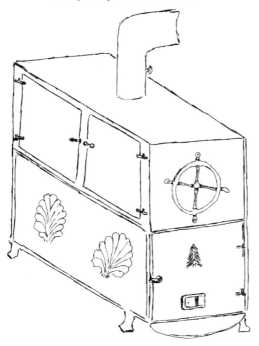

A typical Quebec stove.

into a house, after his release from prison by an angel. Peter was left standing at the gate. The children, uncharitably, consider that their Rhoda is also rather slow-witted at times. They hope the ducks will be well roasted, stuffed with cranberries and savory dressing, when they sit down at the table after church.

With a shout from Israel, the big team is tugging the komatik over the low hill toward the shore of the bay where the trail is fast on snow-covered ice.

The seven boys use a smaller team since they are able to jump off the sled at intervals and run alongside when the going is hard. The eight younger dogs are wild to get into action. Andrew, the family's experienced part-Eskimo sled driver, cracks his long walrus-hide whip. The dogs make a yelping dash ahead and get tangled in a snowbank. Andrew pulls them out of the snow, rearranges the traces, encourages the lead dog. Soon they are chasing the big team through the tickle, the narrow channel between Bonne Esperance Island and adjacent Grand Island. They try to overtake their parents but with Chimo, a veteran dog in command, the big team is fleeter.

The young dogs pick up the scent of a fox as the boys navigate Rapid Champlain, a twisting passage cut into basaltic rock by an ancient river, in summer a place of turbulent current. Suddenly, the animal breaks into the open—a crosspatch fox, dark gray fur against the snow. The fox runs across a ridge and disappears. The dogs become widly excited. Andrew uses all his skill with whip and voice to hold them on the trail. Soon the sled is on the ice of the last bay. There is enough crust to hold the komatik from skidding and provide foothold for the dogs. In the distance, houses of the settlement look like a straggling line of miniatures; pretty toys painted red, green, or yellow arranged along a shelving terrace—the curving estuary of the river.

When the bay is crossed, the dogs head for the church where they are unhitched and tied up at a distance. They soon bury themselves in the snow to rest. There is a confused din on the Sabbath air. All the settlement's dogs, sitting on their haunches around the wigwam-shaped woodpiles near each house, howl like a pack of wolves, to whom they are surely related. Whether the howling is a welcome or a threat seems of little concern to the visiting teams.

The boys quickly join their father when he gets out of the coach-box. He is a big man, six feet tall with long arms and huge hands. In his black bearskin coat and otter hat he looks like some strange animal from the forest. He helps the girls and his wife, a small dainty figure even when bundled up for winter travel. All go into the church. The service is Anglican. The interior walls of the church consist of plain wide pine boards nicely fitted, tongue and groove style, and painted stark white because the head carpenter who built

Winter travel by dog-team was the most popular form of transport on Labrador, far safer than crossing wide bays in small boats during summer.

Runners of a Labrador komatik were shod with strips of steel or whale-bone. Bone was best at low temperatures. Women and small children had blankets and fur robes to keep warm in the coachbox lashed to the sled.

the structure was a New England Congregationalist. The village women and young girls have something bright on their bonnets; men wear white, red, or blue parkas. Everyone enjoys singing familiar hymns, assisted by a tiny organ pumped by the organist's feet. After the sled ride in the open air, the warm church makes George so sleepy he can scarcely stay awake; finally the last hymn is sung. Outside, the boys have a few minutes to talk with friends among the village children. Andrew and Israel have the dogs harnessed and are waiting. The dogs are impatient; when they are in their traces they tug at the shoulder straps and want to go, go, go. Soon the two teams set off for the journey home—home to the roast duck dinner and for dessert, steamed raisin pudding and hard sauce!

"Well done, Andrew!" the boys cry, as the skilled driver guides the komatik over rough spots on the trail. Nearing home, the dogs begin to howl furiously. Perhaps they sense that they too are going to eat a good meal. The team pulls hard over the "ballycaters" where sea ice, squeezed against granite shoreline, breaks into pieces and piles end-over-end in pressure ridges. When they pass the eastern wharf, going up the hill and over the ridge to the "Big House" as the Whiteley home is known to everyone along the coast, they notice a strange team of dogs tied up to the pilings.

The boys help Andrew and Israel take off the coachbox, tie up the dogs and stand the whalebone-shod komatiks against the storehouse. Presently, ten children of various ages sit around the large dining table, all hungry from the morning's activities.

Rhoda enters from the pantry, answering my grandmother's table bell. "You may bring in the ducks, now, Rhoda."

After an awkward pause, the girl blurted: "Yes, ma'am. But there is no dinner, ma'am. The four men in the kitchen, the travelers from the westward, ate it all, ma'am. I offered them a bit of duck, but they took all the birds. And they looked over their plates for more. That's what they did, ma'am."

After a pause, Rhoda added, plaintively, "They ate the puddin' too!"

Hard-to-get magazines and newspapers were put to good use on the kitchen walls of this Eskimo River home.

It took a second or two for my grandmother to ponder what the crestfallen girl had said. The children, open-mouthed, stared from one to another. Grandmother looked sharply at Bossie who was about to expostulate. Then, gathering her composure, grandmother said: "Very well, Rhoda. There is a cold roast of venison in the outside pantry. Bring that to the table, please."

Turning to her disappointed family, grandmother said: "My dears, it is good for us to be disappointed, once in a while. These men, having come a long way, probably needed a hot meal more than we do. Rhoda is a good girl with a Christian spirit."

Certainly, Rhoda was an amiable girl and developed into a good cook. But that afternoon, when the boys looked through the big window into the kitchen and saw the men who had eaten their dinner enjoying a smoke before continuing their dog-team journey, they did not agree with Rhoda's idea of Labrador hospitality.

3

A Chase

In the years following his marriage in 1858, W. H. Whiteley, with a
small crew of hired hands, continued his attempt to wrest a liveli-
hood from both forest and sea. He traded in fur with both the Moun-
tagnais Indians when they came out of the hinterland of Labrador to
the coast, and also with local trappers, but the fishing business
claimed his chief attention.

As is the case with primary producers everywhere, Nature did not
always cooperate. Adverse winds, drifting ice, the uncertain movements of marine mammals and the migration of fish sometimes produced an abundant harvest, sometimes a failure. Being an indepen-
dent businessman was not an easy life but there was plenty of activity
and occasionally a reward for all the work.

In the 1860s and '70s the Bonne Esperance fishing effort was directed to the capture of seals, salmon, codfish, and mackerel. The
water was too cold for lobsters or for shellfish.

Seals were caught during their spring and fall migration in nets set
from the shore: the products were oil and skins. Nets of smaller mesh
size, set out from points on the numerous islands, caught salmon.
Mackerel and codfish were caught by hook and line or by purse
seines which needed the combined effort of two boats. In search of
shoaling fish, a six-oared seine boat would often row ten to fifteen
miles.

In the late 1860s my grandfather got the idea of making a "codfish
trap"—a device with which his name has since been connected.
After experimenting for six years, he developed a large net in the
shape of a square box with net walls and net bottom. From the shore
or from a shoal a straight net led to the door of the trap: this was
called the "leader." When the net bottom at the door was pulled up

A cod trap is a large box with walls and floor of netting. Fish enter by a narrow door guided by a long net or leader. To secure the catch, bottom near door is raised preventing escape of fish which are forced into the far corner and dried up by under-running the netting.

(weights normally kept it and the walls in place), the fish inside were forced to the back of the trap. By pulling up the bottom and sides in and at the same time letting the slack fall back into the water, the catch could be "dried up" in a corner and the catch transferred by dipnet to a waiting boat. The cod trap made the shore fishery much more profitable.

The marketing of salmon and mackerel involved pickling the fish in tubs. Codfish were preserved as they had been for hundreds of years: the gutted fish were kept in salt for several weeks, then washed and air dried. Europe had been the market for this product for centuries. At first, the Bonne Esperance catch was sold to Newfoundland or Canadian brokers. Eventually, it was shipped direct to market in Portugal, Spain, or Italy.

To meet the educational needs of the older children, the Whiteley family, beginning in 1866, spent several winters in the city of Quebec where a house was rented. However, since most of the fishermen employed in the business were now recruited in Newfoundland and brought to Labrador each spring, my grandparents decided that a

Seals and salmon attracted the Basques to Labrador in the 1500s and for a century these were the commercial products of greatest value.

The Whiteley premises at Bonne Esperance.

winter home in St. John's, the capital city of the island of Newfoundland, was a more appropriate choice. When my father was twelve years old, in 1886, the spring and fall migration between Bonne Esperance and St. John's began.

Four of the Whiteley boys turned to the sea early in life. Three began as junior deck officers; James went to Scotland to study marine engineering. Sailing and seamanship had been as much a part of their lives as learning to walk. The oldest, William Henry, Jr., at age twenty-nine, bought an eighty-eight-foot, seventy-three-ton schooner in England and sailed her around Cape Horn to Vancouver, British Columbia. The voyage of 116 days established a local record. Prior to the Cape Horn passage, William and his brother Jack had engaged in various commercial ventures using a schooner they had built in British Columbia to trade in the northern Pacific, plying between Canadian ports and Japan.

Before George, my father, was eighteen, he had sailed as mate and supercargo to Spain, Portugal, Italy, and Brazil in various types of ships taking dried codfish to market.

Cod are transfered from trap to waiting boat, then taken to land to be cleaned, washed, and salted.

Young William Whiteley, Jr., bought the schooner *Mermaid* in London, sailed her around Cape Horn to Vancouver, British Columbia, Canada, in the record time of 116 days. The schooner was used in his Alaskan trading ventures.

On one voyage, the ship was the barkentine *Czarina* of about 240 tons bound for Leghorn, a port in the Gulf of Genoa, northern Italy. Owing to contrary winds, the vessel had been obligated to make long tacks back and forth across the Mediterranean, trying to gain distance to windward.

Early one morning, the *Czarina* lay becalmed as the sun, a ball of fire, rose out of east casting a crimson glow on the placid sea. The ship had been more or less motionless throughout the night, several miles off the coast of Africa, in the vicinity of the port of Algiers. With the coming of full daylight, the square sails on the foremast, high above the deck, began to catch a favorable windshift, enough to move the ship slowly through the water.

About this time, the first mate reported to the captain that two feluccas, long narrow African boats, manned by several oarsmen, seemed to be rowing in their direction. The watch had spotted them at dawn as they moved along close to the land. The two boats were

Preparation of dried salt codfish is labor intensive. Having been caught and eviscerated with part of the backbone removed, then washed and salted in a succession of layers, the cod have to be washed again after a month in salt, then sun dried for weeks, then allowed to mature in piles before final sun-drying and shipping.

now seen to be heading directly toward the ship. Handing the mate the long spying glass, the captain told him to climb to the main crosstrees. "Take a good long look at those boats," he said. In the meantime all the crew were alerted and many eyes scanned the horizon.

Everyone knew that pirates were not uncommon along the Algerian coast. These freebooters were capable of seizing a vessel and towing the prize to a hideout on the coast. After plundering the cargo, the pirates either murdered the crew or held them for ransom.

When the mate regained the deck, he brought an unsettling report. As far as he could judge there were many more men in the boat than the six oarsmen, and the men at the oars were really putting their backs to the work. No question but the feluccas were heading for their ship. Very likely mischief was afoot.

The captain gave orders to bring up the four muskets he kept in his cabin. The watch armed themselves and laid out ammunition.

Barkentines may have three or more masts but with square sails only on the foremast; the other masts are fore-and-aft-rigged.

Some of the crew were detailed to loose all the square sails and prepare to trim the yards. The fore and aft sails were hoisted in order to spread all canvas to catch the slightest breeze.

On came the strange-looking native boats. One of the watch stationed at the masthead shouted that he could see many black men crouching in the bottom of the foremost boat, as if trying to hide from sight below the gunnel. He said the boat was filled with men.

By this time, the leading felucca was less than one hundred yards away. Powerful strokes of the six rowers forged the boat ahead. To the great relief of all on board *Czarina,* the upper topsails began to catch a smart breeze. As the square sails filled, the yards were braced and the barkentine began to move briskly through the water. The two feluccas surged toward the ship. The men who had been hiding now showed themselves, and a wild-looking gang they were, dressed in loose-fitting smocks dyed a variety of colours. Some were bareheaded, others had wound cloth around their heads to form high turbans. These pirates lined the gunnels, shouting to the oarsmen. Now and again one of them would try to leap into the air waving fists. Dozens of knifeblades caught and reflected the morning sunlight . . . the spectacle was guaranteed to put fear into the hearts of helpless seamen.

On board the ship, there was little the crew could do except pray for the wind to increase and anxiously watch the approaching boats. As the chase continued, however, it soon became clear that the ship was moving forward about as fast as the pursuers. Cries of rage came from the leading boat as the rich prize seemed to be slipping out of the trap. The oarsmen redoubled their efforts and closed the gap to less than twenty yards. On *Czarina* the crew crouched near the weather rail, keeping very quiet as if to cause no possible interference with the trim of the ship as she slowly gathered speed. The murmur of the bow wave was a joyful sound. With a burst of frantic effort the lead boat began to gain foot by foot. As the boat closed with the ship, one of the pirates suddenly leaped to the cuddy, carefully balancing himself on the narrow shelf. In his left hand he held a coil of line attached to a small grapnel. Whirling the grapnel over his head, he threw it toward the mizzensail; one of the tines caught in a lashing at the end of the mizzenboom. A great shout came from the pirates as men in the bow of the boat began to haul in the line.

Quick and agile as a cat, one of *Czarina's* crew, Johnny Pico, from Portugal Cove, Conception Bay, ran out the length of the mizzen boom as the sail billowed outwards. He was able to seize hold of the grapnel and cast it off. At the same time, the four guns of the watch sent a volley over the heads of the men pulling on the grapnel. The men on the cuddy fell back on top of those pressing close to them, and the struggling group fell back on the oarsmen. The felucca swerved broadside, colliding with the oncoming boat. Shouts and recriminations could be heard as the two crews struggled to renew the chase; but the freshening wind drove the barkentine further and further offshore. Frustrated and angry, the pirates turned away. Danger of attack had passed. The captin gathered the crew together and read a short prayer to give thanks for their escape.

My father said he had recurrent pirate nightmares for quite some time after that experience, but the chase was very exciting while it lasted.

4

Newfoundland
Maritime Matters

In 1496 a Genoese mariner whose anglicized name was John Cabot, obtained a charter from Henry VII, king of England, to discover new lands in the West, on the condition that the king was to share the profits of the voyage but on no account bear any of the expense. Cabot is believed to have discovered Newfoundland on June 24, 1497. This voyage was a second attempt. In the previous year, the expedition turned back at the behest of a restless crew. On his return to England, the explorer reported extensive shoals of codfish in the ocean around the new land.

Cabot's voyages and those of his son, Sebastian, have been a continuing puzzle to maritime historians interested in this period of transatlantic discovery. Sabastian's reputation as a truthful mariner has been seriously questioned. John Cabot, together with two supporting ships, disappeared without a trace in 1498 when he sought to extend his knowledge of the New Found Land.

Whereas Columbus, and at a later date, Jacques Cartier, kept detailed logs of their voyages so that we have a record of activities and plans, no log of Cabot's historic voyage has every been found. All we know is gathered from comments in letters written by contemporaries.

A boyhood fantasy of mine was to find myself in a room in the old Custom House of Bristol, England. Books in ancient bindings extended from floor to ceiling. As I pulled out the musty volumes and tried to read the stained pages, I would finally realize that the docu-

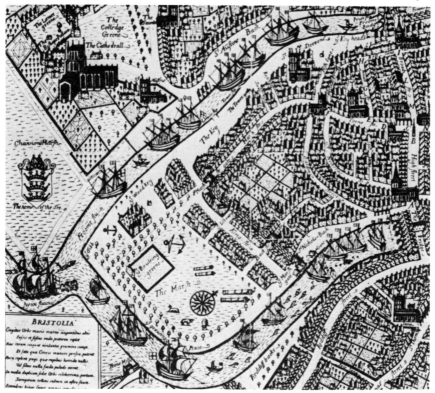

The city of Bristol in 1671. A busy port on the river Avon, in the West of England, Bristol enjoyed a leading position in the fish trade with Iceland in the fourteenth and fifteenth centuries, but after Cabot's discovery of the New Found Land, merchants turned to the new source of supply.

ment in my hands was the long lost log of John Cabot! The famous Library of the Treasure Galleons in Madrid has yielded a variety of unexpected information about the fate of convoys en route from Panama and other far-flung Spanish possessions. The Spanish government kept meticulous records of ship movements. One wishes that the English had been as careful. However, lack of early English records may have been intentional. The New World had been divided between Spain and Portugal. English seamen were interlopers. Henry VII of England took the abitrary position that land discovered north of latitude forty-five degrees could be claimed by anyone. Perhaps it was not prudent to have detailed evidence of English cruises. A shadowy claim would be less likely to anger Spain or Portugal. Another explanation to account for the disappearance of Cabot's log might be the caution of the West of England merchants, who had backed the expedition with their gold. They did not want to report discovery of a potentially rich codfishery. They had been having difficulties with the Iceland authorities about fishing rights around that island. The West of England now sought to develop a new source of supply from across the Western Ocean.

By the mid 1500s English ships were crossing to Newfoundland in search of codfish. They were joined by fishermen from Spain, Portugal, and France. In 1527, John Rutt, who had sailed to Newfoundland in the *Mary of Guilford* on an exploring, trading voyage, wrote a letter to his sovereign, Henry VIII of England, who owned the ship. Rutt reported that there were eleven Norman vessels, one Breton, and two Portuguese fishing out of the harbor of St. John's at that time. Rutt's letter was written in haste in order to catch a ship belonging to Master Grube of Plymouth, England, who was trading in Newfoundland and returning to England with a cargo of codfish, cod oil, furs, and timber.

Later in the sixteenth century, opportunities to trade in Newfoundland, away from the inquisitive scrutiny of customs officials, brought ships from France and Spain with cargoes of port, sherry, olive oil, salt, cork, and dried fruits to exchange for West of England cloth, cordage, and Newfoundland timber, although buying and selling codfish always formed the bulk of the commerce. When Basque seamen arrived from northern Spain in early April or May to hunt whales in Newfoundland waters, they also found that there were numerous seals swimming in the water among the scattered ice floes.

For more than a century after the discovery of Newfoundland, West of England merchant traders were able to exert influence on Parliament to make illegal any permanent settlement in the island. They wished to prevent the colonization that had taken place in Virginia and Massachusetts. Settlement in Newfoundland would result in local fishermen securing the most promising fishing locations. By 1700, however, clandestine settlement began. Desire to own a piece of land, a condition then often denied individuals in England or in parts of Europe, circumvented inhibiting laws. Isolated fishing stations slowly formed in the numerous bays of Newfoundland's extensive coastline. Settlers on the east coast of the island discovered that during March a seal fishery could supplement their income. At first, the fishermen used strong large-meshed nets to catch seals in open water during fall and early winter. Later, bold hunters ventured directly into the icepack with small boats to catch seal living on or near the floes as the ice drifted across the mouths of northeast bays.

Shallops of five to ten tons' burden, decked fore and aft, with a pound or small hold amidships covered with loose boards were then

The town of Brigus in Conception Bay, settled in the 1600s, became a trading and shipbuilding center which contributed to its general prosperity. Captain Bob Bartlett, who assisted Admiral Peary in his dash to the North Pole, was born and grew up in Brigus.

tried. Fore cuddies—small platforms in the bow—provided crew some protection if the boat was caught at sea overnight. Occasionally, an ambitious skipper would venture beyond the headlands working his boat as far as possible into the loose ice of the pack. Captain William Bartlett from the harbor of Brigus, a distant relative of the well-known arctic navigator Captain Bob Bartlett, took his shallop sealing one spring in the 1790s. Finding neither ice nor seals at the mouth of Conception Bay, the bold skipper decided to sail on toward Cape Bonavista, and from there headed seaward toward Funk Island without meeting ice or seals. Securing provisions from a northern village, the eager mariner continued sailing until the shallop reached Spotted Islands, off the Labrador coast, more than four hundred miles from Brigus. Bartlett finally found both ice and seals, loaded the shallop, and returned safely to the home port.

By 1796, in many Conception Bay harbors, fore-and-aft schooners of about 50 tons' burden were being built for the dual purpose of employment in the spring seal fishery and the summer cod fishery. There was doubt, at first, whether a sailing vessel of 50 tons could make effective progress through the icepack. Success of these schooners, however, soon led to the construction of even larger and stronger craft until, in 1819, Captain William Munden of Brigus, built the 104-ton *Four Brothers.* Many sealing captains ridiculed the construction of such large vessels, contending it would be impossible to turn such a craft when in danger of being frozen in or crushed by the ice floe. *Four Brothers,* however, was quite successful, and had a fifty-four year life before she was sunk by raftering ice—huge, rapidly moving pans, which on meeting any resistance, such as the hull of a ship, pile in a confused mass to a towering height and crush by sheer weight whatever stands in their path.

Construction and operation of wooden sealing ships brought considerable wealth to coastal towns of Newfoundland. Owners, skippers, crews, ship's carpenters, sailmakers, blacksmiths, riggers, mechanics in small shops that built punts, oars, gaffs, and other sealing equipment all shared the general prosperity. This favorable economic state lasted for about a century, notwithstanding the uncertainty of the seal fishery, in that ships and crews were sometimes lost, the main seal herd was often completely missed, and the ships were hampered and damaged by extremely rugged ice conditions.

In 1837, 206 sailing vessels put out from harbors in Conception Bay alone, carrying nearly five thousand men to the seal fishery. Towns in Trinity Bay and Bonavista Bay likewise outfitted ships to engage in sealing. Skins for leather, and fat for oil were commercially valuable. Total catch for the industry in a year of average ice conditions, when vessels were able to maneuver reasonably well, might be as high as four hundred thousand pelts. Of course, the fishery was almost a blank in years when the fleet jammed in heavy ice. A prolonged malevolent northeast gale drove heavy floes tight to the land in the spring of 1852. Forty sealing ships, caught in the relentless squeeze, were crushed and sank; many more, set on fire by overturning stoves, burned to the waterline. Such losses hastened the decline of sail.

The sailing-vessel seal fishery was a challenging occupation. Skippers had to be daring and often ingenious; crews hardy and zealous. Ships left harbor, often never to return, like the schooner *Active.* She sailed from Cupids, Conception Bay, on March 18, 1823. That same night in a howling blizzard that swooped down upon her from the north she struck Baccalieu Island. Out of a crew of thirty, only four managed to scramble ashore.

To work vessels through loose ice, crews often had to use brute

At the town of Harbor Grace in Conception Bay, Captain John Mason, one of the founders of the state of New Hampshire, established a prosperous codfishery around 1615. The town was also thriving in the 1800s. A folk song describing a homesick Newfoundlander has a refrain: "Me eyeballs, dey grows loose, when I thinks I sees the BRUCE*; Harbor Grace and Carboneer, take I there, Oh! take I there."

force to aid the sails. Armed with long poles, ice saws and axes, some of the men would pry and heave the unwieldy pans away from bow and stern, and at the same time a gang on a long line from the bow, pulling as if for a tug-of-war, would warp the ship along.

Since all craft were built locally, practice of naval architecture developed by trial and error. Shallops with apple-cheek bows were replaced by a sharp-stem type. Captain Richard Taylor of Carbonear, often called the Thoughtful Man, installed iron plates on the stem and each side of the bow for protection. He also strengthened vessels by the use of false beams to withstand ice pressures. A Conception

*the ferry from Canada to Newfoundland.

The first one-hundred-foot schooner developed for ice-navigation at the seal fishery was built at Harbor Grace.

Bay shallop, in the early days of sealing, was returning home in clear weather with a full load of pelts when, nearing harbor under full sail, a sudden down-draft from the headland struck the vessel, causing her to heel sharply. The load of greasy seal pelts shifted position, capsizing the ship within sight of people on shore. From then on, cargo space was divided into many separate pounds.

Other changes in ship design included taller spars, to improve ability to sail more easily among loose icepans. Then, the foresail was replaced by square sails; this rig was called a Beaver Hat schooner. On ships over one hundred tons, a square topsail on the foremast and a top gallant on the mainmast were sometimes used; this innovation created a jackass brig. Eventually, the normal brig sail plan—a two-masted vessel with square sails on both masts and a large gaff and boom mainsail on the mainmast proved to be most efficient. In 1858, on March 23, the brig *Glide* was the first ship to return home from the seal fishery with a full load of pelts. *Glide* hailed from Carbonear, Conception Bay, and each man's share had a value of $214—a lot of purchasing power for a three-week voyage.

The fading ink of a ship's log records a bare account of one sealing vessel and the zeal of a typical skipper. Brig *Providence*, Captain Frank Taylor, left Carbonear in January, 1837, for Oporto, Portugal, with a cargo of dried codfish. The skipper was determined to go sealing when the ship returned from Europe, so he shipped a crew of twenty-two men with guns and complete sealing outfit to enable *Providence* to proceed direct to the ice after leaving Portugal. In the Bay of Biscay, *Providence* was boarded and seized by a French man-of-war on the lookout for a pirate ship that was harassing commerce in that area. Seeing the large crew, the guns, spiked poles, and other sealing gear, the French commander was convinced he had captured the pirate. Prize and prisoners were taken to Bordeaux. After considerable difficulty, Captain Taylor succeeded in reaching a British consul who was able to convince the authorities of their mistake and arrange for the ship's release. *Providence* proceeded to Oporto where the cargo of codfish was eventually sold. With a partial load of salt as ballast Captain Taylor headed across the Western Ocean. Fortunately, spring was late that year. When the ship reached the ice off Newfoundland, seals had not yet taken to the water. *Providence* was loaded with five thousand pelts and proceeded safely to St. John's.

In the eighteenth century, when arctic whaling was at its peak, ships from New Bedford, Nantucket, and other East Coast ports, vied with ships from Dundee, Scotland, for a share of the Right Whale Catch. Dundee ships also hunted seals in the Arctic. By 1860 discovery of oil in Pennsylvania and elsewhere made whaling unprofitable. In 1862 *Bloodhound*, a wooden sail and steam-driven Dundee whaler sailed from Scotland to take part in the Newfoundland seal hunt. Several similar ships followed in subsequent years. Although initial

St. John's waterfront in March. Steam-powered whaling ships built in Dundee, Scotland, were first used as sealers in 1862. A disastrous storm in 1864 that wrecked twenty-six schooners and damaged more than one hundred hastened the decline of sail in the seal fishery.

S.S. *Thetis* in drydock being prepared for the seal fishery. Hulls sheathed with greenheart, a wood noted for toughness, with bows protected by steel plates, these wooden ships could withstand tremendous pressures while crunching through ice floes.

results were rather disappointing, Newfoundland sealing firms bought these vessels and the three-masted, bark-rigged, carvel-built sealer, solidly constructed of oak and greenheart gradually replaced the Newfoundland-built schooners and brigs. Eventually, twenty-five of these four hundred-ton steam-driven ships made up the sealing fleet. When one of the ships was lost, a replacement was built in Dundee. From years of experience in Arctic whaling, Scottish shipyards had learned about designing hulls for ice navigation. But the prosperity of northern coastal towns declined with the growth of the steam-driven sealing fleet. St. John's, the island's chief seaport, became more and more the center of commerce and home port of the sealing ships.

Newfoundland became the last refuge of these steam-driven bark-rigged sealers which were an anachronism in an age turning to high-pressure steam. But because of the unique character of the ship, they were still preferred for high-latitude exploration. Admiral Peary went north in the sealer *Kite* for his 1891 trans-Greenland expedition. The sealer *Tigress* rescued members of the ill-fated Hall Arctic expedition after their eight-month drift on an icepan. S.S. *Terra-Nova* was probably the best known of these bark-rigged sealers. Chartered in

1904 by the British Admiralty to rescue explorers Scott and Shakleton and their men overdue a year in the Antarctic, she was again selected by Scott for the successful 1909 expedition to the South Pole, which, however, ended fatally for him.

In 1905, Alick Harvey, a St. John's entrepreneur, had a steel icebreaker built in Scotland on new lines. S.S. *Adventure,* despite contrary opinion, proved to be a capable sealer. The success of this powerful ship led to the construction of ten steel ships of various tonnage by other firms. Most of these fine ships were lost to enemy action or were sold out of Newfoundland during the Great War. Six of the old wooden steamers and two modern icebreakers continued the hunt in the 1920s through the 1930s. Introduction of spotting airplanes, helicopters, and the European factory-ships finally led to reduced catches and restrictive legislation. The Newfoundland seal hunt has now practically come to an end.

In the days of schooners, half the net proceeds from the voyage was divided among the crew, and since vessels usually carried about thirty men, living conditions on board were bearable, although there was always a high degree of risk from many dangers. The wooden low-powered steamers carried larger crews; each man made lower wages; living space on board many of the ships was incredibly

Early morning, March 10, sealing steamers begin to leave St. John's harbor for the icefields. In the foreground is the famous ship, S.S. *Terra Nova,* that took Sir Robert Falcon Scott to the Antarctic in 1910.

cramped and often unbelievably filthy, especially after a few weeks at sea. Conveniences were unheard of. Yet, in spite of discomfort, hardship, and perils of sea and ice, men from the northeast coast of Newfoundland gladly walked as much as fifty miles through snow and bitter cold to seek a berth on one of the sealing ships. There was something elemental about the sealing adventure that held a strong appeal for these hardy men.

In the late 1800s William and Arthur, oldest of the Whiteley brothers, went on several sealing voyages with Captain Samuel Blandford in the S.S. *Neptune,* a sealing ship built at Dundee, Scotland, in 1872. With a strong reinforced wooded hull and fitted with sails to augment the power of her engine, *Neptune* was a fine craft for the Newfoundland fishery. A story my father used to tell me about an incident involving his brothers during the spring of 1888 illustrates the keen rivalry among captains and ships so characteristic of the seal hunt.

Fifteen ships, fewer than usual, ventured the seal fishery in 1888 because only five ships had made successful hunts during the preceding spring. William Whiteley was signed on as one of *Neptune*'s ice navigators or "barrelmen"; Arthur, two years younger, had advanced to the responsible post of watch officer or masterwatch. Both brothers, although still in their twenties, had gained considerable previous experience as seal hunters.

Before the ship sailed, there was much speculation in the Whiteley home concerning the probable location of the greatest concentration of harp seals, the main patch, as it was locally called. My grandfather, by using the scanty weather-reporting services then available, kept weekly records of wind direction, air temperature, and ice conditions along north Newfoundland and southern Labrador coasts. He was of the opinion that northern Newfoundland bays had been free of ice when the young harp seals were born on the whelping ice off the Labrador coast, and that northerly winds, since then, might have pushed the whelping ice close to Belle Isle (an island at the mouth of the strait bearing that name). From there, northeast winds could have forced the ice into the open mouth of White Bay, north Newfoundland.

The sealing fleet left St. John's harbor on the usual date, March 10, accompanied by wailing sirens and cheering crews. By daylight next day the formation had spread over a wide area of the ocean. *Neptune, Eagle,* and *Aurora* were more or less in the lead, with *Esquimaux, Ranger,* and *Falcon* astern on the eastern horizon. The remainder of the fleet trailed. Each of the ships on the horizon seemed to be steering a course that would take them outside or to the northeast of the Funks.

Steel sealers in heavy ice. Steel ships especially designed for ice navigation were introduced in 1905. Within a decade the fleet had increased to ten ships, probably the finest icebreakers in the world. Outbreak of war in 1914 produced a quick change. Russia bought some of the largest ships; others were destroyed by enemy action or shipwreck.

By the evening of the second day at sea, the three leading ships had been in drift ice all afternoon. This ice became increasingly heavy, and by noon on March 14 all were at a standstill in very tight floes within sight of each other.

William Whiteley had mentioned his father's weather observations to Captain Blandford. Following considerable discussion with the afterguard, Blandford decided to pass inside or to the west of the Funks and to cross Notre Dame Bay on the northwest course as far as drift ice would allow. *Eagle* and *Aurora* were evidently of the same mind; at any rate they kept company with *Neptune*. All three ships were now firmly jammed.

Captain Jackman was the first to worm a path out of the icy thicket by judicious blasting and getting all of the *Eagle*'s crew overboard on a long line to her bow to pull the ship's head into narrow open leads. Jackman evidently intended to keep Partridge Point (the far side of Notre Dame Bay), under his lee and to skirt the southeastern shore of White Bay; perhaps to enter the bay directly. Apparently he had made the same deduction as my grandfather about the location of the main patch of seals. Only a daring shipmaster would run the risk of

When a ship is jammed and there is danger to the propeller from sunken ice, the crew on a long line can sometimes pull the ship toward an open lead without help from the engine.

being trapped in narrow cone-shaped White Bay, only fifteen miles wide at the mouth. In the past, ships caught in heavy ice there had remained jammed until the floes were blown seaward in mid-May. These ships completely missed the seals.

While *Neptune* and *Aurora* made futile efforts to free themselves from the ice-trap, *Eagle* steamed out of sight. Before Marconi's invention there was no way ships could communicate at a distance.

On March 17 a southeast gale created a swell that helped efforts being made to free *Neptune*. She proceeded northwestward. Blandford was still undecided about his next move. His strategy was to cross to the coast of the Long Range Peninsula. Should they meet the seals, fine! if not, proceed northward in case the main patch had been swept offshore to the northeast. Then suddenly, while *Neptune* crossed the mouth of White Bay, he called William down from the barrel. "Do you see any sign of *Eagle?*" he asked. "No sign. No sign of seals either." "Nevertheless," continued Blandford, "we are going

Crew working to free ship jammed in heavy ice. Direction of wind and tidal current can cause ice to pack around a ship. In 1862, one ship held fast in the pack for twelve days was carried by the moving ice from St. Anthony to Cape Race before getting clear.

into the bay. I have had a feeling. Change course and keep your eyes open."

Neptune made some progress in this new direction, but by noon of the next day she was jammed solid again. Two days passed during which various methods traditionally used to try and free a ship failed to release her. From the high barrel, William finally caught sight of *Eagle,* far ahead. She appeared to be jammed also. No smoke came from her funnel. Only at sunset, after a clear day, could the outline of the ship be discerned on the distant horizon. William was selected to lead about two hundred of the crew over the ice to see what was happening aboard *Eagle.* Jack Griffen, an old and trusted worker in the employ of the Whiteley family, had been given a job in the *Neptune*'s engine room. Jack begged to be allowed to accompany the expedition, which William was able to arrange. Jack really considered himself responsible for the two brothers.

The *Neptune*'s gang walked all day and made a crude camp on the ice at nightfall—a cold unpleasant experience. The smooth ice made for easy walking, but wind had swept away so much snow, there was little left with which to make snow-houses to help keep the men warm. Next morning, the gang continued the tiresome trek and reached *Eagle* about early afternoon. Captain Jackman was on board. He called for William. Had they lost their ship?

"No. The men were just out for a walk. Any sign of seals?"

"Not a hair of a seal. Nothing in White Bay except rum and poverty."

William said his men were not in need of rum but would be charmed to find a few seals. At any rate, Captain Jackman gave permission for the *Neptune*'s crew to stay on board for the night. Meanwhile, the cooks could not very well refuse the gang a hot drink of strong tea, but that was the extent of hospitality. At dusk, *Eagle*'s crew returned to their ship. They had bloody hands and greasy jackets and were surprised to find a lot of strangers crowding the decks; as to finding seals there was total silence. Jack Griffen, however, sought out some old buddies among the crew, including a second cousin once removed. Eventually, he drew William aside: "White Bay is lousy with seals. *Eagle* has most of a load on pans."

Next morning, before dawn, *Neptune*'s men were over the side and away. The ice was as level as a curling rink. William and his men found the seals, worked all day and returned at night to *Eagle* where they were grudgingly given space. Two hundred extra men in a ship already crowded with a crew of three hundred created problems. William was hard put to keep the peace. Three men were sent back to the *Neptune* with a note for Captain Blandford requesting food and other essentials.

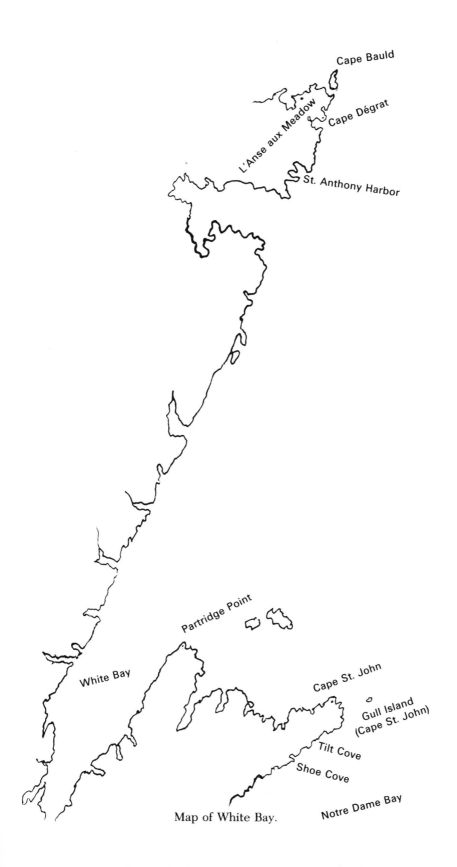

Cape Bauld

Cape Dégrat

L'Anse aux Meadow

St. Anthony Harbor

Partridge Point

White Bay

Cape St. John

Gull Island
(Cape St. John)

Tilt Cove

Shoe Cove

Notre Dame Bay

Map of White Bay.

Meanwhile, William organized his sealers to ensure that no individual strayed away from his group since the watches were now widely scattered over miles of ice. The men toiled from dawn until oncoming darkness forced them to gather together and return to the rough welcome aboard *Eagle*. Food eventually arrived from *Neptune*, which helped to ease tension. By Friday night, *Neptune*'s gang had killed and panned a shipload of pelts. William was now concerned with the problem of transporting this valuable cargo to *Neptune*. To man-haul the pelts over the miles of ice would be backbreaking work, and there would probably be little hair left on the hide by the time the ship was reached. Although the seal's fat was the most valuable commodity, the crew also shared in the sale of the skins, which, if tanned, made good leather.

While the crew was having a bite to eat, Jack Griffen had climbed into the rigging for a last look around before complete dark. William had noticed a swell developing under the ice sheet all during the day. The ice behaved like a pulsating living body, rising and falling in a wavy motion under the men's feet. This sort of movement had not been present earlier in the week. As he now looked upward to see what Griffen was doing, he saw the man throw his cap into the air and shout something.

Jack slid down a backstay. "Sure I'm crazy with delight," says he. "Go aloft and see for yourself."

William raced up the ratlines. There was *Neptune* coming up the bay under full steam, with all canvas flying and ablaze with lights. On and on she came like a battering ram, stopping only when she had burst through the barrier of ice that imprisoned *Eagle*. A change of wind into the southwest had decreased pressure on the northern ice floes and had allowed the ship to butt her way further into the narrowing reaches of White Bay.

Neptune's crew lost no time in boarding their ship. After thanking Captain Jackman for his help, William joined them. Both ships picked up pans during the days following. Then a howling gale from the south forced ice and ships seaward. *Ranger, Falcon,* and *Esquimaux* were finally able to reach what was left of the large patch of seals. They were fortunate enough to secure paying voyages. The ships that passed outside the Funks and continued northeast found some hood seals but ended with an unsuccessful fishery. The element of luck as well as good judgment made sealing a chancy business.

Meanwhile, *Eagle* and *Neptune* finished loading and proceeded to St. John's with their hard-won cargo.

5

To the Icefields

Years ago in Newfoundland, when a person said that he had "a berth to the ice" it meant acceptance as one of the crew of a ship about to sail on a sealing voyage. Stories of perilous adventures told by his brothers so stimulated the imagination of young George that as soon as he was of an age to qualify, he was eager to find a captain who would accept his application.

One morning in early March, 1893, he walked the harbor's waterfront, inspecting ships. A feeling of excitement filled the brisk air. Scores of men were busy carrying equipment from dockside storerooms to the sealing vessels. Others hoisted punts, nesting them on decks; gathered flags, boathooks, barrels, and puncheons; and stowed coils of line for hauling seal pelts, boxes of food for hungry crews, and kegs of black powder for blasting a passage through thick ice floes.

The S.S. *Neptune*, with tall spars and tapering yards, lay at Job's wharf. *Neptune* was bark-rigged then with steam auxiliary power to assist sails. To George's young eyes she seemed an immense ship. His brothers had praised her seaworthiness and speed. Next to her was *Hector*, then *Nimrod*; fine-looking barks with bows protected by thick steel plates; hulls sheathed with greenheart planking along the waterline. At other wharves more ships were being prepared. He inspected them carefully: *Wolf, Leopard, Eagle, Terra Nova, Walrus.* On March 10 the fleet would set out with thirty-three hundred men aboard fifteen ships.

While walking home, George made up his mind to seek a place in one of those ships. He looked forward to sharing the dangers of the seal hunt.

At the suggestion of his father, he decided to call at the residence

of Captain Sam Blandford, skipper of the *Neptune.* Just as well to try
for *Neptune,* George thought. And Blandford was a renowned sealing skipper. In a daydream, he saw *Neptune* under full sail, yards
trimmed to the breeze, engine full speed ahead. A great ship smashing through ice floes, splitting and churning pans! What a sight! To
be in her high barrel on the mainmast spying for seals and conning
the steamer. . . . What an experience!

Reaching Captain Blandford's house, George waited for a few minutes before gathering enough courage to ring the bell. A maid came
and looked him over. He asked to see the captain.

Years later, he recalled the tone of the interview. "We crossed a
wide hall," he said. "She knocked at a door and entered; to reappear
a few moments later. Beckoning with her head, she said, 'Captain
Blandford will see you. Go in.'

"Captain Sam was walking to and fro in front of a coal fire burning
in the grate. Occasionally, he turned to talk to Mrs. Blandford, who
was knitting a muffler in a chair by the fire. She looked up as I entered
and said, 'Sit down, young man.'

"The captain drew up in front of me. 'Well, son, what is on your
mind?'

" 'I came, sir,' I said, 'to ask you for a berth to the ice in the
Neptune.'

" 'Hummm,' he growled. 'What is your name, boy? How old are
you?'

"I answered his questions; then kept quiet. I noticed he was working on a quid of chewing tobacco. This he now removed from his
mouth. He then commenced a parade, back and forth across the
room, discoursing all the while about the worthlessness of most
young men who wanted to go on a sealing voyage. As far as he could
judge, these young fellows were worse than useless; they were a
nuisance to the ship. Not like when he was a young man. Nowadays,
boys were careless; did not pay attention to try to learn anything.
They were headstrong and foolish.

"As he walked, his hands were folded behind his back, and when
he turned, he gave a flip to the long tails of his morning coat. Blandford was a man of medium height, with a thick chest and powerful
shoulders. His round, red-cheeked face was clean-shaven. He walked
with a quick step, agile and sure-footed, and his head jerked from
side to side as he walked, like a hungry gull searching for a fish. I tried
to be as solemn as a clam although he looked a bit comical.

"After ten minutes or so of this lecture, the captain paused. I
thought that was the signal for me to depart. I rose slowly and moved
toward the door. There was, evidently, no chance of a berth for me

on the *Neptune*. I was about to open the door, when Mrs. Blandford, who had been silent during her husband's observations, exclaimed, 'Surely, Sam, you are going to give the young man a berth!'

"Her words stopped me from opening the door. I looked around at Captain Blandford. He eyed me sharply, then said, 'Very well. Go down to the ship in the morning and tell the clerk to sign you on!' "

So began George's nine years of adventure on board the S.S. *Neptune*.

The Honorable Samuel Blandford was an unusual man. Born in the isolated village of Greenspond, Bonavista Bay, he had little formal education, although he was very well read. He had a remarkable memory and good judgment tempered by the flame of experience. He profited by mistakes; other men's mistakes as well as his own. He was a sincere man, a sealing skipper who went out of his way to teach any eager young fellow how to hunt seals and how to handle a ship in the icepack. Blandford's father had been the local blacksmith and the young man learned to assist in the shop. For this reason, he stayed home during the summer instead of sailing north to Labrador in a cod-fishing schooner, as was the local custom. Blandford's powerful physique probably came from his early years at the anvil.

In the 1840s every large northern Newfoundland town sent a fleet of sail to the seal fishery. Blandford began his sealing experience in the days of the large fleets of sailing vessels. To work a wind-driven craft through the icepack requires judgment, leadership, steady nerves, and some intuition. Blandford learned fast. Soon he was master of *Hebe*, a new brig of 120 tons, and was marked as one of the young skippers who had the qualifications to be a successful sealing master. After ten years in sail, he won command of *Tigress*, a steam-driven Scottish whaler built in Peterhead, especially strengthened for sealing in Baffin Bay. Some years later, when the 465-ton *Neptune* came out from Scotland, built for Job Brothers, a St. John's firm, under the watchful eye of Captain William White (a notable sealing skipper who owned a quarter interest in her) she was the most powerful ship in the Newfoundland sealing fleet. On the death of Captain White, Blandford was promoted to *Neptune*. He was enormously proud of his command.

Selection of a sealing crew was sometimes a haphazard arrangement, unequally divided between owners, skipper, and other interested parties. *Neptune*'s three hundred seal hunters were, however, personally chosen by Captain Blandford. In those days, there were at least three applicants for each available berth, hence *Neptune* always carried a lively crew. Success as a sealing captain led Blandford into politics and eventually he became a member of the Upper

House of Assembly, a status somewhat similar to the position of Senator in present-day government. As a favor, Blandford would sometimes accept a man recommended by a local politician to be one of *Neptune*'s crew. But woe to the individual if he did not measure up to the captain's standards.

When young Whiteley joined *Neptune*, there were twelve experienced seamen in the afterguard who slept and ate in the big main cabin: masterwatches, barrelmen, quartermasters, chief steward, and the first mate, sometimes called the second hand. This individual was the captain's chief support and second in command of the ship. Blandford's brother, James, filled this post. Second mate and chief bridge officer was Arch Blandford, the captain's nephew. Both of these men were qualified masters in the coastal trade. *Neptune* also had an experienced Labrador pilot, Tom Doyle, in case the search led as far north as coastal Labrador. The masterwatches, who acted as battalion commanders, were in charge of a section of the crew when men were away from the ship, widely scattered on the ice in pursuit of seals. Each of these veteran sealers had been with Captain Blandford for many years.

Every Sunday night, when the ship was in the icepack, the captain would invite certain young men of the crew to come aft to the main cabin for a lecture on the art of sealing. This was a serious discussion. Charts were spread on the cabin table and the operations of past seasons were reviewed. Captain Blandford drew imaginary circles on the charts to illustrate his opinions: last March this particular area of the ocean was the probable location of the main herd of seals; winds in February had been mostly in such and such direction; icepack had been loose there, but packed tight here. The group sat around the big table, under the swinging oil lamp, and tried to lap up the captain's great experience.

Eventually, the captain might start walking the deck with hands folded behind his back as George had seen him on that first visit . . . walk the full length of the cabin, pass through the open door of his stateroom, reverse, and reenter the cabin still talking and flicking his coattails. Blandford always wore an old morning coat on Sundays and a sealskin waistcoat with a heavy gold watch-chain draped across his wide chest. He would urge the young men to log everything that happened during each voyage; to note velocity and direction of winds between December to March; to study the habits of young and old seals. He would often wind up his lecture by standing before the group. If he was excited about some idea that had been discussed, he might lapse into the broad dialect of his Dorset, West of England, ancestors: "I hope youse young gaffers ruminate on the honor 'tis to

be on board this gert ship *Neptune*, three hundred men, Sam Blandford, master. Be on youse guard, me sons! Let no man take your cake
of hard bread without a fight!"

One Sunday, he told them the story of the ill-fated Hall Polar
expedition. A group from the United States had chartered the sealer
Polaris to explore the Polar Sea. There were fears for the ship's safety
since she was long overdue. Blandford was second hand on *Tigress*
with Captain Isaac Bartlett who was making his last voyage before
retiring. *Tigress* was on her second trip for that season and was
searching for old hood seals. For a week, fog had cocooned the ship
in a damp white web, but the gunners had worked the punts among
the loose ice and had picked up a few hundred seals. On the morning
of April 30, *Tigress* lay with engines stopped waiting for the fog to
lift. The ship rolled from side to side slowly as long swells moved
through the icepack. Presently, fog began to clear. While the afterguard were at breakfast, a shout from the deck reported that the
barrelman had sighted a large black pan of ice with people on it; pan
was flying a flag—the Stars and Stripes of America. Getting under
way, the sealer steamed up to the pan and took the castaways on
board, nineteen in all, including two Eskimo families.

Charles Hall, who had organized this Polar expedition, was an
experienced Arctic explorer. He had been commissioned by the
United States government to try to reach the North Pole, had actually achieved a new northern record of eighty-two degrees, eleven
minutes, north latitude before turning back. While trying to get
south before another winter set in, *Polaris* was caught and jammed
by raftering ice in Baffin Bay. Efforts to escape from the ice failed.
Thinking the ship doomed, hurried attempts were made to transfer
provisions to a suitable ice floe before abandoning the ship. In the
midst of this vexatious activity, while the hull of *Polaris* cracked and
buckled, buffeted by the squeezing icepack, a whirlpool of current
twisted the ship away from the large pan and the floe party found
themselves suddenly borne away from the ship, as if in the grip of
a raging river.

The catastrophe had isolated ten of the crew and nine Eskimos on
the big pan and there they lived for one hundred eighty days, drifting south more than eighteen hundred miles . . . something of a
record. *Tigress* had picked up the group near Gready, off the Labrador coast. The seal hunt was straightway abandoned and the ship
returned to St. John's. The lives of the castaways had been saved by
the skill of one of the Eskimos who had counseled the group to stay
together on the pan when there was a strong urge to try to make a
dash to land. The Eskimos had also been able to catch seals, providing

Wilfred T. Grenfell, M.D.
In 1892, Dr. Grenfell was sent out from England in a ninety-ton ketch by the London Deep Sea Mission to assist schooner fishermen on Labrador and north Newfoundland. From this beginning a widespread medical service developed in this area under the leadership of the International Grenfell Association. (Jim Dunning)

food when the group was on the verge of starving.

Hall and the remainder of the ship's company tried to reach Ellesmere Island to survive the winter. The group suffered extreme privation. Subsequent investigation, years later, showed that cannibalism was practiced. Charles Hall perished, a victim of arsenic poisoning, planned by one of the ship's company. There were few survivors in addition to the castaways rescued by *Tigress.*

As my father was going on watch one night, on board *Neptune,* Captain Blandford handed him an enormous black buffalo-skin coat. "Wear this, my son, it will keep you warm. This fine coat came from the *Polaris* expedition."

My father had many memories of the old "Nipshun," as the northern crew called her—exciting, ludicrous, tragic. One sentimental memory he used to recall took place as the ship was homeward bound, with a full load of thirty-eight thousand seal pelts stowed below deck. It was Sunday, the ship's coal bunkers were nearly empty and the ice was tight. The captain decided to await a change of wind or current that might loosen the ice floe. With engine stopped, *Neptune* lay motionless in the warm April sun, a rather grimy ship reeking with the smell of melting seal fat, blood, and unwashed humanity. As far as the eye could see a continuum of dazzling white ice and glittering pinnacles surrounded the solitary hull.

Dr. Wilfred Grenfell was the ship's doctor that spring. He had come out from England some years before, and had set up a medical practice in northern Newfoundland and Labrador with cottage hospitals to care for coastal families and men of the coastal fishing fleet. For this humanitarian work he was eventually knighted.

Around six bells in the forenoon, Grenfell and Captain Blandford were walking on the poop deck.

"Doctor, do you think we could have a Sunday service, like they have in the British navy?" asked Blandford.

"Yes," said Grenfell, "I think that could be arranged."

"Very well," said captain. "James, call all hands. We will have a church service."

Solomon, the chief steward, came up with a new Union Jack which he spread on the wheel box. The entire ship's company gathered in the waist of the ship or along the rail, wherever there was sitting or standing room. My father wondered whether such a service had every been held on a sealer. *Neptune* lay quiet in the ice; there was hardly a sound to be heard over the wide white ocean of ice. Dr. Grenfell, standing near the wheel box, began the service with a familiar hymn: "Oh, God, Our help in ages past. . . ." The crew sang with vigor, a growling joyous chant, thrilling to hear. After a prayer, taken from the naval service ("Protect this ship in which we serve . . .") spoken by Grenfell in his resonant English voice, the Bible was handed to the captain so that he could read the Lesson, Psalm 95.

As the captain read the line, "the Sea in His, and He made it", Darius Green, standing next to my father, whispered to him rather loudly, "and, for my part, 'E can 'ave it." Young Whiteley was uneasy that Darius was overheard, but Captain Blandford read on to the end.

My father said he had attended many kinds of religious services— simple ones in village churches, elaborate ones in great cathedrals, but he would always remember the coming together on the deck of the old *Neptune* as a very special occasion.

6

A Narrow Escape

One event during that first season in *Neptune* nearly put an end to young Whiteley's career as a mariner. Due to Whiteley's lack of experience on ice, Captain Blandford had an eye on him; saw that he was busy with tasks that kept him on board the ship. Whiteley's chief job was to stand watch on the bridge to relay orders from the barrelman to the men at the wheel in the stern of the ship. The barrelman conned the steamer from his perch at the top of the foremast by shouting orders to the bridge. These directions were then called back to the two men who wrestled with the huge double steering wheels.

Early one morning, the barrelman reported a large group of seals about eight miles into the nor'east. Hunters immediately went over the side heading in the direction of the herd. The crew were soon spread out over miles of frozen sea.

According to my father, who had the morning watch on the bridge, the ship was virtually jammed in thick ice. When Captain Blandford was no longer fully occupied with overseeing the navigation of the ship, the lad was emboldened to approach him. He asked permission to follow the hunters, saying that the voyage would be over before he would have a chance to get on the ice. The captain evidently considered the weather clear enough for the young greenhorn to see what sealing was like, without getting into trouble. Quickly collecting the gaff and a coil of line he had put in a secure place for just such an occasion, George jumped over the bulwarks before Blandford might change his mind.

As he cleared the ship's side, he heard the captain shouting something about staying with the crowd . . . not going off by himself. He really did not pay attention to this counsel, being occupied with leaping from icepan to icepan, anxious to catch up with the crew.

A sealer's gaff is an eight-foot-long boathook. Seals are killed by a solid blow on the head using the gaff as a weapon. The iron-shod boathook also serves as a stout pole by which to vault across narrow lakes of water between pans. George finally caught some stragglers who had begun to work on the first seals they had encountered. The majority of the crew continued walking several more miles further west. George stayed with the stragglers all day. They killed and he hauled the pelts to a large pan. The coil of line each sealer carries over his shoulder is used in hauling. Dragging heavy pelts over rough ice is hard work; the lad found it a tiring but interesting experience. The unlimited expanse of the icefield induced an exhilarating sense of freedom; the glistening frozen waste stretched to the wide horizon; icepans of all sizes slowly undulated in response to swells generated by distant atmospheric forces. Reflection of sunlight from the vast expanse of ice was blinding. George was glad he had brought his dark goggles to guard against snow or ice blindness, even though brilliant days were rare.

After the group had secured many pelts on one pan, they walked on until another patch of seals was located. At sunset, George was surprised to find that they had walked the ship hull down. Only the upper topsails of *Neptune* were visible on the horizon's rim. Suddenly he began to feel ravenously hungry; he had eaten nothing for nearly ten hours. At dusk, the scattered bands of hunters began converging toward one another in order to return to the ship. Presently, about sixty men of the group George had joined began to march a single file in the direction of *Neptune*'s masthead light glimmering in the distance. The light shone on the far horizon like an early rising star. Jumping from pan to pan, finding a way around a hummock of ice, the men were a long winding string of black bodies with the masterwatch leading, heading for the light like insects drawn to a flickering lamp.

Presently, large flakes of snow began to drive before a keen wind. Any wind blowing over an icefield has a bite to it, even in bright sun; now, the cold seeped into sweaty clothes. The column had not gone more than a mile or so, when the gang in front stopped. On reaching the group gathered together on a large pan, they found that an old man had become weak. All hands were waiting until he regained his strength. This was the custom among sealers. Someone produced a bottle of Radways Ready Relief, a patent medicine held to be a stimulant, and the old man took a hefty swig. After a while George was shivering and feeling hungrier than ever. Arch Garland, a young

When the seal pelts have been hauled over the ice to one place, the collection is marked by the ship's flag. This laborious process is called making a pan.

sealer he knew, not much older than himself, approached him and said, "What do you say if we two go on? The others will soon catch up to us. I'm cold standing around." They were on the fringe of the gang. George surely wanted to get on board the ship and, without thinking carefully, agreed to go with Garland. Snow was falling, but you could still see some distance ahead. As they drew away from the gang, another man joined them, a big, strapping fellow named Fitzgerald, an experienced seal hunter.

They had not been walking more than twenty minutes when the gently falling snow rapidly turned into a blizzard. The wind, increasing to gale force, drove the wet flakes into a swirling drift. The stinging blast beat into peering eyes, snatched breath from mouths and bowed heads. Should they stop and wait for the gang to catch them? Too risky. The other men may have stopped or perhaps not even started. *Neptune* was somewhere ahead. She was jammed. She would not come to them. They must get to her. With the help of Fitzgerald's pocket compass, they tried to set a course. The storm was so disorienting that without the compass, they would have completely lost their way. George remembered feeling intensely miserable although not fearful. He was possessed by the delusion that if they kept walking long enough, they would no doubt reach the ship. By the light of a flickering match, they tried to check, from time to time, Fitzgerald's estimate of the ship's bearing. The thoughts of his older companions were probably quite different from the young lad's. Few words were spoken; they saved their breath to fight the storm.

"As we were staggering along, Garland suddenly broke through a seal's blowing hole. We quickly pulled him out; scraped the ice and slush from his clothes with our sheath-knives. Fitzgerald, who from this incident forward assumed command, bade him take off his skin boots and wring out his socks. A cold task—which Garland was somewhat loath to undertake, but Fitzgerald was insistent. Twenty minutes must have passed before we were ready to set out again. The spindrift blew and the gale lashed our faces. Clothing damp with sweat and smeared with seal's blood stiffened and froze into armorlike mail. Snow beat inside our collars; down our necks; inside our pants; and into our jacket sleeves; and froze or melted according to what would produce most uncomfortable sensations.

"We trudged on as warily as we could until finally Fitzgerald stopped. We huddled close to catch what he was about to say. He said that he was sure we were lost. We had walked our distance and beyond it, and there was no sound of the ship's siren. The captain would certainly keep the siren going as long as men were on ice. We might be to leeward or to win'ward of the ship; there seemed no way to tell where we were. We talked together for a few minutes and decided to go forward as long as we could walk."

Now the ice began to loosen. This might mean they were approaching the outer edge of the floe. Reaching a wide lead—a pool of water across which they must ferry, a small pan was pried free; they stood on it cautiously and paddled with gaffs to the opposite side. Each broke through thin ice as pans began to sink under their weight. George got soaked several times. Each time Fitzgerald made him take off some of the wet garments and wring them out. Fitzgerald stood in front of him holding open his jacket to break the force of the storm. He said it was better than freezing solid in wet clothes.

"While crossing a string of rotten ice, the honeycombed surface suddenly caved in and Garland, less agile than we were, completely disappeared. He was nearly exhausted and hadn't much spring left in him. When he emerged, Fitzgerald luckily was able to hook his jacket collar with my long gaff and between us we half dragged, half rolled our comrade on to firm ice and finally got him on his feet to scrape and wring his clothes. Garland was so weak he could scarcely help himself. Suddenly, his knees gave way; he fell over on top of Fitzgerald and lay gasping on the ice. 'I'm dying,' he said. 'Save yourselves. I can go no farther.' We shook him and at last got him to his feet again. Fitzgerald pleaded and swore alternately. I found some pieces of hardtack in my pocket and pressed him to eat them. After a while we started again, but made slow progress, half carrying Garland between us. Hope was almost gone from me, when out of the drifting snow ahead there was a glow, a light. I can't remember who shouted first. I can only recall that suddenly I found my body tingling with excitement. Then Fitzgerald yelled: 'A light sure enough!' He almost broke into a run. We eagerly pressed on, dragging Garland after us if he seemed to falter. Then I had the awful feeling that we might be seeing a mirage; our desperation was creating an illusion. I yelled desperately until my throat become hoarse. As we drew nearer the light, we thought we could see figures around the glowing center. We all shouted together. Presently a few men separated from the crowd and ran towards us. This was real; no mirage. We were brought to the fire, where we sat down in the snow, exhausted. Seeing Garland's condition, a man found a bottle of Sloans liniment and poor Garland was given a vigorous rubdown to restore his circulation."

They had not been on the large pan more than fifteen minutes when the whoop of a siren brought all to their feet. Presently the sealer burst upon them, the driving force of her wide, iron-plated stem crushing the ice around her bow. Lights glowed all over the hull. Acrid smell of live steam mingled with the odor of seal fat and coal dust. This was an exciting moment for George and his companions. The men they had encountered were from the S.S. *Wolf*, commanded by Captain Kean. The men had been waiting since sunset for the ship to pick them up, together with the five hundred seals they had killed and hauled to the large pan. *Wolf* had missed the herd on her way north and had finally turned back on a southwest course. Seeing *Neptune*'s smoke, she had proceeded in that direction and had met the patch of seals. Two watches had been put out amongst the loose ice to kill and pan what they could before nightfall, while the ship ventured further in order to estimate, if possible, the size of the patch. Captain Kean had expected a snowstorm and had marked the large pan as a meeting place. *Wolf* had been delayed in returning, having encountered heavy ice. It was now nearly 2 A.M. Soon, the rattle of steam winches filled the night air, as seal pelts were hoisted on board. Masterwatch in charge of the gang shouted to the captain that three men belonging to *Neptune* were on the pan. They were ordered to come on board.

"After speaking to Captain Kean, we were taken to the main cabin where a platter of seal's flippers—the forepaws of the seal—were put

At day's end, a ship has to force passage through the icefield to locate pans and hoist the pelts on board. When ice is loose, picking up pans can be dangerous work.

before us, along with dumplings, bread pudding, and a jar of Barbados molasses. Never did food taste more satisfying. Even Garland managed to build up a pile of bones around his plate. *Wolf* stopped for the night where she had picked us up. Freezing weather and snow continued for most of the next day, clearing around four o'clock in the afternoon. *Wolf*'s barrelman reported *Neptune* in sight about five miles away with her flag at half-mast. Having thanked Captain Kean, we set out for our ship. The day happened to be Sunday. As soon as our identity was established, as we approached *Neptune,* the ship's flag was raised all the way to the peak. Our crew lined the rail. Captain Blandford was waiting for us at the gangway. He delivered a scorching lecture for our benefit in the presence of the ship's company. But after that was finished, and I was at the cabin table having a solitary supper, Captain Blandford came out of his stateroom and said, 'Never mind, my boy. You will have many more escapes before you are able to skipper a ship. But you will remember my warning as you were leaving. I told you to keep with the gang, and to come on board with them. You had a narrow escape by not obeying my orders. What would I be able to explain to your good father when *Neptune* reached the wharf in St. John's? He would ask me, "Where's my son, George?" And I would have to say, "I lost 'im!" '

"I never determined what impulse led Fitzgerald to join us, as Garland and I began to walk away from *Neptune*'s men, but without him we would surely have perished."

7

The Four Punts

One of the most dramatic episodes that took place on board *Neptune* during my father's association with Captain Blandford impressed on him the importance of maintaining constant vigilance concerning the whereabouts of crew, as long as men were away from the ship on ice or in small boats. This practice he followed resolutely on sealing ships he subsequently commanded.

To mark the sixth season my father had gone sealing in *Neptune,* he was promoted to the position of barrelman—one of three. The barrelman is the eyes of the captain. On three-masted ships like *Neptune,* there is a barrel on the foremast and a sometimes second barrel located near the top of the mainmast. From this crow's nest, which is actually shaped like a barrel, secured to the mast one hundred feet or more above the deck, the barrelman can see about fifteen miles around the horizon. When the ship is passing through floating pans of ice, the barrelman directs the course, taking advantage of the widest leads—panels of open water—selecting what he suspects is the thinnest ice in order to help the ship crunch and butt a passage through the ice pack toward the seal herds. A barrelman must learn to judge appearance of the icefield that covers the ocean to avoid placing the ship in a vulnerable position. Huge pans of ice squeeze together with tremendous force under influence of wind or tidal currents. Hulls of sealers have been mortally pierced, ripped open, like a knife going through butter, by the shearing action of thick icepans. When hunters are scattered widely over the ice, the barrelman must try to keep positions in mind; alert also to possible changes in weather conditions, lest a blizzard engulf both ship and crew in a blinding, directionless whiteout. Hunters are urged to stay

The barrel or lookout station can be situated on foremast or mainmast. Entry is gained by trapdoor in the bottom. The barrelman has to be an alert, resourceful individual to keep in mind the location of the working crew spread over miles of ice.

together wherever a storm catches them, to increase the chance of their being picked up by the ship. Every barrelman remembers tragic incidents where divisions of a ship's crew froze to death, because all were not picked up at the start of a blizzard.

During the hunt, seals are killed, skinned, and the pelts collected on large pans of ice marked by the ship's flag. Before day's end hunters walk back to the ship, often a distance of ten or more miles, although sometimes the ship can move about and pick up the crew. In a good hunt, over a period of a week, as many as five thousand pelts will be collected on pans to be hoisted on board the ship as quickly as she can maneuver.

George had enjoyed his first season as a barrelman. Fortunately, weather had been generally fair and the hunt successful. Blandford had found a large patch of harp seals by mid-March; now, nearly loaded with twenty thousand pelts, *Neptune* was finishing up in early April by looking for old hood seals that had taken to the water amongst loose ice. The Newfoundland seal herd consists of two species: Harp seals, which have a harplike black patch on the back, and a larger animal, called a hooded seal or "hoods"—from a pouch of skin on the head that can be inflated. Small boats called punts are used to hunt hood seals when these have left the ice and are swimming in open water. Each punt carries a rifleman and four sealers who row. Seals are shot and hauled up on pans where pelts are collected.

On a clear spring day, from the barrelman's lofty perch, the immense ocean of loose ice was, at certain moments, an awesome sight, beautiful in its cold dazzling whiteness. Suspended between sea and sky, he felt as if he was in a different purer world than a part of the grimy ship below.

As my father recalled the incident, he said: "On the morning of that eventful day, we had dropped groups of punts all over the ocean. The ice was loose enough for *Neptune* to go anywhere. During early afternoon, I turned the ship around and headed toward a small patch of seals about fifteen miles distant. I had spotted the seals with my telescope. When we reached this patch, the seals were in the water. The active animals were diving to catch fish. We put out four punts —all we had left—in charge of Jim Powers, an experienced sealer. *Neptune* was then put on a course to the southeast to begin picking up all the boats and men we had dropped earlier in the day. The punts had scattered widely, but I had logged the positions as well as I could. However, we spent a good deal of time before all the boats were rounded up and the seals that had been killed were winched on board. Snow was falling in the growing darkness as the last group came over the rail. Now, only Jim Powers and his four punts remained to be located and recovered; I knew this was going to be a difficult job.

"*Neptune*'s high barrel was equipped with a three-inch compass—small for real accuracy. We had cruised in a dozen different directions while collecting the other boats, but I tried to keep track of my fix on the four punts. I felt sure of the direction in which they lay, although they were out of sight over the horizon, now indistinguishable in the darkness. I called down the course to the bridge.

"From the barrel I could now see nothing at a distance. My little world was circumscribed by darkness and snow. Below me, the forward part of the ship was a glowing pool of whitish yellow from deck lights that provided illumination for crew busy stowing pelts. A searchlight projected an intense cone of light forward over the bow so that I could see the kind of ice the ship was about to hit. To con *Neptune* effectively was almost impossible. At full speed, the iron-shod bow of the ship smacked into whatever kind of ice lay across our heading to the punts.

"I was very conscious of my responsibilities and limitations—a young barrelman untried in situations requiring a high degree of navigational skill. From past experience, I knew crews were often highly critical of barrelmen who committed, in their opinion, errors in judgment. I began to sweat from the tension, although air temperature was below freezing. After we had been under way for about ninety minutes in the direction I had set, Captain Blandford hailed the barrel and asked me to come down. When I reached the bridge, several of the afterguard were talking to the captain.

"The old man turned to me and said, 'George, Skipper William, here, says you are going in the wrong direction. The last time he saw the punts they were bearing west-sou'west.'

"Captain Blandford was obviously extremely agitated. For a moment, taken completely by surprise, I couldn't say a word. Eventually I stammered, 'Well, sir, I am sure I had a good fix on the boats.' However, conversation was abruptly ended by the captain, who said, 'Skipper William, you take the barrel.'

"William went up the ratlines. Captain Blandford walked to the win'ward side of the bridge. I remained on the lee side. The ship swung around more than four points from the course I had established. *Neptune* started in the new direction.

"As I walked to my side of the bridge, I slowly began to feel unsure of myself. Perhaps I had been wrong. For the man in the barrel, there are always several events happening simultaneously which require some attention. I might have made an error in laying off that last bearing on the boats. A three-inch compass does not present much of a sighting surface. Yet, as I considered and reviewed the circumstances of the afternoon, I became convinced that no mistake had been made. Now, to contradict, or even to reason with, Captain Blandford required tremendous nerve. I was a young mariner of limited experience, while Captain Blandford spread an aura of inviolable authority about himself. The feeling of being in the right began to consume me, however. I was like a blazing tree in a gale-fanned forest fire. My heart pounded violently. Rivulets of sweat ran down my forehead. In spite of the freezing wind and driving snow, I was burning up—about to explode. Finally, after *Neptune* had been under way on the new course for about thirty minutes, I could no longer stand the tension. I felt I must speak to Captain Blandford in spite of what might happen to me.

"I walked over to the weather side of the bridge. 'Captain,' I said, 'If we lose those twenty men, I will not be responsible. I know we were steering the correct course when you called me down from the barrel. Skipper William could not possibly have seen those boats from the surface of the ice. I could barely see them from aloft.'

"The old man swung around. I thought he was going to strike me. Instead he tore off his fur cap and fur gloves. Flung them on the deck and jumped on them. 'For God's sake,' he cried, voice cracking with emotion. 'Find the men! Find the men! That's all I want.' He turned abruptly and left the bridge.

" 'Very good, sir,' I said. 'I'm going aloft.'

"I swung into the rigging and raced aloft. When I reached the stays below the barrel, I called to Skipper William, 'Go below. Let me into the barrel.' Neither of us spoke as we passed in the rigging. I climbed up through the trapdoor and prepared to take charge.

"My problem was to set a course that would correct for the thirty-minute interval *Neptune* had been heading in what I considered the wrong direction. How much compensation must be allowed in setting a new correct course? I swung the ship back to the original direction, west by north; then, I allowed three points to a new course of nor'west. We had been heading west-sou'west on the doubtful course William had set.

"By this time, every man on board appeared to be on deck. Some were on the foredeck along each side; others gathered in groups on the fo'c'sle head. The engine-room gang seemed to have raised the ship's speed. *Neptune* drove through thick icepans like a harpoon going into a plaster wall. I could catch snatches of talk from men in the rigging. Some were cursing me: 'Damn young fool; doesn't know what he's doin'! We'll never see them punts 'gn'!'

"Alone in the barrel, I sent up a prayer for help. My whole life, I felt, depended upon finding those men. After running for eighty minutes, I altered course four degrees to the west. Snow had stopped. With the night binoculars I searched the horizon. We should have been seeing something soon, if my calculations were correct. As I was carefully scanning whatever I could see on the ice in the darkness that lay ahead, I heard a sudden shout from men on the fo'c'sle head. 'A light! There's a light!' Turning quickly, I spotted a glow—a light, sure enough—just off the port bow. Course was changed toward the flickering yellow gleam. Shortly after, *Neptune* came up to the pan with the four punts pulled up on the ice, surrounded by the hunters and their catch of seals. The men had made a fire using seal's fat and gaff handles. The pelts and boats were soon hoisted on board. The twenty men were glad to have *Neptune*'s solid oak deck under them once again.

"Someone rattled the main halliards against the side of the barrel. 'Come down and have your dinner,' called the chief steward. I was more exhausted than hungry, although I had not eaten anything except a large bar of chocolate since noon. I was filled with a great sense of thankfulness, however.

"Later on, as I sat at the main cabin table, Captain Blandford opened the door of his stateroom and, looking across the cabin at me, said, 'Well done, my boy. You did a good job.' That was all he said. But that was enough. I could only imagine what he said to Skipper William."

8

A Happening at Funk Island

Off the northeast coast of Newfoundland, fifty miles out to sea, a small low island and a nearby islet, collectively called "the Funks" by local people, lie along the path of the drift ice on which seals breed. Ocean currents sweep the field of ice southward past the island and the surrounding shoal ground that have been the graveyard of many ships.

In the spring of 1900, my father was again on board *Neptune* with Captain Blandford. The sealing fleet encountered extremely heavy ice on the way north. When *Neptune* had reached about twenty miles north-northwest of the Funks, pans of arctic ice, one hundred yards or more in length and width and ten feet in depth closed tightly around the ship like a puckered mouth around a strawberry. Blasting and various other tactics had no effect. The ship *Newfoundland,* owned by Captain Farquhar of Halifax, Nova Scotia, was inside and astern of *Neptune.* She was also jammed. The two ships were at a standstill in the solid icepack.

At length, a furious gale out of the north smote the ships, day and night—a full gale. Fortunately, weather remained clear; no snow. But the wind was cold enough, in the opinion of *Neptune*'s Scottish chief engineer, "to freeze the fires of Hell." All hands stayed below, except for the watch. Due to ocean currents and the strength of the gale, the field of ice began to growl, creak, and move at a faster rate. Sealers refer to this phenomena as "running ice." Of course, *Newfoundland* and *Neptune* moved with it.

At first, *Neptune*'s crew simply tried to keep warm. But after a day's drift, snow- and ice-covered Funk Island was visible on the horizon. Word soon got around the ship that she "was bearing down

The sea beats upon Funk Island incessantly, and in winter grinding ice tossed by the waves erodes its flanks.

on the Funks." A lot of eyes began to watch that sliver of solid rock, less than fifty feet high, come closer and closer. *Neptune* was being carried stern-first straight toward the island; borne relentlessly to her possible destruction by the drifting icepack. As *Neptune* drew closer, the crew saw what the fate of their ship might be. Wide pans of running ice, thick massive pieces, went aground on the sloping shoreline at the north end of the island. Tremendous pressure from behind forced these pans to grind against each other; to twist over and over, upend, and, having been thrust into the air for twenty feet or higher, finally topple with a crash, scouring the granite backbone of the island like an avalanche—an awesome demonstration of nature's destructive power.

Neptune carried a crew of 285 men. Some of the sealers began to get out on the side-sticks—a series of fore-and-aft poles secured by lines to the ship's rail, forming a kind of ladder used by the hunters to stand on when leaving or boarding. Many of the crew were carrying belongings in boxes or seabags. Captain Blandford was on the bridge now. As a junior officer, Whiteley had great admiration for his captain. He felt Blandford could accomplish any feat of seamanship by reason of his long experience as a sealing commander. Blandford shouted to his crew on thesticks, warning them not to get excited; to do nothing without orders from him; to be sure every man had a coil of line and a gaff, should they have to jump from the steamer. Captain Sam had a throat and lungs like the toughest leather; when he raised his voice in a bull-like roar, the hair on a man's head twisted into a knot.

The *Newfoundland,* jammed to the west and astern of *Neptune,* was the first to strike one of the outlying ledges. The aft section of the ship was suddenly pushed out of water, depressing the bow. Then the hull was flung sideways. Spars canted at an alarming angle; the ship was almost on her beam's ends. Some of her people were thrown on the ice floe. Surely the ship's rudder had been smashed or the hull pierced! The surging mass of ice bore the ship over the shoal; she slowly righted herself. In the loose ice behind the ledge, Captain Farquhar was able to let go an anchor. Crew began clearing away the mess of displaced stores and equipment. By a combination of luck and good seamanship, *Newfoundland,* although leaking and damaged, was still afloat and navigable.

Newfoundland's maneuver may have given Blandford an idea. He told the mate to check both anchors and lay out enough chain for quick action. Whiteley was sent to tell the chief engineer: "When you hear the engine-room telegraph call for 'Full Speed Ahead' give the engine every pound of steam you can develop."

By now, the noise of shattering ice on the island was quite audible. Aboard *Neptune* the question in the minds of all was whether the ship could survive a direct assault. Fortunately, the barrelman saw a small lake of open water behind the island. He shouted this information to the bridge. The low island was acting like a rock in a fast-flowing river, parting the running ice to left and to right, but leaving an ice-free wake a short distance behind it.

Neptune drew closer and closer to the island; her broad stern pointed directly toward the maelstrom of ice. Would she be caught and broken asunder? The crew noticed that the ice-jam accumulated in front of the island was pushing to one side the huge pan in which the ship was locked. *Neptune*'s stern was being gradually thrust to starb'ard. By a narrow margin, the ship, now being pushed sideways, cleared the point of the island. As soon as the steamer began to slant sideways, Blandford shouted order in rapid succession. As Funk Island came abeam, he rang the engine room for full speed. *Neptune* responded and after some hesitation broke out of the trap; changing pressures on the ice, as it met the island, had loosened the icy grip. By charging the slackening floes at full speed, the ship was able to enter the pool of open water to leeward. The captain maneuvered *Neptune* as close as possible to the island; there was deep water all the way to the face of the rock. A punt was lowered, and after considerable difficulty, a suitable place was found to wedge securely an anchor. The crew gave a wild cheer when the ship was finally in a safe haven. Running ice continued to stream past.

Neptune lay to her anchor for five days. In course of time, the gale blew itself out. On the third day, the little lake around the ship was alive with old seals; sleak black heads popped out of the water in all directions. The running ice had brought them south. Next day, young harp seals were everywhere on the ice which still continued to pass by the ship. By the fifth day, a large number of both old and young seals had been observed, inside and outside of the Funks. Finally, Captain Blandford could not stand being idle any longer. It would have been prudent to wait several more days; hunters would not have had to walk as far. But the quantity of animals greatly excited the old seaman; he wanted to secure a shipload before another storm might change the entire situation.

The mooring was taken aboard. The ship struck out into the moving pack. *Neptune* loaded in ten days and returned to port. Captain Farquhar kept the *Newfoundland* afloat and also secured a voyage. The remainder of the fleet, swept far to the south by gale and drifting ice, did not fare as well.

Over the years, many sealers were wrecked on the Funks or were crushed by ice near the island. In 1896 two strongly built ships were lost, one after the other. The *Wolf* was caught in raftering ice—rapidly moving floes that pile against a ship's side, if she is jammed, tumble over the rail, crush the deck beams, and sink the vessel by tremendous weight. Fortunatley, other sealers, located not far from the stricken steamer, were able to rescue the marooned crew who had taken to the ice. *Windsor Lake* was pinched between two pans which cracked some plates of her hull, although she was a steel ship. When the pressure slackened, the strickened ship sank like a stone. The sealer *Labrador* happened to be within walking distance but little of the ship's stores or personal belongings of the ship's company were saved.

Newfoundland was fortunate to have escaped the Funks without greater damage. And *Neptune* was just plain lucky.

9

A Visit with Captain Jackman

The recollection of an event that took place during my father's last year with Captain Blandford invariably brought a twinkle to his eye.

Neptune had happened upon a large herd of seals with no other ship in sight. The fleet were jammed in heavy ice more than thirty miles eastward. In ten days, *Neptune*'s hunters, working long hours, panned twenty-five thousand pelts. The ocean of ice for miles around was spotted with crimson piles, each pan marked with the ship's flag.

Eventually, a few ships freed themselves from the ice barrier and forced a passage through the floes. Several were now in sight on the horizon. *Neptune* had not been able to pick up all her pans—no more than half of them, because the heavy ice slowed progress. Captain Blandford was worried lest some of the recent arrivals would steal *Neptune*'s seals. Temptation to steal was great, since the season was advancing; soon all seals would take to water, heralding the end of the sealing season.

One evening, Whiteley was called to the captain's cabin. He was told to take a man with him next day to make a survey of all remaining pans belonging to *Neptune,* at least as many as he could find; to secure the flags on the pans and make an estimate of the number of pelts on each pan. He was to walk as far from *Neptune* as possible, and at nightfall he was to board the *Eagle*— the barrelman had reported her position as being the nearest ship—and ask the captain if they could spend the night on board.

As soon as daylight made search possible, the two men left *Neptune.* They worked all day checking the pans and securing flags. Nightfall found them far from their own ship but near some of *Eagle*'s hunters. They walked to the *Eagle* with these men and boarded the ship. *Eagle* carried two tall masts and had a high bow and forecastle head, presenting an unmistakable profile.

The two men from *Neptune* were met at the gangway by Mickey Walsh, the short, one-eyed chief mate, who always accompanied Captain Jackman, veteran skipper of *Eagle.* Mickey was well known as a "hard case." As he squinted at the two strangers, he loosened a string of oaths, interspersed with questions. He wanted to know the names of the men . . . from what ship . . . what were they doing on ice . . . were they lost . . . what did they mean by coming on board *Eagle?* Mickey was chewing a large quid of tobacco; the brown juice ran down his whiskers. He looked like a much soiled, grizzled, ninth-century Viking—tough as water-logged oak. When he had satisfied his curiousity, he walked aft to report to his captian, who immediately ordered the two men to appear before him.

Captain Jackman was seated at the head of the cabin table. He was a broad-chested man with enormous shoulders. He wore a blue guernsey. Over his heart a large anchor was embroidered in red wood. His hair was standing on end, and he had not shaved for weeks. His large hands, like the paws of a polar bear, were folded on the table in front of him. In a threatening growl, he demanded to know why the men had come on board his ship together with a number of other questions. Whiteley told him that he had been on ice all day counting pan and securing flags and had come on board for shelter because *Neptune* was too far away to reach before nightfall. Captain Jackman asked my father his name. "Are you W. H. Whiteley's son?" Jackman said he was well acquainted with the young man's father. Finally, after some minutes of silence, the two were told to make themselves comfortable for the night in the main cabin.

After a meal, Whiteley fell asleep on the cabin settee. He woke about midnight and found that the ship was under way at full speed. She kept going all night. He wondered how they would get back to their ship.

On deck after breakfast, Whiteley asked the barrelman if he could see anything of *Neptune.* The man replied that he thought he saw her smoke about twenty miles west. Later, Whiteley noticed that *Eagle*'s course had changed. The ship was steaming in the direction of *Neptune*'s position. Captain Jackman brought *Eagle* to within one hundred yards of *Neptune* at about two o'clock in the afternoon. All on board *Eagle* were on deck having a good look at the ship, deep in the water with a load of seals. Captain Jackman leaned over the rail of the bridge. He called Whiteley aft; he wanted to talk to him.

"Now, my son," he said. "Go on board your own ship, and tell that old son of a bitch that I would not steal his seals even if they were the last and only pans on the ocean, and if I saw my men coming on board with seals that I thought they had not killed, I would put them in irons. Tell him, also, that I can find my own seals. If I saw him or any of his northern bastards . . . coming towards me (Jackman was born in St. John's; Sam Blandford came from north Newfoundland) I would turn my ship around and go in the other direction. . . . Be sure to deliver my message. Now, go on board your ship."

The two men got out on the ice and, in due course, boarded *Neptune*. Whiteley delivered the message, word for word. The old man heard him out. Then he asked, "Did he really say that? Then he's a blackguard!"

Blandford immediately climbed to *Neptune*'s bridge . . . blew a blast on the siren three times. The signal was answered by *Eagle*. The crew of each ship roared into cheers. The captains waved in the most friendly fashion. *Neptune*'s engines throbbed into life, and the ship moved off to finish picking up her pans.

10

Loss of the Stella Maris

My father married May Canning in 1898, and although after the marriage he went on sealing voyages less frequently, he was eventually able to satisfy his desire to have a command. The excitement of the hunt, the elemental power of wind, ice, and ocean fascinated him, although he also understood the dangers and privations under which the crew often worked.

In 1925 his ship was the *Stella Maris.* I remember very well returning from school on March 13 to find my mother seated by the telephone in our front hall. She looked somber. Hanging up the receiver, she turned to me with a worried look in her blue eyes. "The Marconi Company picked up a message this morning," she said. *"Stella Maris* sinking about eighty miles north-northeast of Cape Fogo—that was the message. Attempts to reply failed to get response."

I put my arms around my dear mother and hugged her. "We will just have to wait and hope," she said grimly.

Far at sea, the following events were taking place.

Early in the morning of March 13 on board the *Stella Maris* in the lee of the canvas windbreak, on the starboard side of the bridge, Captain Whiteley was drinking a mug of cocoa, thanks to the attention of the pantry steward. Fred Ballard, chief engineer, suddenly appeared, climbing the ladder to the bridge two steps at a time, a worried frown creasing his usually cheerful face.

Ignoring a greeting, the chief drew close: "Captain George," he said quickly, "there's something dreadful wrong with the ship."

"What do you mean?" asked the captain, startled.

"There's a hell of a lot of water in the engine room. Pumps can't seem to keep the level from rising."

Captain George Whiteley, the author's father.

"Make a sounding: see exactly how much water there is in the hold. If there is damage below the waterline, we may be able to shift coal to change trim, as we did in *Viking,* a few years ago. By getting the leak out of water, a patch might be possible."

The chief left for the engine room; the captain looked around the horizon. *Stella* was a 250-ton wooden ship with a crew of ninety men. Suppose the ship had to be abandoned. Was there a pan of ice in sight large enough to hold ninety men safely? The ship had been cruising slowly in close-packed ice yesterday, but was now at full speed, following the edge of a loose string of pans that had separated from the main icefield. Sea was calm. The subarctic sky had a cold gray complexion.

From the bridge, the captain saw the chief step out of the engine-room door. He ran along the deck to the ladder.

"I crawled into the starboard bunker with a flashlight," he gasped, "but had to back out fast." His face was streaked with sweat and coal dust. "There's a wall of water entering the bunker. She must be hurt bad." He shook his head, puzzled.

"How long do you think she can last?"

"She's going fast, captain."

"Look after your men, Fred. We'll lie alongside the ice and get the crew out of her."

There was a large pan with a small hummock or ridge on it about two hudnred yards distant, not far inside the edge of the loose ice.

"Port a bit, helmsman. See the large pan with the hummock? Bring her broadside to it."

The captain rang the engine room for slow speed. *Stella Maris* began to poke into the heaving skein of drifting floe. He called to one of the men on the foredeck: "Tell Fred Cram the captain wants to see him at once." Fred, one of the masterwatches, had been with him for many years. When Fred arrived, the captain said: "We are in desperate trouble . . . probably sinking. Don't make any fuss; find the first mate, Mr. Barbour. Tell him. Then get hold of food or anything else which may be useful on ice. There's a half barrel of kerosene on the aft deck. Get everything to the rail on the port side. Mr. Barbour is to alert the crew. Avoid panic." As Fred left the bridge, he called to him: "Send up the wireless man, immediately!"

Before Tony had both feet on the deck of the bridge, the captain spoke decisively: "Send an SOS at once. *Stella Maris* sinking; probable position eighty miles NNE Cape Fogo." The lad stared, blinking, a quizzical look on his face. "Get it off, now! At once!" the captain yelled at him.

Tony, the wireless operator, was a young English lad from the Canadian Marconi Company's Montreal office. This was his first trip on a sealing steamer. The captain had asked him, earlier in the morning, to be sure to have the wireless generator working properly, since he planned to send a message to one of the other ships.

By looking forward from the bridge to the bow of the ship, the captain could see that the stem was dipping a little lower each time the bow rose and fell, in response to long swells drifting through the icepack. *Stella* was sinking . . . no doubt about that. Part of his mind was numb, scarcely believing what his eyes registered, events had followed one another so swiftly. At the same time, questions tumbled over and over . . . of many items needed, if they were to be cast away, the limited time remaining to secure them. No more than ten minutes had elapsed since the chief engineer had come to the bridge.

Stella was alongside the large pan. Engine room was signaled: STOP . . . FINISHED WITH ENGINES. All hands seemed to be on deck now. A number of men jumped with their kitbags. The captain called to his crew: "Food is more important than your gear. Gather all the wood you can find loose—poles, planks, anything that will burn.

Throw things on the pan." Unfortunately, the ship was iced-up so much that little material was available. Lifeboats and nested dories were masses of ice, frozen solid from the driving spray of the last gale.

"Check the ship, please, Mr. Barbour. Everyone out on the ice."

Turning to the helmsman, the captain said: "Now lad, go help Fred Cram get those boxes of food over the rail. And watch out. She's liable to go under any minute."

The stern was now at a noticeable angle . . . the bow a foot or two from the surface of the ocean. The ship looked ready to dive forward. With a muffled thud, a bulkhead gave away below deck. The captain rushed to the side of the bridge, prepared to jump. But with a jerk, the crippled steamer settled to an even keel. Were there any distress flares, the captain wondered? He raced down ladder to his cabin under the bridge. Water was beginning to lap over the high sill. He pulled several drawers before locating flares; impulsively, he also picked up his sextant. At the rail, the articles were handed to one of the men. Then he remembered binoculars. He had used them in the crow's nest barrel earlier in the morning, before *Stella* left the thick ice. They would be useful. Jumping into the rigging, he raced up the ratlines to the barrel. "Come on, skipper! She's going," cried one of the men. Swinging the case around his neck, he slid down a backstay, ripping his leather gloves. The ship seemed to vibrate. He jumped over the rail and sprang to the ice. The rail was almost level with the pan. With his back to the ship, he looked for mate Barbour. All hands present and counted, the mate reported.

The captain's eyes swept over the wide forbidding expanse of ice and returned to his little group of men. Would he be able to save their lives, or was that question now in other hands?

"I turned around to have a look at the ship. The top of her funnel was just disappearing. In a few seconds, there was only a thin scum of coal-dust on the water, a few boards floating, the small lifeboat, and three dories, manned by some of the crew. The remains of the ship drifted in a small lake of water formed by the sinking hull. *Stella Maris* had vanished as peacefully as the morning star fades at sunrise."

Three days before, *Stella Maris* had cleared from St. John's for the northern seal hunt with twelve other ships. Built for the British navy in a South of England shipyard, constructed of oak, and copper fastened, the sturdy gunboat, as H.M.S. *Starling*, had served in the China Sea for fifty years. Sold out of the navy, she gradually moved westward, converted to a freight carrier. On a fateful day in 1917, she was in the harbor of Halifax, Nova Scotia, proceeding into Bedford Basin, where a wartime convoy was being formed. Two of the ships ahead of her collided. The S.S. *Mont Blanc,* loaded with picric acid and TNT, caught fire and blew up. The tremendous explosion devasted Halifax; caused ten thousand casualties, killed and wounded; and blew the superstructure clean off the old gunboat. Rebuilt and renamed, the ship was bought by a Halifax shipping firm and used in the Newfoundland trade. During winter she was outfitted as a sealer. During the previous spring hunt, *Stella Maris* proved to be a strong, able craft. Now she was at the bottom of the ocean; the ship's company adrift and helpless on a pan of ice, eighty miles from land.

" 'Put the men to work, Joe,' I said. 'Make some kind of snow-wall, a shelter from the wind. Keep them busy.' Then I looked for Fred Cram. 'How much food were you able to save?' 'Not a great deal,' he said. 'Some bags of hardtack, a barrel of salt beef, cans of cocoa, a little sugar, a couple bags of potatoes, and a keg of molasses. Also a big kettle to boil water, and I have my gun.' 'We'll do our best with that food,' I said. 'Give the rifle to Jim Ash; he will guard the supplies. This grub may have to last us a long time.' "

The captain had not seen the wireless operator since he had sent him to transmit the SOS signal. He found the young man helping to look after two of the stokers. These poor devils, wearing next to nothing in the hot boiler room, hadn't been able to get below for additional clothes. Fortunately, a member of the crew had an extra woolen sweater which he contributed and a few other jackets were located. Someone had the novel idea of using a large puncheon, saved from the wreckage, as the basis for a snow-house. The shivering stokers crawled into the shelter to keep each other warm.

The captain could be an impatient man. He wanted to talk to the operator, and finally he was able to draw Tony aside. "Did you get out the SOS?"

"Yes, captain," the young man replied. "I know the signal went out. To be ready for the message you had planned to send, I asked the chief to start the auxiliary engine for the wireless generator. The set had good spark. But before I was able to repeat, the generator must have shorted . . . from water flooding into the engine room. I wasn't able to transmit or receive after that."

During the long, cold, dreary night, the captain questioned the lad about twenty times. Tony was most patient. Always, he replied, "I know the SOS went out, captain."

Next morning, the crew returned to the task of finishing the windbreak. Hands were the only tools, and snow on the pan was not well suited for wall-building, but the group was kept busy. Everyone participated, and the activity helped to maintain alertness. Having had little to eat for more than twelve hours, the men made repeated requests for permission to start a fire. About three o'clock, the captain decided to see what could be prepared. "Let's all take a blow and boil the kettle," he said.

Some of the wood rescued from the wreck was collected on a corner of the pan. The wood was wet, but with liberal use of the kerosene oil and chunks of fat from a few seals the men had killed, a blaze finally started; although there seemed to be more smoke than flame, enough hot water was collected to boil potatoes and to make a mug of cocoa for all hands. Fortunately every sealer carries a tin cup and a sheath knife on his belt. The cook also produced a slice of salt beef and a cake or two of hardtack for each man. The crew sat around the fire, munching the tough bread like dogs gnawing bones, silently keeping thoughts to themselves. It takes very little time to return to a primitive state.

There had been sunny intervals during the day but in the late afternoon high cirrus clouds began to sail across the sky, probably harbingers of unsettled weather. Several times the captain climbed the hummock on the pan to study the horizon with binoculars. Nothing but an empty ocean of ice met his gaze. No sign of a black smudge hovering on the line between frozen sea and gray sky to indicate the presence of a distant sealing ship. On the pan, the crew sat huddled in groups, each group representing a good many households back home. The captain prayed that "somewhere, someone had heard that SOS".

The second night was harder to get through as the men were hungry and the wind whistled a somber tune. When daylight came it brought great relief. To keep warm, men hugged together after beating arms across chests to keep blood circulating, but there was not much activity now because the pan was too small for the entire crew to exercise even in groups. During the morning, ten of the younger men came to the captain to ask whether they might set out over the ice. The floe looked tight to the southwest, the probable direction of land. Perhaps they might meet sealers from another ship, which then would come to the rescue. By dragging a dory, they might reach land.

After some consideration, the captain said the plan was too risky; he was responsible for their safety. The group should stay together. The SOS had gone out. They would be rescued; he was hopeful of that.

There was some grumbling, but no one left. To walk over the ice with the expectation of securing help was not wise, whether the ship's company were to be rescued or not. The captain felt sure about his decision, for in the past, crews that stayed together after a ship foundered had the best record of survival.

Over and over in his mind, the worried commander tried to reconstruct the events of the past few days. Why had the ship gone down so quickly? Could anything have been done that was not done? Sealing ships are usually lost by being crushed by the weight of raftering ice or by fire. In other cases, pans of ice, like sharp knives, cut into planking when forced against the hull of a ship, and a fatal leak develops. But on this trip, they had not once been jammed in heavy ice.

In order to avoid missing any link in the sequence the captain reviewed happenings from the start of the present voyage.

A clear morning saw the fleet leave St. John's harbor on March 10. A brisk wind gradually developed—hauled into the northwest—blew hard—but *Stella* made fair progress. Next morning, wind increased to a gale, as the ship rolled and labored heavily and took on a lot of water. Before noon, a heavy sea broke on board flooding the engine room and carrying away a length of bulwark on the port side. The ship was hove-to dry out the engine room and stokehold. With air temperature below freezing, rigging, dories, and superstructure were soon coated in layers of ice, but *Stella Maris* was a good seaboat and lay-to like a duck. After a few hours, the engines were started again at half speed owing to heavy seas. At sunset, the ship encountered loose ice, entered it, and made progress until midnight, then she was stopped so that all hands could catch a sound sleep, safe in the shelter of the ice.

"I lay down on the settee in my cabin, just as I had come down from the bridge. Did not even bother to untie my fur hat or take off my gloves. In a disturbing dream, I watched a ship gradually turn into an iceberg, drift away slowly, and then disappear. The dream probably woke me, as the cabin clock struck six bells—3 A.M. I went to the bridge for a look around. A cold clear night. I climbed the foremast to the barrel. From this crow's nest, I used a telescope to observe the horizon. There was a low, bright light in one direction; too low for a star, I thought. Probably the masthead light of one of the large steel sealers. Joe Barbour, my second in command, had the early-morning watch. I asked Joe to come up and take a look—'That light looks as if it might be the masthead light of the *Prospero*,' I said. 'If we could reach her and take her wake, the broken ice would help us work north to the patch of seals I believe lie to the northwest of us.' "

Leaving Joe Barbour in the barrel to keep watch on the light, the captain returned to the bridge and got the ship under way. As *Stella* was rammed through the loose ice, she occasionally had to be stopped and put astern in order to have space to gather forward speed for ahard butt into a thicker barrier of the floe. After a while, the captain was called to the barrel for another look. On the way to the mast, he passed the door of the wireless room. He asked the operator to be prepared to send a message to another ship later in the morning. Power for the wireless transmitter came from the main engine. The engineer had to open a valve and divert steam to the auxiliary engine which ran the wireless generator. The procedure was uncomplicated, but it usually took a few minutes to get things running smoothly.

When the captain reached the barrel, Joe said: "The ice is getting tighter ahead, skipper. I think that ship is jammed solid. She hasn't moved since I began to watch her. If we go in much further, we may get jammed also."

After he had surveyed the situation carefully, the captain agreed with the mate's opinion. "We will reverse course," he said. "When we reach open water, we can work north along the edge of the pack."

"I went to the cabin to have breakfast. Joe turned the ship around and picked up our wake. *Stella* made good progress towards open water. Then the masterwatch took the barrel. Joe came to breakfast and I went to the bridge. When I reached the bridge, I noticed the ship was steaming down a long narrow lead between two enormous sheets of ice. It seemed to me that these two huge pans were swinging and would come together, forced by a powerful tidal current. I called to the barrelman, asking him if the ship could pass through before the pans crunched together and closed the lead. He said the ship would get through. But before *Stella* reached the far end of the lead, the pan swinging on the port side caught the ship, pinning her against ice on the opposite side. *Stella* stopped short. Shock of the impact jarred her entire structure. There was a secondary rebound of ice from the stout wooden hull and, with engine going full ahead, the ship slipped out of the viselike trap. In the previous spring, *Stella* had been subjected to severe ice conditions, so I did not pay much attention to this punch."

During the morning, *Stella Maris* cruised in open water along the edge of the ice. A few of the crew on watch were moving part of a deckload of coal from the stern to a new pound on the foredeck. When the captain noticed that the ship's trim seemed to be somewhat by the head, he stopped the shuttle. To keep stern and propeller as deep as possible was important, in order to avoid damage to blades by icepans sucked into the wake, especially when she went astern. A ship had to reverse a great deal when being navigated through heavy ice.

When, some hours later, the chief engineer reported out-of-control leaking, the captain did not think of that squeeze. But he pondered it now. How could that blow have caused the fatal wound to the old ship? She had tackled heavier ice before! He fretted over the loss of the ship, as he searched the horizon again and again, hoping to see some sign that their position was known by a searching ship. But the horizon was bare.

Later on, a couple of the young men, scouting around, spotted seals and after a chase succeeded in killing a couple. The crew forgot their plight as they shouted encouragement and gathered around the hunters when the animals were skinned. "Make a fire and have something to eat," the captain said. There was not much left that was burnable, but by using the kerosene and strips of seal fat, the splintered planking ignited. Men tried to roast the seal meat. Without suitable cooking gear, their efforts were not highly successful, but the dark meat provided some nourishment, and the activity kept everyone busy.

Since the sky was beginning to thicken with haze, the captain thought the time had come to use some of the distress flares. A ship might have seen the column of smoke from the fire and be alerted by the red flares. Fred Cram ignited half a dozen of the rockets. By the time the men had finished munching the hardtack and the bits of seal, darkness covered the face of the frozen ocean. Light snow began to drift down softly. The bite of Arctic wind added to the chilling effect of the surrounding ice. A cold miserable night was fast approaching. The men gathered in groups, sang favorite hymns, and burrowed into the snow to make a crude shelter. To huddle together to keep warm, like eskimo dogs in a blizzard, seemed an instinctive reaction.

"As I sat talking to the masterwatches—the group leaders—discussing what steps we might take if the situation became desperate, one of the crew walked up to me, 'I've been standing on the edge of the pan over there,' he said. 'I think I can hear a voice, a cry, very faint.' I looked at the man, thinking, I hope we're not going to have trouble—a poor chap loosing his sanity—not that such a state of mind was without a reason. We were on the ice without much food, and with slim hope of rescue. 'Take me to the spot,' I said. We walked beyond the hummock to the far edge of the pan. The surging of the vast ice-filled ocean, like the hissing sound of air suddenly inhaled between half-closed teeth, was the only sound on the night wind beating into our faces. 'There!' the man said suddenly. He placed his fingers on the margin of his left ear, as if the better to collect any sound with his open hand. 'I've heard it better than that,' added the man, turning his head into the wind. 'Now! That's it!' he cried. 'Didn't you hear that cry?' Perhaps there *was* something out there in the snow and darkness. I was as happy to find that my man was perfectly sane as I was to grasp at the straw of possible rescue. Crouching on my knees, I put my ear to the surface of the ice. I once had a crew member who was part Eskimo; he claimed he could hear the thump of a ship's propeller by listening close to sheet ice. The man knelt and listened. 'I think I hear a ship, skipper. Well, your ears are better than mine. Stay here. I'll go for some young fellows; they have keen ears.' In a few minutes I returned with two Trinity Bay men. 'Can you hear anything on the wind from that direction?' We all stood tense, waiting. 'Look there!' one of the lads pointed to the left. 'Is that a light?' "

A dim diffused glare shone thorugh darkness and spindrift. Then it disappeared. The glare was again visible; then it disappeared once more. The probing of a searchlight, the captain guessed. "There may be a ship near by. Let's give them a hail!" All together, the crew of the *Stella Maris* yelled as loud as they had strength left in their bodies. Again and again. Gradually the sound of a powerful steamer could be heard, quite plainly, as she ground her way into the icepack. The glow of deck lights shone through the murk. Before long, the jibboom of the S.S. *Prospero* was high over the edge of the pan, and the hull of the ship surged into camp. *Stella*'s crew had to scatter before the steamer slowed.

Rescuing survivors. Sealing ships have been destroyed by ice pressure, fire, explosion; fortunately crews have been rescued in many cases.

Yelling with excitement, the shipwrecked mariners scrambled up the side-sticks to the *Prospero*'s solid deck. When all the crew was on board and counted, the rescue ship continued her progress but eventually stopped her engines for the night.

"We were in the captain's cabin. Captain Burgess was in his bunk, and I lay on the sofa. 'I think the weather is going to storm, Skipper George,' said Captain Burgess. 'Gale and snow—good job we found you.' After a while, I noticed the steamer was rolling heavily and bumping among the pans of loose ice. So I said to Burgess, 'Why don't you move further into the icepack, where it will be smooth? We all need a sound sleep.' Captain Burgess took down his speaking tube to the bridge and said, 'Steam her in another three miles. Whiteley wants to go to sleep—' "

Next morning, Captain Whiteley was having his first real meal in many days, a breakfast of bacon and seal kidneys, when Joe Murphy came into the saloon. Joe was the lookout in the barrel who spotted *Stella*'s smoke signal. "What are the conditions out there now, Joe?" "Well, Captain George," said he. "You would have to be a seal to stay on that ice today. The wind and swell we had last night broke up the ice. Where we found you, I don't think there are pans as big as that tablecloth."

11

Working on the Offshore Banks

By 1898, three of the Whiteley boys were operating the business at Bonne Esperance. Jack, the oldest of the team, lived in British Columbia and came east each spring, Edward lived on Labrador year round, while my father and mother made their winter home in St. John's.

I was brought to the Labrador Island, where my father had spent his boyhood, when I was less than a year old and every summer thereafter, until age seventeen. Thus my life, at least during summer, was strongly influenced by the sea and the many-sided activities of the families' marine products business. While this was not an ideal situation, being rather one-sided, island life had much to offer a growing boy: the opportunity for hard manual labor, the freedom to exercise one's ingenuity, to develop responsibility in handling boats, and to come to know uncertainty of economic return that continually hovers over primary producers, farmers or fishermen, so dependent on natural forces beyond human control. Moreover, the sea-girdled islands, apparently unchanged for eons, the inland lakes and untrodden hills, created a love of wilderness that has never left me.

In 1931, after living in Canada for several years, I returned to Newfoundland to work as a marine biologist. Newfoundland was then a Dominion, a member of the British Commonwealth. The government of Newfoundland had recently joined with a corporation funded by the British government to establish a Marine Labora-

William Whiteley with his sons, in 1895 (W.H.W., Jr, was at sea). George at left, second row.

tory for the purpose of carrying out a survey of the fishing grounds of the northeast Atlantic and of investigating the feasibility of applying technological innovation to age-old salt codfish industry.

To estimate productivity of a particular marine species, such as cod, haddock, salmon, or lobster, it is necessary to determine as accurately as possible the age of the individuals in the annual catch —individuals that support the commercial fishery. Fishery biologists have found, for example, that if fishermen are making large catches of cod, the bulk of the catch probably consists of relatively few age-groups or year-classes.

That is, one or two year-classes, even a single year-class, might dominate the catch; large numbers of seven-year-old fish, for instance, might produce eighty percent of the landings. Conversely, low-yield year-classes will result in a period of scanty catches and hard times for fishermen. Many commercially valuable species depend on the vigor and numbers of specific year-classes.

Population data is collected by the time-consuming process of measuring thousands of individuals; or, in the case of cod, haddock, and salmon, by selecting about a dozen scales from the tail region of

A Spanish trawler working near *Democracy*. For centuries Spanish, French, Portuguese, English fished the Newfoundland and Nova Scotian offshore banks. After World War II the Soviet Union and its sattelites sent hugh fleets of trawlers and factory ships.

each fish. The scale samples, placed in separate envelopes along with identifying notes, are eventually examined under a microscope in the laboratory; the age of each fish can be determined by certain structural detail on the scale. Hence, basic research demands that investigators go to sea to collect this sort of raw data as extensively as possible. Sampling catches at sea is the first step in a study that may eventually lead to the capability of predicting fluctuations in the productivity of fishing grounds.

The Grand Banks of Newfoundland, a submarine plateau to the southeast of the island, larger in area than the total of Massachusetts, Connecticut, and Rhode Island, has yielded a supply of cod, haddock, flounder, and other fish for nearly five hundred years. This area, and the adjacent Nova Scotian banks, together with Brown and Geroges Banks in the Gulf of Maine, are now considered overfished, chiefly because of the large fleets of Russian trawlers, joined by factory-ships from other Communist countries, that invaded the banks in the postwar period.

Historically, French, Spanish, and Portuguese vessels joined Newfoundland, Canadian, and U.S. fishermen to reap the harvest of Continental fishing areas and, in spite of biological fluctuations from time

St. John's harbor from the south side. A Soviet mothership with a trawler alongside occupy a space at the north quay.

to time, the overall productivity of the fish stocks remained remarkably constant over the centuries. Not until the postwar period did serious decline in total landings begin.

I am convinced that the huge fishing fleets of the USSR and her satellites were part of a planned attack on our seafood resources. From the air, I have seen a portion of this fleet extend to the horizon in all directions north and east of Cape Cod; an armada of large, modern trawlers and factory-ships. Overfishing by these fleets have decimated the north Atlantic fishing grounds. But the two-hundred-mile limit and the use of licenses which both Canada and the U.S. have set up will no doubt decrease the intensity of the foreign fishing effort and the depleted stocks of fish may eventually recover.

It is also reasonable to assume that the Soviet government was interested in more than obtaining a supply of protein. Oceanographic research vessels, posing as fishermen, were undoubtedly making detailed studies of ocean-bottom topography, tidal currents, temperature and salinity profiles of coastal water, the physical structure of the Gulf Stream, and other aspects of physical oceanography so important to submarine warfare. Naval experts consider that if a war should ever develop, nuclear submarines will be one of the chief offensive weapons. Submarine tactics depend on a sophisticated knowledge of physical oceanography.

Crew of the fishery research ship *Cape Agulhas* have just put the big trawl overboard and the wire towing cables are running out. Captain Fudge in the wheelhouse checks the operation.

When the Newfoundland laboratory began its pioneer work in the
northeast Atlantic in late 1931, economic conditions worldwide were
in a depressed state. In addition to investigating the basic oceanography of the seas surrounding Newfoundland and the Great Grand
Banks and the effect of physical and biological conditions on fishing
success—such as the manner in which various fish species reacted to
fluctuating salinity and temperatures in their habitats—we studied
the effect of currents on the distribution of young stages as well as
mature fish, the productivity and distribution of plankton—micro-
scopic fish food—and the interrelationship between food supply and
successful spawning of commercially valuable fish species. We were
also interested in other related matters; namely, the possibilities of
freezing cod or salmon—instead of producing dried salt cod, salted

After winching onboard the two heavy wooden steel-shod doors which act as paravanes to keep mouth of the trawl open, crew then pulls in the trawl by hand.

The fish collect in the narrow end of the cone-shaped trawl, called the codend. This entire section is now winched on board, a fastening is removed, and the catch falls out on deck.

or canned salmon—and in the economics of utilizing fish species that had heretofore not been commercially exploited.

Clarence Birdseye had recently introduced a quick-freezing method of food preservation, using supercooled brine or blasts of extremely cold air. The methods looked promising. Birdseye had made the discovery by accident. While engaged in fox-farming on Labrador, he caught trout through the ice to feed the foxes and his sled dogs. He found that low air-temperatures quickly froze trout, and in that state they kept their fresh taste for a week or more. I am sure Birdseye had no idea that his fruitful observation would eventually revolutionize the marketing of food worldwide.

To gather data at sea, the laboratory operated a steam-driven, former Grimsby trawler. We investigated fishing areas with this ship from Nova Scotia to northern Labrador. For several years, I spent months at sea. I also used wooden sailing vessels called bankers, a type made famous by the beautiful Lunenburg schooner, *Bluenose.*

My first cruise to collect biological data on one of these fishing vessels was made in March, 1932. Fortune Bay, on the south coast of Newfoundland, was the home area of a fleet of sailing bankers. These fifty schooners were the last of a once-famous north Atlantic fleet of

After the catch is examined by biologists, the crew clean the fish which in this case are to be salted and stowed below deck.

salt-cod fishermen that used to range over the offshore banks from the Virginia Capes to Labrador. But East Coast fishermen, both U.S. and Canadian, were turning to the fresh-fish trade, and diesel draggers were supplanting the sailing banker.

The ship in which I sailed was named *Democracy*. She had been built in 1912 at Essex, Massachusetts, and her hard-pine planking and tall spars were still sound after twenty years of hard work. In length about one hundred twenty feet, with a displacement of one hundred fifty tons, she was able to stow two hundred thousand pounds of salt cod. Our crew consisted of captain, cook, twenty fishermen, and a deck boy. *Democracy* carried ten dories, with two fishermen manning each dory.

The first spring fishing trip is known locally as a "frozen baiting." Shore fishermen who live on the fjords at the head of Fortune Bay carry on a March herring fishery. Herring is the best bait available at this time of year. We bought eighty barrels at $1.50 per barrel. Placed on racks overnight the herring froze solid. In this condition, they were stowed in the ship's bait lockers.

We sailed from the harbor of Fortune at noon on Good Friday, March 25, with all sails set to a fresh northwest wind. During the

Deck of a sailing banker. Notice the large cable coiled near the bow used in anchoring on the banks in fair weather. Dories have their sails set to dry.

Without auxilliary power, a banker depends on her crew in dories to tow her out of harbor.

afternoon, we put into the harbor of St. Pierre, a French possession, located south of the Burin Peninsula, about forty miles from Fortune. The captain wished to pick up a spare storm staysail and a truckload of empty whiskey cases; firewood for the cabin stove. The St. Pierre waterfront was busy loading rum runners with cases of liquor for deserted beaches on Long Island and other hideouts along the coast of the U.S.A. Captain Hannrigan, *Democracy*'s skipper, a short burly man, active in spite of his sixty years, picked up information from one of the smugglers that the Nova Scotia banks were free of ice. He thought we would probably head in that direction to begin fishing.

My journal states: "We are under way again; course SW by S from St. Pierre's Gallantry Head; wind fair at ten knots. How pleasant to feel the ship under sail, moving with a gentle lifting motion. The mainsheet strains; blocks creak softly. A swirling pool of water marks our wake. We sail into the sunset of a peaceful evening. The main cabin is the gathering place for most of the crew. The ten dory

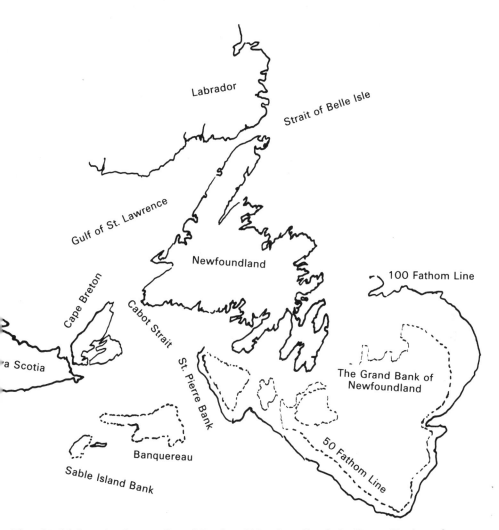

The chief fishing banks are: Grand Banks of Newfoundland, St. Pierre Bank, and the banks off the coast of Nova Scotia.

skippers sleep here in cubbyhole-like bunks along each side of the cabin. The captain and I share a large wide bunk in a tiny stateroom on the starboard side. Crew not on watch busy themselves in various ways seated on a narrow shelf in front of the bunks; one fixes his lignum vitae trawl roller; another bends a new flag on his trawl buoy. Radio has just given weather report: 'fresh NW wind becoming strong SW with snow tomorrow.' On deck, wind is bitter cold. Seawater temperature must be close to thirty-three degrees. Sighted drift ice just before dark. We tacked to the south and east."

The Nova Scotian fishing banks lie about one hundred fifty miles from Fortune Bay. Given average weather conditions, a vessel can reach the area in a day or two. We took nine days.

Day after day we met drift ice whether we tacked to the west or to the east. The ship had to heave-to in a series of gales. Captain Hannrigan decided to head northwest—to get inside the icepack near the mouth of Cabot Strait on the Newfoundland side. We skirted the ice-edge only to find that the heavy floes extended all the way to the coast. The ship was put about again to sail southward until drift ice was no longer a barrier. Constant fog had prevented Captain Hannrigan from getting a noon sun-sight or any celestial observation by which to establish a line of position. Having to heave-to and drift made accurate dead reckoning a real problem. We really did not know where we were with any reasonable degree of accuracy. In this uncertain, worrisome state, a sudden lift in the fog, one afternoon, disclosed that we might be nearing land. A sounding was made, but before the ship could bear off, we found *Democracy* surrounded by breakers; the schooner struck several times, but fortunately there was a heavy swell running which carried the ship over the back of the reef into deeper water. The grounding must have taken a slice out of the keel but there seemed to be no other damage.

Thankful for our narrow escape, we bore away south, resolved to continue in that direction.

Next morning, the fair wind dropped to a cold damp wheeze. Towering swells, like whaleback mountains, now beset the ship from several directions, creating a confused pattern. *Democracy* drifted with all sails set among thousands of small pans of ice like grossly overgrown white lily pads floating on the surface of the ocean. The schooner rolled first to one side, then to the other; rising up, up, on the swelling oily wave, then twisting and settling into the deep trough. The mainsail filled as the ship reached the crest, hung limp as the hull descended, then filled again with a thunderous report. The main boom swung outboard, wrenching the sheet bar-tight with such a jerk, I wondered how long the deck bolts securing the mainsheet blocks would hold. A diesel-powered trawler, out of New York, fishing for halibut, passed under our stern. She hailed us for any fishing news. When she reduced speed to speak to us, her hull and superstructure would completely disappear from sight as she sank into the trough of a sea. Moments later she would reappear on the back of a wave as if she were about to be launched into the air like a rocket.

The dreary day passed slowly until, at sunset, the night wind pushed us forward again.

On April 4 *Democracy* rounded the extreme south end of the icefield, and by tidal eddies on the surface of the ocean the captain judged we were nearing the edge of Banquereau, a Nova Scotian

Democracy, a ten-dory banker, is becalmed in loose ice on the way to fishing ground.

fishing ground. During the night, we came upon a small fleet of eleven Newfoundland schooners at anchor. Crews on most of the vessels were cleaning the day's catch. Around two small tables on the foredeck a team of three men gutted the cod, removed the head, and then cut out the backbone. The splitting tables were red with blood and gurry while on each side of the big deckhouse, in glistening black or yellow oilskins, fishermen armed with flashing knives were chopping mounds of frozen herring—tomorrow's bait for thousands of trawl hooks. In the rigging, like tea-kettles with two flaming spouts, small tin kerosene lamps cast over the shadowy scene an orange-tinted glare that mingled with reflections of green and red navigation lights in the dark ocean.

We sailed slowly through the fleet, Captain Hannrigan at the wheel. He ranged *Democracy* close to certain vessels to exchange fishing information. At midnight, we anchored in ninety fathoms.

About 3 A.M. next morning, our dorymen were roused by the captain. After a quick mug-up, the crew began to chop frozen herring to bait the long-line trawls. Each trawl consists of twenty eight stout lines, and each line has about one hundred fifty hooks attached to it by short leaders. Before daylight, the dories were hoisted overboard and the dorymen rowed away from the ship to set trawl, each on a given compass course. *Democracy* was fishing at last.

During my four years with the Marine Laboratory, I gained a great deal of pleasure from various seagoing assignments by being an attentive listener. Many fishermen or sailors, afloat or ashore, were eager to describe incidents in their lives which may not have been too unusual in their view, but which, to me, were fascinating. I also found, in some cases, events meant a great deal to an individual, as if, at one point in time, this ordinary person, often inarticulate, even illiterate in the general sense, had achieved a high level of personal awareness and sense of worth.

During one rough night, when I was on deck, sheets of spray swept aft as *Democracy* plunged into and pushed aside the wind-blown crests of breaking seas. An elderly doryman, on watch at my side, said: "I mind [remember] a terrible August gale when I was a young man. We were anchored on the eastern edge of Grand Bank; three hundred fathoms of cable out. Gale sprung on us without any warning. While we were at anchor, the schooner's riding sail was up, to help keep the vessel's head to windward. Somehow, the force of the first blast of wind tore the sail adrift from the sheet and the sail began to flog the main rigging. There was no way to muzzle the sail whipping around like that; it would cut off a man's head; so what with the

Crew cutting frozen herring into small pieces to bait the trawl hooks.

rearing of the vessel in the seas and the strain on the rigging, the spar commenced to weave like a spintop. Before we could do much of anything to relieve the strain, the force of the sea and the twisting ship broke off the mainmast not much above the deck. There must have been a weak spot there. Anyhow, blue water poured over the bulwarks like a raging river. The captain, in his cabin below decks, thought the ship was sinking and wouldn't come on deck. I got an axe and cut the mooring cable (hated to see that fine cable go); called all hands to man the pumps; cut away the main rigging so the mainmast wouldn't punch a hole in the side of the ship. The broken spar lay across the deck, lodging on the bulwarks. With every sea it was like a battering ram, chewing up the taffrail; a threat to the vessel's survival. Somehow, we were able to clear away the mess of rigging and roll the spar overboard, so the sea could carry away the wreckage from the ship. Then, we turned to the foresail and double-reefed it; if we got the sail up, we could heave-to properly or run before the gale. But before we were able to rig the canvas, a great roaring monster of a wave broke over the bow. We all grabbed something solid for dear life. The sea broke up the nest of dories on the port side —swept them clean away, and drove one of the crew through a fish box. He was badly bruised but no broken bones, thanks be to God!

In fine weather, a ship may anchor so that dories will set trawl in a starfish pattern using the ship as a center.

A wild night, that way, boy! But we saved the schooner for the owners and for ourselves, I suppose. And they thanked me."

The life of a Banks fisherman is filled with many hazards, especially during sudden winter storms that sweep over the cold ocean waters. On such a night, the laboratory's research trawler *Cape Aquihas* was hove-to on the Grand Banks. Our ship, although old in years, was a stout craft and we were in no danger. Captain Gabe Fudge and I shared a cabin located directly below the ship's pilothouse. A narrow ladder on the wall was the only means of entering or leaving the cabin and it led directly to the ship's helm. A gimbald overhead compass on the ceiling recorded the trawler's heading. Gabe glanced at the compass occasionally as he reminisced about his years in sailing bankers.

Gabe said: "We had a rough time, one winter fishing trip. I remember it well. From Belleoram, Fortune Bay, we sailed the first day of February—a mighty cold day—with bait lockers filled with frozen herring. The *Santos* was about one hundred thirty tons, a fine-looking schooner, practically new, only two years old, built in Shelburne,

Nova Scotia. For gear we had the best of everything—spanking fine sails, new running rigging, miles of trawl, spare equipment, ice axes and ice pounders and lots of grub. We sailed as far west as Rose Blanche Bank, swung over the dories, and each dory set a few tubs of trawl. The day started out fine, warmish for February. By the time the dories had taken back their gear, the sky was clouding, and before we had all the dories back on board, I could see the weather was making up for a dirty night. Soon, fog shut down thick . . . southeast wind with snow flurries. Later, the wind chopped around to the north and began to freshen fast. By dark, a living gale had hold of us. Salt spray froze on everything. No canvas could stand that wind. We wrestled the sails as best we could. The big mainsail had been furled early on. We handed the staysail but the foresail was iced up so much we couldn't get stops on it. We tied down the gaff as securely as possible and put a vang on the boom to ease strain on the foresheet, and I made sure every opening on the deck and cabin house was covered and snug, booby hatches and any other place through which water might enter the hull. Even though hove-to, the violence of the sea made any physical movement a slow strenous effort, almost a struggle for existence.

"All night, under bare poles, we ran before the seas. While the vessel was hove-to, when we snugged her down, the man at the wheel, watching the breaking seas instead of the ship's head, let her broach a bit and a few big ones came on board. Two of the crew were thrown against the windlass and were injured. We did the best we could for them at the time. In the freezing weather and flying spray *Santos* iced up quickly. The foredeck was soon like an iceberg; the nested dories a solid mass. We had to take the cook out of the fo'c'sle. All hands gathered in the cabin with the hatch battened down. *Santos* was logging about ten knots but we couldn't do anything to slow her down. The vessel was deep in the water from weight of ice. Force of the gale tore off the tops of the seas and flying sprindrift beat like hail on the helmsman.

"From our general heading, to be safe, we had to clear Seal Rocks off St. Pierre. For seven hours I took the wheel myself. When the schooner was heading to windward while we snugged down, a man couldn't stand more than five minutes at the wheel; a face would freeze, even in that short time.

"When I was steering, my big sheepskin coat and collar, covered by oilclothes and sou'wester, were so coated with ice the wind didn't seem to get at me. Not that I was not uncomfortable, but I was not starving with cold. The worst nuisance was the slippery deck. When the ship would rear up on a sea and then plunge into those clumpers, it was a struggle to hang on to the wheel and at the same time keep a steady footing.

"And, of course, it was pitch dark.

"One of the crew, Jim Smith, stood by me (if I was near starving with limited food I couldn't refuse that man my share of grub). Jim crawled out of the cabin somehow and got the door shut between the worst seas. He tied himself to a ring bolt in the deck; with a piece of oak he beat the spokes of the wheel, freeing them from the encasing ice. Otherwise, I would not have been able to continue steering. Jim was a Roman Catholic in a crew of Protestants. Every now and again, when he would feel the schooner rise on the back of a sea and catch sight of a terrifying mass of water foaming down on us, he'd make the sign of the Cross on that sea. I'd say to myself: 'All right, old man. If you think that sign does any good, keep it up. I'm for you.'

"Down in the cabin, the cold must have been as perishing as it was on deck. There was no fire; the stovepipe was stuffed shut. When *Santos* would bury herself in a foaming graybeard, the deadlights in the deck would reflect green sea, as water filled the scuppers and sluiced down the deck. The noise of rushing water must have sounded ominous to the men below. I'd hear a muffled shout from someone in the cabin, 'She's gone this time . . . gone this time, boys.' But I'd say to myself, as the stern rose again, 'No, she's not gone yet. . . .' But oh my, it was rough!

"One time, Smith looked forward and said, 'Skipper, I can't see any dories on the port side.'

"I kept looking between seas. Sure enough, the entire nest, all those six dories nested together, were clean gone. Certainly, I never saw them go. When the ship would be smothered by a sea, pieces of ice torn from the mass on the foredeck, pieces as big as a growler, would surge across the waist. With the air full of sea smoke, spray, and frost, I couldn't make out anything forward of the cabin house.

"Smith and I rigged a clever dodge to keep the compass-hole clear. The compass was in a tiny lighted space on the back of the cabin house, opposite the wheel. The opening to the compass was closed by a sliding wooden shutter. With all that water surging around and freezing where it landed, we'd never been able to keep the compass-hole free of ice. Smith found a long-handled string mop wedged in the scuppers. When the deck would fill with a sea, he would plug the compass-hole with the mop. Then, after a while, we would take a peek to see how the schooner was heading. It was a job to keep the mop from freezing stiff but somehow Smith would stamp off the ice. Anyhow, we kept the opening free enough so that we could check the course.

"Towards morning, I was beaten out, completely pooped. Had to lie down for a spell. I called George Mills, whom I could depend on, to take the wheel and to call me if he thought the schooner wasn't riding well. In oilclothes, sheepskin coat, rubber boots, I fell into bunk. But I wasn't down for long before George woke me to say the ship was listing badly to starboard. We had better do something quick.

"The nest of dories that remained on the starboard side was a mountain of ice and made the ship list quite a bit. Forward, she was as much like an iceberg as a vessel could be.

"I called the crew to come on deck. All hands turned out except for two men; the biggest fellows too. My God! I said things to those two men that I'd find hard to repeat. But they stayed in bunk, sniveling like spoiled children. They were frightened to death. 'She's going to sink,' they said, 'there's no use doing anything to try to save her.'

"Well, with the rest of the men working with ice hammers; breaking ice loose from dories, stanchions, scuppers, running rigging, and getting it overboard, all the while watching out and hanging on so as not to go overboard themselves, the ship was lightened considerable.

"When sea and wind began to moderate, I said, 'Now boys, let's get the jumbo on her.' Some job to set that staysail! We set a course for St. Pierre and, at dusk, even in light snow, caught sight of Gallantry Head light.

"Next morning, after jogging around all night, I thought we'd get into St. Pierre roadstead but I'damned if the wind didn't come down nor'west again . . . hard. We had to run off once more, but we hove-to that night and got some sleep. Next day, wind moderated and veered, permitting us to head towards Fortune Bay and our home port, Belleoram.

"I forgot to mention, that when we set the jumbo after that long struggle, the cook was able to get down into the galley through the forward booby hatch. We had some deer meat in a locker and the cook prepared a big meal; the first real food we had eaten in several days. I can tell you, that feed of venison was a tasty bit.

"After a few days home in Belleoram, we put on fresh supplies, picked up six new dories, and set sail again."

The *Cape Agulhas,* our research trawler, carried a crew of twenty-five, including the engine-room gang. All the fishermen had formerly served as dorymen in sailing bankers during some period of their lives. These men often commented on the strong feeling of personal safety each one experienced living and working on a trawler com-

In winter when sudden storms often occurred, the captain might decide to make a flying set in which dories are dropped in a long line as the vessel sails a compass course and then reverses to pick up the dories.

pared with the rigors of dory fishing. Of course, steam or diesel trawlers were not immune to accidental loss. Sometimes they caught fire. A trawler could pile up on ledges trying to make harbor in fog just as easily or more easily than a sailing vessel, because of their speed. And trawlers sometimes disappear with all hands—never return to port—overwhelmed by a rogue sea or by some other hazard. But the life of a sailing banker doryman, in winter or summer, is beset by particular dangers. And of these dangers, fog is foremost.

During any time of the year but chiefly in winter a practice known as "making a flying set" is often used to reduce the chance of losing a dory among drift ice or in fog. We made a number of flying sets from *Democracy*. In practice, the captain selects a course to cover whatever area of the bank he considers productive. Under all sail, the vessel proceeds along this course, hoisting out one dory after another at intervals. The men have to scramble quickly into the boat and let go the falls while the schooner sails right on. Trawl is immediately set at right angles to the ship's course. The schooner continues on this course until all dories are away. Then she sails back to the position of the first dory, a distance of eight or ten miles, and begins to pick up dories and men who have, by this time, set and hauled their gear and have a load of codfish or haddock . . . maybe. Flying sets give the skipper a definite line to follow in event of a sudden gale, snow squall or fog. Sometimes, even with this precaution, a dory and the schooner miss connection.

One of the trawler's crew had a brother-in-law who found himself in this perilous situation.

"Not too many years ago, this was," Morgan told me. "In the month of August."

"The skipper of the schooner decided to make a flying set because a greasy look to the morning sky gave him misgivings about the day's weather. Sure enough, before the dories were all aboard, a blanket of fog suddenly rolled down, thick as mud. Ned Forsey was a dory skipper; he was an experienced fisherman, but his helper was a young lad, only eighteen, on his first trip to the banks. Ned had taken him as a dory mate because the young fellow had begged to go with him, and he was a strong, husky chap that had the makings of a good fisherman.

"When Ned saw the curtain of fog shutting-in his horizon, he decided to stop overhauling the trawl, drop the gear, and row directly in the general direction of the schooner; the trawl could be picked up next day or later. This decision turned out to be unwise. In the fog, they never found the ship.

"Before the realization that they were lost hit them, both men rowed vigorously; laying on their oars, now and again, to listen for the schooner's horn. No sound broke the stillness except for the lapping of gentle waves against the sides of the dory. They shouted again and again but there was no welcoming reply.

"By nightfall they were still adrift.

"Fortunately, the sea was calm as often happens in thick weather. By some mischance the dory's sail had been left aboard the schooner, otherwise they would have considered the possibility of sailing to land. Next day, in spite of the persisting fog, they had strong hopes of being rescued. The older man kept up the young fellow's spirit by telling him that he was sure the schooner would find them. (The ship did actively search the area for three days, but the dory must have drifted beyond reach in the fog.)

"On the morning of the fourth day, Ned decided to open the emergency food and water rations that all dories carried. They had

Following a centuries-old tradition, Portuguese vessels sail westward to New-foundland to fish for cod.

eaten nothing since breakfast four days previous. To their intense disappointment, the food was contaminated and putrid. Evidently the cannister had rusted through in several places along a seam and had not been inspected before the ship left port. The bitterness of the men gave way to rage and black feelings of despair. But they turned again to the oars, vowing to row to land.

"Ned still tried to encourage the younger man whose strength was weakening. After a week without food, the fierce hunger and thirst was replaced by a gnawing feeling in the gut. The foggy weather which had persisted all week was followed by day after day of clear, blue sky, bright sun, and a gentle breeze. The castaways longed for rain even if it took a gale to bring a refreshing shower. But no rain fell. Ned tried to joke, "If we were this long adrift in winter, we'd be froze stiff by now,' but there was little cheerfulness left in them. Mechanically they both kept on rowing most of each day, but vigor had long gone from the stroke. The dory was not making much headway towards land.

"To keep up sagging spirits, they sang hymns and songs and wore out their eyes on the sharp rim of the horizon. Tragically, there was no hook or line in the dory they could use to catch a fish. The boy's flesh seemed to fade away. Ned dipped his wool mitts in the sea and each sucked the moisture. He had a feeling if they drank salt water it would destroy their minds, but couldn't help trying to relieve thirst by sucking the mittens.

"After fourteen days, the condition of the boy was serious. His eyes were sunk into his head and skin barely covered his skeleton. And he was badly constipated.

"On the morning of the fifteenth day, he died quietly.

"Ned's spirits touched rock bottom. He took in his oars and rested; wondered what he should do with the body.

"Next morning, as he sat on the thwart and tried to get some circulation in his arms and legs, his eyes swept the horizon as they had searched, hour after hour, for sixteen days. At first, he did not comprehend what his eye picked up. He kept looking intently. A three-masted sailing vessel with yards on her foremast and under full sail was converging towards him. Seizing the oars and summoning all his waning strength, he rowed in the direction of the barkentine.

"A Portuguese fishing vessel, homebound, ranged alongside and hoisted abroad the dory with Ned and the dead boy.

"On board the ship the Portuguese cook, not unfamiliar with castaways, fed the survivor liberal amounts of gruel in spite of Ned's insistence that he needed solid food—a square meal. A day or so later, a Newfoundland banker was sighted; Ned was transferred to her and eventually he was landed in Fortune Bay.

"After a month's rest in a hospital, he had recovered much of his lost weight and strength. Glad to be alive, he said he figured fishing was his way of earning a living. Come next spring he would like to sail again."

One member of the trawler's crew, Levi Parsons, delighted in relating tales of strange and mysterious happenings at sea and on

The Portuguese use small one-man dories, about half the size of those found on Nova Scotian or Newfoundland bankers. The advantage is that many more fishermen are setting trawls and covering an extensive area.

land. He firmly believed in his yarns. They were proof, he considered, of the definite limits surrounding human knowledge of reality, or as he observed, "We people don't know everything."

While the ship was hove-to, one Sunday afternoon, to give the crew a rest, Levi confied to me an incident that had taken place some years ago when he was a doryman on the sailing banker *Paloma*.

"We went to sea in the early part of January," he said. "And in a gale on St. Pierre Bank sprung the foremast a couple of inches, so the skipper decided to run for shelter and repair the damage. We made into the village of Harbour Buffet, a snug port on the south end of Long Island, Placentia Bay. While *Paloma* lay at anchor there, a man came aboard with a hardship story: he had been sick during the past summer; most of the codfish he had caught were sunburned on the flakes when he was drying the catch; he netted herring in the fall but hadn't enough to feed his family all winter; they were short of food, near starving. So the skipper gave him a barrel of flour, a few pounds of tea, salt beef, beans, and molasses, and the poor fellow rowed away overjoyed. A day or two later we sailed for the banks again, having put the ship to rights.

"Now, the weather that winter and spring was the worst you ever saw. Gale after gale; nor'east, sou'west, no matter the direction; wind, sea, and cold made hell of a doryman's life. Twice the western boats from Rose Blanche were caught in a norther. Coated in ice, with canvas shredded, several went aground and were broken up on the long beach of Miquelon.

"In spite of rough weather, our fishing was good. *Paloma* worked over the eastern side of Green Bank, that is, to the eastward of St. Pierre Bank. Whenever the sea was civil enough to set gear and we were able to underrun our trawl twice in a day, we'd have a full doryload of cod every time. The skipper wanted the vessel loaded before we returned to Fortune Bay but our supply of bait ran low, so he decided to put into Harbour Buffet again to pick up enough herring to finish the voyage. Buffet is a great place for herring.

"*Paloma* had logged more than fifty miles heading landward when a howling nor'easter brought snow squalls and thick fog. The wind was on our starboard quarter. We could keep going fairly well under reefed foresail and reefed jumbo or staysail. The mainsail was snugged down before the canvas froze still. We had ample sea-room except for Lamb Rock—a three-fathom spot on our course in the middle of the ocean—and a treacherous breaking reef called St. Mary's Cay offshore from Cape St. Marys. Many a ship had been lost on that breaker.

"The old *Paloma* was making pretty good weather in the storm,

Levi could tell a good story.

although she was rolling quite a lot without the steady effect of the
mainsail. An occasional sea broke over the bulwarks with a surge of
white water across the deck. A bucket or two slopped over the high
sill of the fo'c'sle companionway. I was off watch with five of the crew
and the cook in the fo'c'sle. We lay in bunk all standing, you know
—oilclothes and everything on, just in case we had to jump quick.
The other fellows were asleep but the rolling and pitching made me
nervous. The fo'c'sle's oil lamp flickered in the draft from the scuttle.
Jackets and trousers, hung on a line to dry over the stove, swayed
back and forward and twisted around with the motion of the vessel
as if they were in some way live things.

"After a while, the ship's motion increased as if we were getting into shoal water or had changed course. I climbed out of bunk and stuck my head out of the companionway to have a look. In spite of the thick fog and the late afternoon, there was still enough daylight to see around. The wind had kicked up a savage sea. My dear man, the breaking crests of those combers were coming aboard with every roll now. Spray was flying. With the main boom tied down I couldn't see aft very well, but when the fore boom lifted, every now and then, I saw the skipper at the wheel. He was steering. He always liked to steer in a storm. Then I caught sight of another figure crouching in the wind near the captain. I thought to myself, now, that is queer. The captain had said he wanted the watch on deck to stand right in the eyes of her, on the bow, to catch sight of anything ahead that would bring danger to ship.

"I crawled out of the hatch and looked forward. She was burying her bowsprit now, every time she pitched by the head. I counted the watch . . . one, two, three . . . three to port and three to starboard. That's peculiar, I said to myself. Six on watch, and two aft. Going below, I counted the sleeping crew; five and myself made six, and the cook. We only had fourteen all told on board, including captain and cook! Perhaps I was mistaken about seeing a man aft with the captain, although I was almost sure I saw one. As I was mulling over this puzzle, holding on the fo'c'sle ladder, I felt the schooner heel, a kind of shudder. Jumping up the steps, I heard the captain shout, 'Hard down hard, sir,' as if repeating an order.

"On deck there was noise and confusion. The schooner had jibed. Foresail and staysail booms crashed to starboard as the wind came over the stern. Before the ship settled on port tack, the booms swung back and forth with canvas rattling like cannon. The men on watch were yelling and pointing to starboard. About seventy five yards astern, just visible in the fog, huge seas curled high and broke—a fearsome sight. Those breakers could only be the Key! St. Mary's Cays!

"I stood in the companionway and watched as we drew away from danger. Then I looked aft at the captain. He was standing at the wheel. But he was alone. Just the captain at the wheel.

"I ran aft as he brought *Paloma* back on starboard tack, on our course to land.

"What happened, skipper?" I cried, grabbing a handhold on the wheelbox.

"My God, Lev," he said, "that was a close one!" We were heading straight for the Cays, straight for the breaker, when I felt a touch on my arm. I glanced around. I could swear that a man stood by me . . . 'Hard down,' says he. 'Quick!' So I put the wheel over and she jibed. When I looked again . . . he was gone. We may have been well paid for that flour, I think!

"I didn't know what to make of all that. But we just missed a bad job on the Cays, that's for sure.

"Two days later we reached Harbour Buffet. It appeared that they were holding a wake in one of the houses. Who had died? The very same poor fellow the skipper had helped with the food. And, would you believe it! The hour of his death was just about when he saved us from the Cays!

"Now adjust your mind to that."

12

Coastal Cruising

While engaged in various biological projects in Newfoundland, I had many opportunities to work along the perimeter of the island, as well as the offshore banks. In fact, I managed to travel, either on foot or by small boat, the entire length of the sourth and west coasts and certain bays of the northeast shore. I grew to love the rugged escarpment facing the sea and the warm-hearted, hard-working people.

In 1951, after an absence of fifteen years, I visited Newfoundland in my own boat, a sixty-four-foot motor sailor, designed and named *Seal* by William Hand, a noted designer of New Bedford. Two of my sons, my elderly father, and some lads of college age made up an enthusiastic crew. From Woods Hole, Cape Cod, *Seal* visited several harbors along the Maine and Nova Scotian coasts, since this was a new cruising ground for most of the ship's company. Then we decided on a west to east circumnavigation of Newfoundland.

For various reasons we ran out of allotted time, however, and had to leave the south coast leg for another year. We were able to do that in 1952.

For some time I had been collecting information about a tragedy that had taken place on the south coast on 1942: Two U.S. Naval vessels ran ashore in a snowstorm with great loss of life. I had read all the Court Martial reports of this incident and wanted to visit the specific site. Owing to a sudden storm and dense fog, we nearly wrecked *Seal* in the same spot where the ships had been lost. I was, however, able to collect some eye-witness accounts of the wreck and rescue operations.

One of the chief projects on *Neptune*'s 1977 cruise to Newfound-

Ramea Island is one of the largest south-coast trading centers.

land was to visit again the scene of the tragedy, as well as to call at some of my favorite harbors alongshore and on the Labrador coast.

Having made landfall at Cinq Cerf Bay, we turned to cruise eastward. I knew there was a fish-freezing plant at Ramea Islands, a small archipelago about ten miles off the mainland. We looked forward to getting fresh cod or flounder. Since refrigerator ships make regular trips to Halifax or Boston, the general store might stock vegetables hard to find elsewhere on this coast.

The fog of early morning had not burned off as much as I had hoped. *Neptune's* log states: "Rough . . . confused southeast lop; visibility about two hundred yards . . . used fathometer to follow depth contour lines . . . located lighthouse at the western end of the largest island. A passage between islands leads to the village. About one hundred houses, mostly square boxes with flat roofs, scattered alongshore and the sides of low hills, form the settlement. Four windows and a door indicate the front of a house; the flat roof implies light snow accumulation from winter storms. The landscape is bleak; no trees soften the hills. Patches of gray granite push aside brown and green mosses; clumps of curly dock, scurvy grass and wild celery struggle for roothold. In some northern communities, brightly painted houses compensate for lack of color in landscape, but paint salesmen have yet to reach Ramea. We buy excellent fresh fish and are under way again."

Ten miles due east of Ramea, on the mainland, a tide-swept channel between high hills leads into a fjord named Grey River, although the actual river does not begin to assume its form until the northeast arm has penetrated the interior for another eight miles. Then, some ten miles further on, above tidewater, the Grey descends from the high upland plateau in a series of beautiful falls, which few people have seen, for although the Grey has splendid upriver salmon pools, terrain is rough and, in places, almost impassable.

Since the outer coast is wrapped in a cocoon of fog, we spend two days in this many-branched arm of the sea. The steep-sided narrow river valleys, overlooked by ranges of brooding desolate hills, establish an awesome sense of isolation. The landscape presents a face that has scarcely changed in twenty thousand years . . . since the last glaciers departed.

Dawn of July 4 promises a clear exhilarating sail; we are soon under way. Appropriately, we sight an eagle soaring above the rugged cliffs of the fjord where the bird probably has its nest. The seacoast in this area is spectacular: deep water allows a vessel to sail close to the shore which rises abruptly to a fourteen-hundred-foot high plateau. Narrow waterfalls drift down the mountain sides; sometimes glistening like a single rope of pearls, sometimes woven into a complex braid. Splendid craggy capes, like Cape La Hune, extend into the sea, guarding entrances to numerous extensive bays. So much of the coast invites a closer look: U-shaped valleys eroded by glacial scourings, limestone hills probably containing Paleozoic fossils. A yacht's crew could spend an entire summer investigating the inlets and island-studded bays of the south coast.

Neptune entered one of the smaller bays to visit the town of Francois. In spite of the French name, most of the families are of English descent. Years ago, on another cruise, I made friends with several of the villagers, unfortunately two of them have since died and the other family has moved to Nova Scotia, but I want my crew to see the village, so we point *Neptune*'s bow toward the tiny lighthouse perched on the side of the towering headland and eventually tie up to a wharf.

Francois, a string of small houses and fish shacks that look as if they were nestling against the interior wall of a volcano's crater, is a typical south coast fishing settlement. Years ago, the village had no outside communication with the rest of the country, except for the fortnightly visit of a mail- and freight-carrying steamer. The twenty-five years since my last visit has brought some changes: fishermen now sell their cod and salmon to a freezing plant instead of salting and drying the catch; and descending from a precipitous slope behind some of the houses, a cat's cradle of wires suggest a TV aerial or a radio-telephone antenna. After an hour ashore, we set sail again planning to spend the night in one of the many small bays of the huge fjord called Bay d'Espoir, which extends inland for forty miles. During afternoon, a front is obviously overtaking us. Clouds begin to accumulate; rain pelts down; fierce gusts sweep the bay; we steer *Neptune* into coves, skirt islands, and cautiously thread narrow passages until toward sunset the weather clears. We anchor for the night in an attractive place called Roti Bay. *Neptune* is now nearly twenty miles from the ocean. Rolling hills of moderate height covered with groves of small spruce interspersed with rocky ridges characterize this inland landscape. Again, the sense of isolation is impressive. I found many delicate insectivorous pitcher plants and small bog orchids during a ramble ashore. There is no sign of land mammals. Moose, common on the south coast, are usually encountered much further inland.

Next day, after further exploration among islands, we turn *Neptune* seaward again. Hermitage Bay is full of fog, but with few offshore dangers on our course we eventually find our way into Harbour Breton, a fishing village well known from the sixteenth century to the present.

I draw my crew's attention to a group of substantial brick buildings across the harbor from *Neptune*. That's the former Newman & Company premises, I tell them. Newman's of Dartmouth, a very old Devonshire trading firm, was one of the first West of England companies to exploit Cabot's discovery that codfish were plentiful in Newfoundland. Newman's had prospered in the French wine trade during the mid-1400s and had built a fleet of cargo-carrying ships. Newfoundland dried salt cod were taken to Portugal, a good customer for such product, and bartered for port wine for which there was ready sale in England. After defeat of the Armada in 1588, a struggle which had interfered with trade, the company, now Newman and Ropes, expanded and imported wine, salt, cork, and dried fruit from Portugal and sent back wheat, wool, sugar, and manufactured goods. The history of commerce is more interesting than people imagine. Here is another example: One day in the autumn of 1679, a Newman vessel left Oporto bound for London with a cargo of port wine. In the Bay of Biscay the ship was sighted by a large

Francois village nestles at the base of a high escarpment.

French privateer which gave chase. Rather than fight an unequal battle and risk the cargo (Newman's ships were permitted by the government to carry guns for defense) the Englishman spread all sail and ran before the wind. The ship evaded her pursuer but was now in mid-Atlantic buffeted by an October gale. The captain decided to continue westward to Newfoundland where he would find shelter at Harbour Breton. When in the following spring the cargo of wine was examined in England, bouquet and fine flavor were so exceptional, the wine experts concluded that a transatlantic passage and winter layover improved the wine. Ever since this incident Newman's port has been sent to Newfoundland for storage and eventually returned to England.

Another footnote to Harbour Breton history is linked to the war of 1812. Newman's brig *Duck,* en route to Newfoundland to pick up a load of dried cod, was also ferrying forty young men to work at Harbour Breton and other Newman and Ropes plantations. These were indentured workers; that is, hired to stay in the colony for three years and two summers, after which they could remain on the island or be returned home. They were given free passage both ways. This custom provided a supply of apprentices and led to a start in business for many young men. The brig *Duck,* unfortunately, was captured by an American privateer, but before the prize crew reached a New England harbor, *Duck* was recaptured by an English ship. About the same time, Captain Broke of H.M.S. *Shannon,* on a cruise out of Halifax, Nova Scotia, found his frigate extremely shorthanded. He had captured many American ships which had to be returned to Halifax. The number of his ship's company had been greatly reduced by the necessity to supply each prize with a crew. By chance, the English privateer with *Duck* astern came over the horizon. Since an engagement with the U.S.S. *Chesapeake* seemed imminent, Broke knew that her crew greatly outnumbered his reduced company, so he ordered the English ship to heave-to. Broke was surprised to find so many capable replacements; he quickly "borrowed" twenty of the *Duck*'s passengers. The young lads fought so well in the famous naval battle with the U.S.S. *Chesapeake* on June 1, 1813, that Newman & Co. was subsequently allowed to fly the British naval white ensign from the flagstaff at Harbour Breton.

For *Neptune*'s crew, an unexpected event in Harbour Breton was the discovery of a telephone. Since we had been out of touch with home for several weeks, the ability to communicate by long distance was appreciated. Alex Bell would have been pleased to hear our cries of delight in praise of his remarkable invention. Harbour Breton had also recently been connected by a road to the Trans-Canada High-

way. No longer was this section of the south coast completely isolated. Refrigerated trucks carrying frozen seafood produced at the
local freezer could now be driven to Port aux Basques, to reach the
mainland across Cabot Strait via government car ferry. We were
invited to visit the freezing plant and bought delicious fresh cod and
salmon.

After several days at this historic harbor *Neptune* again ventured
beyond the headlands into the fog. In spite of the cold cloudy
weather, visibility improved as we crossed the wide mouth of Fortune Bay. By afternoon, when the low silhouette of the French island
of St. Pierre came into view on the southern horizon, patches of blue
sky welcomed us to this unique island—a small remnant of the once
extensive French empire in North America.

A small incident reveals the sensitive nerve of French nationalism.
As we cautiously approached the stone wharf adjacent to the custom-
house, I noticed, among a group of bystanders who had gathered to
inspect the arrival of a foreign yacht, a smartly dressed gendarme
eyeing *Neptune* intently and somewhat critically. During the time
we had been in Canadian waters, we had been flying a courtesy flag
from the starboard spreader—a Canadian flag, red and white with
maple leaf emblem. The Canadian flag had evidently attracted the
gendarme's attention. He began pointing, shouting and waving his
arms. George Campbell, fluent in French, gathered that he was or-
dering us to remove the Canadian flag. "You are now in France," the
gendarme reiterated. "You must fly the flag of France!" When we
finally got some lines ashore on the bollards, which were large can-
nons half buried in the concrete surface of the wharf, George was
able to communicate with the excited official. After an apology for
our lack of a tricolor, George promised that as soon as customs had
finished our entry papers, the captain would most certainly secure a
suitable flag. The episode ended by my buying a fine French tricolor
for ten dollars at the shop nearest to the wharf and seeing that the
boys flew the flag properly from the spreader.

The history of St. Pierre and the larger but sparsely populated
island adjacent to it, called Miquelon, reflects events that convulsed
Europe from 1540 down to 1940, when Charles de Gaulle appealed
to Frenchmen everywhere to join him in opposing the Vichy government. At that time, St. Pierre became a free French port.

Like the mother country in 1789, St. Pierre experienced its Revolu-
tion, Reign of Terror, Jacobin Club, and, under the Empire, a minia-
ture coup d'état. Over the centuries the island suffered extraordinary
vicissitudes of fortune: such as wild prosperity during the U.S. prohi-
bition experiment and deep depression during the 1930s. In the 1500s

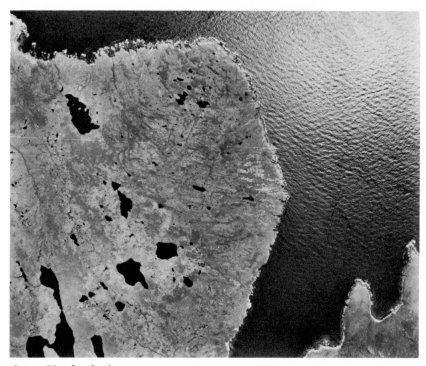

Lawn Head, a high promontory, slopes gradually toward a formidable wall of rock thrust into the ocean. Air Photo Division, Canadian Government.

Basques, Bretons, and Normans (who probably gave the island its name) found shelter in the harbor when threatened by storms on the nearby fishing banks. France formally took possession of the island in 1662, when they also erected a fort and established a town at Placentia in Newfoundland. French influence at this time was spreading rapidly over North America. About 1689 Frontenac, governor of New France, realized that the English colonies had to be destroyed or else France would risk losing all that her explorers, missionaries, traders, and armed forces had won. As a result of this decision, French forces with the help of Indian allies began to attack English settlements all over the continent; from Newfoundland (key to control of the St. Lawrence) where St. John's was burnt to the ground, to communities in the Ohio and Hudson River valleys. The Deerfield massacre in 1704 typified the ferocity and horror of Indian border warfare. In the U.S. and Canada this worldwide struggle for Empire is known as the French and Indian Wars; a struggle in which young George Washington learned something of the art of soldiering while attempting to capture Fort Duquesne.

St. Pierre was taken by the English in 1713 and remained in their hands for fifty years. By the Treaty of Paris, the island was given back to France to serve again as a port of refuge for her fishermen. The

British government was well acquainted with the value of St. Pierre as a fishing station and especially as headquarters for the bank fishery. They were also well aware that its dangerous proximity to Newfoundland rendered it a menace to the island. Notwithstanding these facts, the property of the permanent English settlers at St. Pierre was sacrificed. Local realities were usually disregarded when global strategic issues were at stake. The French gave up the port of Madras in India, coveted by the English, in return for regaining St. Pierre.

Events at Louisbourg in Cape Breton provide another example of arbitrary judgment by a government far removed from the effects of its decisions. The French considered Louisbourg a choice location not only from which to attack English colonies but also from which to exploit the extensive nearby fishing grounds. So much money was spent on building and fortifying this seacoast town that Louis XIV was said to have remarked that he expected any day to see the great fortress appear on the western horizon, such vast amounts of money had been spent on its creation. In 1745 an army composed chiefly of New England colonists under General Pepperell and Admiral Warren succeeded in capturing this source of harassment, the famous fortress of Louisbourg which had resisted all previous attempts to reduce it. But in 1748 the Peace of Aix-la-Chapelle restored Cape Breton and Louisbourg to France to the indignation of those who had risked their lives in its conquest.

Neptune's crew spent two delightfully sunny days in St. Pierre, the first clear weather the locals had enjoyed in three weeks. The air service to Sydney, Nova Scotia, which had been grounded, flew sorties day and night taking advantage of the fog-free skies. George Campbell's command of the language smoothed our travail with customs and immigration far better than my limited vocabulary would have done. We were soon free to explore the narrow streets, each with its attractive cluster of shops. The island—people, architecture, ambience—is very French. One thinks immediately of a village in Brittany. The cultural contract to Newfoundland is sharp, although the past insularity has been somewhat reduced owing to the number of summer visitors-for-the-day who come by ferry from the town of Fortune, in Fortune Bay.

Long before dawn on July 9 we took in our lines and headed seaward toward Newfoundland. A magnificent red sunrise heralded another splendid day but indicated deteriorating weather for the morrow. With all sails furled *Neptune* motored over a flat calm sea. Our immediate objective was a precipitous headland on the western side of Placentia Bay, about thirty-five miles distant.

13

Wreck and Rescue

Years ago in the predawn hours of February 18, 1942, the weather along *Neptune*'s present course was not clear and calm. A blinding snowstorm had reduced visibility to a few yards and a roaring north-east gale churned up towering seas. Air temperature was far below freezing. The maelstrom of sea and snow surrounded a U.S. de-stroyer, the U.S.S. *Truxtun*, an old four-stacker. The ship struggled against the heavy seas and low visibility rolling beams under. At 0410, *Truxtun*'s navigator and the officer of the deck were standing in the port wing of the bridge, holding onto the rail to keep their footing on the slippery deck. Simultaneously they sighted a dark object about seventy five yards ahead. Snow squalls made accurate observation difficult. Immediately, the navigator ordered engines stopped. This command was followed by the order: Right rudder, starboard engine full astern. As *Truxtun* commenced swinging to the right, the ship struck. Engines were stopped. The hull appeared to rise up as if on a sloping ledge and slid along for a considerable distance. The cap-tain, Lt. Commander Ralph Hickox, came on the bridge immedi-ately. Word was passed: All hands on deck with life jackets. Engines were again put astern to back the ship down, but wind and sea had swung the stern to port and the stern grounded after the ship had moved a few yards. *Truxtun* was hard and fast aground in a raging sea and a whirling snowstorm.

Why was the U.S.S. *Truxtun* in this part of the Atlantic seaboard?

On September 1, 1939, by order of Adolph Hitler, German air and land forces invaded Poland. A world war had begun. After the fall of France in May, 1940, Winston Churchill, who had become Britain's prime minister, sent a message to President Roosevelt suggesting

The coast of Lawn Head near Chambers Cove where U.S.S. *Truxton* went ashore in the blizzard. The stick on the cliff helps fishermen recognize and identify the area when fog makes for uncertainty.

that a loan of fifty older destroyers would help at this critical stage of the war. German air attacks on shipping had depleted Britain's destroyer fleet, so necessary to guard convoys. Four months later, when Germany controlled the whole of Europe from the Channel to the Soviet border and Britain was fighting alone with its back to the wall, the British government granted, with the consent of the territories involved, the right to the government of the United States to establish naval and air bases at locations in the West Indies, Bermuda, and Newfoundland.

Fifty overage U.S. destroyers eventually found their way to England and played an important role in the Battle of the Atlantic.

On January 15, 1941, the first U.S. soldiers assigned to protect the leased bases sailed from the Fifty-eighth Street pier in Brooklyn for St. John's, Newfoundland. Argentia, on the east side of Placentia Bay, was chosen to be the naval base. Argentia was located on a peninsula near the town of Placentia, a French stronghold in the eighteenth century. Argentia's ships and planes were to carry our surveillance of the western Atlantic and guard mainland America. On August 14, 1941, President Roosevelt and Prime Minister Churchill met amid considerable secrecy on the U.S.S. *Agusta* and the H.M.S. *Prince of Wales* to sign the Atlantic Charter in Argentia harbor. The Charter,

The U.S. base at Argentia. The historic meeting between President Roosevelt and Winston Churchill took place on warships anchored near the twin islands at right, known as Mae West.

while not an official document, made a distinct impression on the Axis powers and on the Soviet Union. The waters of Placentia Bay had never seen such a concentration of air and naval forces.

After December 7, 1941, the strategic importance of the Argentia base was fully realized. Build-up of equipment continued night and day. A specialized cargo vessel of the (AKS-2) class, called the U.S.S. *Pollux,* about eighteen thousand tons burden, was used in the work of equipping the Argentia base. *Pollux* had taken supplies to Argentia from Boston on several occasions without destroyer escort. On the afternoon of February 15, 1942 she began her rendezvous with tragedy.

The *Pollux* sailed from Portland, Maine, at 1620, bound for Argentia. Evidence that a German U-boat wolf pack was operating in the area had been picked up by sound gear, hence destroyer U.S.S. *Wilkes* was assigned as escort. Next morning, U.S.S. *Truxtun* (DD229) joined the group in the Gulf of Maine. *Truxtun* took position on the port bow of the *Pollux, Wilkes* on the starboard bow. The ships began zigzagging maneuvers. Commander Destroyer Division 26 on board the U.S.S. *Wilkes* was in command of the group.

At noon, February 16, *Pollux*, steaming at thirteen knots, zigzagging, with a base course of 069 degrees true, was about three miles south of Brazil Rock buoy, off the extreme southern end of Nova Scotia. By 2000 hours (8 P.M.), estimated position of *Pollux* was lat. 45-28 N, long. 57-03 W, speed fourteen knots. This position put the ship some one hundred fifty miles northeast of Sable Island and two hundred fifty miles off the Nova Scotia coast in the latitude of Cape Breton Island. Base course of 069 degrees true was now changed to 047 degrees true in accordance with previous instructions from escort commander. After this course change, contact with *Truxton* was lost, although the lights of the *Wilkes* were seen from time to time. Visibility had sharply decreased due to snow squalls; snow continued to fall throughout the night.

On board *Truxtun* a similar course change was made at midnight and the ship ceased zigzagging. At 0215 on the eighteenth, a radio direction finder bearing of 235 degrees on Sable Island was obtained, but owing to sea conditions the bearing was not considered reliable. At 0230, course was changed from 047 degrees to 048 degrees true. The low-pressure storm had now created huge seas which made life on board the narrow-beamed destroyer exceedingly uncomfortable. At 0300, clocks were advanced one-half hour because the ship had entered the Newfoundland time zone. By 0415 the *Truxtun* was a total wreck.

At the time of grounding, an unsuccessful attempt was made to reach either *Pollux* or *Wilkes* by signal searchlight. Radio silence was still maintained. The ship's estimated position when she hit the rocks would have placed her thirty miles southeast of Ferryland Head. In other words, *Truxtun* was more than thirty miles off course!

At 2140, February 17, after *Pollux* had lost contact with *Truxtun*, regular soundings by fathometer were made. The readings showed that *Pollux* had crossed the fifty-fathom contour bordering the south side of St. Pierre Bank. Subsequent soundings, combined with very unsatisfactory radio bearings on Cape Race and Sable Island, indicated that the ship's course would carry her about twelve miles off land, on the west side of Placentia Bay. The raging sea and the snowstorm interfered with accurate direction finding; even the U.S. Navy at that time did not possess absolutely reliable electronic equipment.

Shortly after midnight, February 18, sounding showed the *Pollux* had passed the northern fifty-fathom line of St. Pierre Bank. At 0130 the ship's base course was changed from 047 degrees true to 057 degrees true. From the estimated position of the ship at 0130 this course headed directly to Latine Point, Argentia. At 0330, soundings suggested that the vessel was just to the southeast of Cloue Rock, a ten-fathom spot well known to French fishermen. Continuous soundings were made under this assumption, and depths no less than thirty five fathoms were recorded. The commanding officer decided to discontinue zigzagging due to proximity of land. Base course of 057 was maintained and an effort was made to transmit this information to the *Wilkes* by visual signal lamp but the attempt was unsuccessful due to low visibility. Radio bearings on Cape Race and Sable Island were again considered unreliable due to night and land effect. Soundings seemed to confirm dead reckoning position.

At 0414 the officer of the deck and all forward lookouts reported searchlights to port. The searchlights revealed the presence of land on the port beam. The commanding officer had just entered the bridge from the charthouse as the searchlights were reported. He immediately ordered engines full astern and hard right rudder. Collision quarters alarm was sounded. Since *Pollux* was on the base course 057, it was hoped that land could be avoided by maneuvering to starboard.

At 0417 the *Pollux* went hard aground and the bow started to sink immediately.

Searchlights that had warned *Pollux*—too late, unfortunately— were from the destroyer *Wilkes*. She had grounded a few minutes before on the rocks at Lawn Point on the west side of Placentia Bay. Both ships were almost forty miles off course. Fortunately for her crew, *Wilkes* was able to extricate herself before too much hull damage had been caused by the surging sea. On *Pollux,* in spite of two bridge officers and a pair of lookouts in the skytop and also in the crow's nest, there was no advance warning of danger until the searchlights revealed land close aboard. Gale-driven snowflakes blending with sea spume swirling in the darkness conspired to blur the vision of sentinels.

As soon as commander of the *Pollux* saw the ship's bow dipping, he rang the engines full ahead to prevent the ship from sinking in the adjacent deep water, for the hull seemed to be hanging on a ledge. Engines and rudder were manipulated to bring the ship into a position for rescue and possible salvage. Thus, by 0420, February 18, tragic events had taken place. Both *Truxtun* and *Pollux* were aground hard and fast not far from each other but out of sight, due to the configuration of the land, darkness, and the whirling snow.

Immediately after *Truxtun* struck, damage control reported water in the aft engine room and a hole in D fuel tank. Soon the sea round the ship was thick with bunker fuel. The destroyer seemed to impinge on rocks on the port side of the aft engine room. All hands were ordered to bring blankets on deck for themselves.

The bitter cold night wind was laced with sleet. An attempt made to lower the whaleboat failed. The forward guy tore out of its hold-down due to the severe lurching and pounding of the stricken ship. The loose davit allowed the whaleboat to smash repeatedly against the side of the destroyer. When the craft finally hit the water, it sank. Continual pounding of the wreck against the ledge weakened the port side of the hull. Keel plates in the aft engine room began to buckle. In a short time the aft engine room was half full of water and had to be abandoned. Forward engine room was still dry and generators were running normally.

In another attempt to get a line ashore, the gig was lowered to the port rail but jagged rocks close aboard presented a fearful sight—at one instant smothered in a surge of foam, then, as water drained away, a kelp-covered, unscalable crag. In the darkness anything could happen to boat and crew. It was decided to leave the gig at the rail until daybreak. Life rafts were cast into the sea in order to move them around the stern to the port bow. Number six raft was lost during this maneuver, so the plan to move number four was abandoned.

Daybreak found the destroyer pounding and grinding on the granite bottom even more violently. Wind and sea had increased in intensity. All the aft part of the ship was flooded—living quarters, engine room, and fireroom. The precipice on the port side was judged unsuitable for a landing. A boat or a swimmer would be helpless in the surf that washed against the rough palisade. The only possible spot was a boulder-covered beach about two hundred fifty yards distant, directly ahead of the bow. Rescue efforts were directed toward this place. All the three-inch manila line and wire cable on board were layed out on the forecastle deck. Enough of the line to reach shore was tied together. Two crew in a life raft carrying the end of a light heaving line were swept to the beach by paddling with the onshore waves. On reaching the beach, the men pulled in the three-inch manila and made it fast around some rocks. Two more rafts were manned with about six men each. They pulled themselves to the beach by means of the big manila line and by paddling. A fourth raft brought in the wire cable to be used to pull the rafts back on board. However, while the rafts were being retrieved, they became fouled in the manila line, and in order to recover the needed rafts the captain signaled to the men on shore to release the big line. During this interval, one of the men on the beach set out to seek aid from a distant fishing village.

At 0830 an attempt was made to launch the gig so that more men could be put ashore. Unfortunately, in this operation the boat was badly smashed and sank. Cresting seas, evolving into furious combers in the shallowing water, beat upon the ship and shore with increased devastating violence. The destroyer's hull began to disintegrate. The crew had gathered at various locations which, for the present, offered safety; some were on the forecastle head, others clustered in the well deck, a few were on the bridge, and a dozen clung to the galley deck house roof. The aft part of the ship had broken away and was under water. Air temperature was about eight degrees below freezing point. As the agonizing hours dragged on, the battered broken hull of the destroyer began to list to starboard, and the list continued at a steady rate, as if the ship was going to capsize. The severe list prevented any further attempt to get a line ashore from the forecastle head. Boilers and generators were shut down. When water began to enter the forward engine room at a rapid rate, all machinery spaces were abandoned. Two more rafts were now manned and nine men paddled to the beach safely. The captain passed word that anyone who wanted to try was free to swim to land. The men ashore signaled that some help by local people was on the way, and shortly after, individuals appeared at the top of the cliff above the beach and began hauling survivors up the face of the rock. *Truxtun* had now listed to starboard so far that crew were driven from the galley deckhouse and well deck to the side of the bridge structure and the forecastle life-line. All were cautioned to keep hands and feet moving to help prevent frostbite. Empty ammunition boxes were thrown into the sea to provide flotation for individuals washed overboard by the breakers that swept the superstructure continually.

By noon *Truxtun* was far over on her starboard side. The hull was fracturing at number three stack. More and more men were being carried into the water by the breaking seas. Most of these sailors began swimming to the nearest point of land on the port beam but wind and sea carried them rapidly parallel to the shore, so that they made for a point about two hundred yards eastward. At this place, the sheer cliff made getting a handhold difficult. A thick layer of fuel oil floating on the water and extending fifty feet from the shore created an exhausting hazard. Most of the men in the water were caught in this tarlike oil layer. Dashed about by the rough seas, they could not help swallowing the oil. A hazardous landing place, paralyzingly cold water, strong backwash from the shore—these factors combined with the men's general debility accounted for the loss of so many swimmers. Some of the crew were lucky enough to be swept further eastward, not far from the beach where the rafts had landed; Newfoundland fishermen who had come overland from the villages of Lawn and St. Lawrence scrambled down the cliff to the beach and were able to rescue these exhausted men by wading into the water up to their shoulders in order to drag the swimmers ashore.

By early afternoon *Truxtun,* now broken into several pieces, was barely above water. All but three of the ship's company had been swept off the remains of the hull or had tried to swim to land. Later a dory, brought by horse and sled from Lawn, a distance of twenty miles, was manned and rowed to the wreck to pick up these remaining survivors. Commander Hickox had stayed on the fractured bridge until washed overboard. He did not make it to the beach.

The rescue efforts that saved so many lives were organized, for the most part, by a man named Joseph Manning, from the village of Lawn, located on the coast west of the scene of the wrecks. Having met and corresponded with Mr. Manning, I became greatly attracted by his personality and laconic style. He was good enough to recall the series of events that occurred on that fateful day and night.

"Well, it was February 18, Ash Wednesday. I went to church, as is the custom, came home and had breakfast. Then I went up the harbor to bail out my skiff, since I had kept her in the water all winter. While I was there, two fellows from Webbers Cove came along and told me there was a ship ashore on Lawn Point and that you could see the ocean between her and the land. I argued with them that you couldn't see a ship ashore on Lawn Point, in under that land, as it was a bit thick and hazy. But in no time after, we got a report that there was an American destroyer ashore in Chambers Cove. We came to the conclusion that the ship they saw from Webbers Cove—that's to the west of Lawn—was a ship standing by the wreck in Chambers Cove. The wreck itself couldn't be seen because it was around the point. You can get a better slant on Lawn Point from Webbers Cove than from the village of Lawn because we are further in at the head of the bay.

"Anyway, about two o'clock in the afternoon I got another report that there was indeed a ship ashore on Lawn Point. But the report was only hearsay, there was no real foundation to it. And to go out there on a fool's errand was a long ten-mile journey. However, I thought there must be something to the report, so Jim and Tom Conners started off on foot. I got the horse and sled and said I would go and have a look. Now, I didn't think I'd be going to see her at a wharf; so I took a new coil of manila line and two brand new fishing lines and two cod jiggers, in case we would have to heave the fishing lines out to the wreck. And I took my axe. Then I started out with the horse and sled. Jim's son was with me and Fred Edwards.

"Well, we drove to what is called Three Stick Ridge and I saw no sign of any wreck. Then I drove further out towards the sea to try to bring her open, if she was there at all. Sure enough, there she was. She looked like a big island from that distance. I watched her for a little while; then I said to myself, if I was under that great high cliff I'd like for someone to come and help me.

"So I started back on my tracks to find a better way to get out there. On my way, I met two more horses; I told the three men that the ship was ashore and we must go out there to help the crew. I had no food for myself or my horse. One of the men I met was Mrs. Grant's son. I asked him if he had any food; he said he had a little lunch and a few oats for his horse. They were out to cut firewood and had not expected to be away for long. Well, we decided to go to help the ship, food or no. I sent Jim's son back to Lawn to look after my store. Fred Edwards didn't feel well, so he went home also, but he had a few pieces of brown bread in his pocket and he gave them to me. Now that was all the food I had. We started on our journey after that. On the path, I picked up Jim and Tom Conners, they had walked all the way. We now had to drive back and around the village of Little Lawn and up over that hill known as Breakheart Hill before we could turn out towards the wreck. On our way, two more men joined us, which gave us eight men and five horses. To get up over Lawn Point was a terrible climb; it is a regular mountain. I don't know whether any horses had ever gone that way before. Waist-deep in snow, we often had to cut an uphill trail so the horses could get through the drokes of fir trees and alders. And all the time there was the gnawing worry that we didn't know for sure whether or not there was a man to be saved, at all, at all.

"We were finally getting well out and I was the leading horse. I ran to the edge of the hill and brought the wreck open. I shouted back to the rest of the boys that I couldn't see a man alive on board. The ship was there in the water below me; a scattered sea swept clear over her; I was looking right down on top of her from the crest of the hill. The other fellows hitched the horses to a tree and walked on. I had to go around a copy of firs to get back to my horse, and that left me behind the rest. Alf Grant had waited for me. After I had picked up the axe from the sled we doddled on. When we broke over the hill, one of the other fellows is running back and shouting to bring a line. There were men ashore down below in a cove waving their arms and yelling. We hurried over to the brow of the hill and looked down on them that were in the gulch among the rocks. They weren't like human beings at all! Poor fellows covered with crude oil, some of them lying out as if dead and more diving around in the breaking seas. It was a hard-looking sight. They signaled to us that the main body of the crew was further out, somewhere in under the Big Head. We finally got to what we call the Big Head of Lawn Point at about twenty minutes after five in the afternoon. Everything on the ground was a glitter of ice and a man had to watch his step.

"God only knows how high it was at the top of the hill, but we had a fellow with us who used to go gunning there for seabirds. He knew the best path to take us to the very edge of the cliff. So we rigged a leading line from the top of the hill down to the edge. We got a good line over the cliff and started hauling up the poor frozen creatures. The cliff was overhung, which was good for hauling the bodies clear, and the life jackets the men wore acted like a pair of slide runners on the glittery ice after we got them over the edge and began hauling them to where we could get a firm hold on each one. By the time we had three up, two sailors and an officer, the last daylight had gone from the sky. We would have to work in darkness from now on. I took the three men further up the bank and started to look for a copse; found a place in a hollow with enough stunted trees for a shelter. I told the men this is where they would spend the night. They thought I should take them to the settlement, but I said the rest of the crew had to come up over the bank first, not really knowing there were so many people to be rescued. But anyhow, that was no time to leave the Head. The main important thing was to get a fire going. There was no dry wood thereabouts what with the trees covered with glitter, but I thought on some good dry boards on my slide, so I went to where the horses were tied up and brought back my horse and sled. Then I pried the boards off the sled and got ready to make a fire. By that time another man from Lawn arrived who worked at the St. Lawrence gypsum mine. He tried to light a fire by using a sailor's life jacket. With my axe I made some splits out of the boards and between us we got a fire going. Then a fellow from St. Lawrence found our spot. Some of the survivors persuaded him to lead them back to the village. They didn't realize how far they would have to go on a very bad trail. On my way back to the cliff, I met another St. Lawrence man helping some poor fellows back to the fire. I told him to try to keep the fire going. When I arrived on the edge of the cliff, there were two other men from St. Lawrence and a chap from Corbin helping the seven Lawn men with the hauling. When Alf Grant saw I was back, he asked me to take his place as outside man on the line. Every time seas would strike the base of the cliff, spray would drift upwards over us. We had no oilclothes; it didn't take long before every man on the line was soaking wet. I stayed outside man until Jim got after me. He said there were more men from St. Lawrence now, with rubber suits; they would take our places. I went back to

Fishermen from Lawn who said their relatives had helped rescue American sailors.

the woods to gather anything that would burn for the fire and to see if any more helpers had arrived. I stoked the fire and then returned to the line. No more helpers had turned up. So the night fled away as we kept on hauling. Someone guessed the hour must be after nine o'clock; a fellow with a pocket watch finally got it out. The time was quarter to midnight.

"About two o'clock we lifted the captain. I can tell you, we were glad. Our arms were about hauled out and backs near broken and we were all starving to death besides. Indeed, between the cold and hunger we were near perishing. Still and all, we were a sight better off then the poor devils we had just pulled up. We were expecting food to arrive from St. Lawrence, but it only came after we had left. When we hauled the captain, we all went back to the fire. Jim Connors looked around at the sailors and said, 'I often hear tell of the Pilgrim Fathers and the bad winter they had; this looks just like that time.' Some of the men were lying down on the ice and snow, some more crouched by the fire and stood around with blankets over head and shoulders. We couldn't get handy to the fire at all. To keep the blaze going you had to throw the boughs and wood clear over their heads.

"There were still about twenty men in the gulch down on the beach that had to be rescued. Our crowd from Lawn that had been working all night were bet out. A few men from St. Lawrence arrived with some American servicemen. An officer from the *Pollux* asked for volunteers from his crowd and, with the newcomers, the work of hauling began again. The men from the beach were in bad shape and it was hard work to bring them up the slope in blankets.

"Most of the sailors trying to help were in bare feet and half frozen themselves. The officer asked for volunteers so often, I finally called on all the Newfoundlanders to come and finish the job. By five o'clock all survivors had been brought up from the beach.

"We weren't short of a job even when that was finished. Wood was getting scarce in the copse after the night's cutting. It took time to collect enough to keep the fire alive. At daybreak an American rescue party arrived with medicine, clothes, and boots. A St. Lawrence

Ledges off these cliffs tore the bottom out of the U.S.S. *Pollux*.

man guided them to our camp. He was the only St. Lawrence man there at daybreak.

"When it seemed we were no longer needed, it was time to head back to Lawn. We were twenty miles from home but only five or six miles from St. Lawrence. We would go there first. We gave the sailors our axes to help keep the fire going, and we took six of the crew besides the eight of us and started with the horses. We didn't know the country and now had no axes to cut a way clear if we got mixed up with trees in a hollow. The going was not easy at all. We were on the way about five minutes when one of the sailors on the slide asked me if we had much further to go, so you can imagine how he was feeling. However, we didn't get lost on the barrens, and when I saw the shacks at Iron Springs—that's the St. Lawrence fluorspar mine— there were doctors and nurses to take care of the sailors. The medical people really saved a lot of lives, I think. We drove on to St. Lawrence to get something to eat; Jim got some dry clothes, as he was perishing with cramps.

"As you know, St. Lawrence got all the credit for helping the rescue; never a word about the Lawn men. Sure, we didn't go out on that ice cliff for glory, but to save lives. The American government is said to be rich, but they haven't enough money to pay me to punch in another night like that one, unless it was to rescue storm-lost sailors. St. Lawrence men did help with the wreck of the *Truxtun* in Chambers Cove. But men from Lawn were there too. Some of our crowd got a dory over the road and over the cliff and rowed out to pick up the last survivors clinging to the wreckage of the destroyer.

"I tell you, boy, February month is no time to run ashore on the coast of Placentia Bay."

14

A Recollection

Ever since the 1952 Newfoundland south-coast cruise in *Seal,* I have maintained an interest in the Lawn Head wrecks. Court Martial proceedings did not answer many questions I had formed about the navigation of the ships, but I did learn something when I became acquainted with Henry L. Strauss through membership in the Cruising Club of America. I had heard that Hank had been in Newfoundland at one time during the war, and when I described what had taken place and of my interest in the events, he quietly told me that he had been signalman on *Pollux* and was one of the survivors Manning had taken back with him on the sled! Hank recalled the eventful incident:

"I had the quartermaster watch in the early evening of February 17," Hank began. "A biting gale-force wind, driving a snowstorm ahead of it, lashed ocean and ship with a furious assault. *Pollux* labored heavily in thirty-foot seas. Visibility from the bridge may have been a few hundred feet, and somewhere in that whirling shroud of spindrift, destroyers *Truxtun* and *Wilkes* were riding herd on us as we approached the rugged south coast of Newfoundland.

"Throughout the afternoon, clamor from wind and sea had steadily risen. In order to check the compass repeaters, and to look for any signals from the destroyers, I had to use both hands to hang on to the rail to keep from being flung to the deck or tossed overboard, as I clawed my way out to the wings of the bridge. When my relief came on watch at eight o'clock, I was tired from the constant strain of holding fast. As I gave the course, speed, and other data to my shipmate, I told him, 'It's all yours, and I don't envy you.' I carefully

Henry L. Strauss, a quartermaster on the
U.S.S. *Pollux*, survived the catastrophe.

made my way below, wondering how the 'old man' must feel. He had
been on the bridge for nearly eighteen hours.

"The compartment where I berthed was comfortably warm in
marked contrast to conditions on deck. The off-watch crew was going
through the nightly routine of acey-deucy or the unending navy bull
session. With a strong sense of satisfaction I climbed into my bunk.
To stretch full length without straining to clutch something; to relax
under a warm blanket; to fall asleep knowing that your present home
was a strong well-found ship—these feelings stood for real luxury.

"It seemed as if my head had just hit the pillow, when, about seven
hours later, I was startled awake by a terrific crash followed by three
successive jolts. As I fell out of my sack someone in the blue glow of
battle lights shouted: 'We've been torpedoed!' A few seconds later,
the banshee wail of our siren signaled 'collision.' This was followed
by the buzzing of general alarm. In the confusion of falling bunks and
stumbling men, the chap next to me gasped, 'We must have run into
one of the tin cans.'

"Fifty feet seemed to be trying to climb into my trousers as the deck heaved and tossed. A bosun's mate fell heavily near me, swearing, 'Why doesn't some son of a bitch turn on the goddamn lights.'"

"Pushing my way past staggering bodies, as the grinding lurches of the ship tried to knock me off my feet, I climbed out of the compartment and ran through the wardroom to the bridge. Overturned stools, books, charts, instruments caromed around the wheelhouse. Carefully, I made my way out to the port wing of the bridge. Roar of breakers drowned out the confusion aboard *Pollux.* About one hundred feet distant, ghostly white in the night's blackness, steep snow-covered cliffs and jagged crags pounded by a wicked sea told a grim story. The hull of *Pollux* took a sickening lurch to starboard as waves swept across the waist of the ship. *Pollux* was ashore and mortally wounded. My watch read 4:52 A.M.

"About a half mile astern, off the port quarter, behind a pile of rocks or a low hill, cones of bright blue from big searchlights stabbed the darkness with wild sweeps. Calling to another quartermaster, I bucked up an icy ladder to the nearest searchlight platform. Every inch of the superstructure was covered with a thin coating of glaze where flying spray had frozen. The convulsive shaking and jolting of the ship nearly threw us off the deck as we tried to operate the lights. We exchanged calls with the other ship and learned it was the *Wilkes.* She was also aground but apparently in better shape than we were.

"We played our lights on the shore around us trying to get some idea of our predicament. I scrambled on down to the main deck to locate a lead line for a sounding. Just before I reached the deck a green wall of water crashed over the ship's side and swept everything before it. Bomb racks in the forward section splintered instantly, spilling their load of thousand-pound bombs. These huge missiles rolled around the deck like ninepins. I fully expected to be a tiny portion of a colossal explosion that would demolish ship and snow-covered cliffs to peanut-size pebbles. But in a few minutes all the bombs had washed over the side, where rail and life lines had already been wrenched away.

"We eventually found a spare sounding line on the bridge. To venture forward to the lead-line locker against that sea was foolhardy, if not impossible. Three of us, working together by grabbing onto handholds, worked along to the aft part of the main deck. We dropped the lead over the starboard side. The line ran through our half-frozen fingers for what seemed an incredibly long time; finally the lead touched bottom. Eight fathoms of line had run out—forty-eight feet of water on the starboard side and ten feet on the port side. The ship was aground on a narrow ledge.

"Just as we had finished sounding and moved away from the rail, *Pollux* gave a wild surge that knocked us flying. The entire ship shuddered. Battered and stove-in along one side, the forward starboard launch—slashed adrift from davits by the seas—spun past us in a swirl of foam. I thought, there goes my abandon-ship station.

"Back on the searchlight platform we found that the radio shack had sent out distress calls and our approximate position. The ship swayed and groaned, pounding harder and harder against the reef beneath her. We toiled with the big searchlight in order to keep in touch with *Wilkes*, still aground somewhere astern of us. Also, by examining cove and cliff with the beam, we hoped to find a suitable landing place. But a careful survey revealed nothing to encourage anyone from leaving the ship. Like most of the crew, I then believed our lives were in no immediate danger. *Pollux* was a big ship; we seemed to be so close to shore.

"Dawn, cold and gray, finally lifted the black veil surrounding *Pollux*. Our position was no longer reassuring. *Pollux* was hard and fast aground; the bow at waterline was stove-in; the forward three cargo holds were flooded. To port, the ship paralleled a steep-sided shallow cove while our entire starboard side was fully exposed to a raging sea sweeping in from the open ocean. Unfortunately, the stern of *Pollux* was floating free so that with every cascade of foam the aft section of the ship swung wildly back and forth like a pendulum. Obviously, sooner or later, the plates of the hull were going to buckle and give way. No metal could withstand for long the fatigue set up by the driving power of those seas. Off the port bow, a promontory of upended sharp rocks extended from shore to within twenty yards or so of the ship's side and about fifteen feet below the level of the ship's deck. Seas continually broke over this ledge. Abeam of the ship there was a narrow strip of beach mostly covered by barrel-size boulders. All around to the left, as well as ahead, a steep overhanging cliff with patches of ice and snow in the crevices presented a formidable wall of brown granite about seventy-five feet high.

"*Pollux* had hit a perilous-looking coast. I no longer felt safe.

"With the coming of daylight, gale and seas increased in force. Enormous waves, surging landward from the open sea, swept across our foredeck with unceasing fury as if anxious to destroy the hull as rapidly as possible. Wooden hatches broke loose and splintered against steel stanchions; life lines were swept away. Around the cargo wenches and king posts, lumber of various lengths battled with cartons of equipment swirling in irregular eddies before being churned overboard. The wheelhouse was a shambles of damaged instruments. Each wave caused the ship to lurch and the succeeding crunch felt like two trains colliding head-on at slow speed. The integrity of the entire hull was being destroyed.

"The captain wanted to try to get a line ashore so that a breeches buoy could be rigged to get the crew off the ship. But a gunner's mate came to the bridge and reported that the armory in the stern was flooded. There was no way to reach the line-throwing gun.

"By this time the *Wilkes*, which had been astern of us, had been able to work free of her grounding and was hove-to on our beam. She lay off, about a mile away, flopping about in the heavy seas like a wounded duck. Her signal light blinked: 'We have taken on water but will stand by until help comes.' She had radioed for aid from Argentia.

"*Truxtun* was nowhere to be seen. We believed she had escaped. Actually, she had gone ashore about a mile north of us, out of sight around a bend in the coastline.

"I went below to my compartment to get more clothing and cigarettes. Bunks and personal gear had been tumbled into a heap by the movements of the ship. When I opened my locker everything fell out onto the deck. I could hear the swish of sea water lapping against the forward watertight door.

"When I returned to the bridge, the hull had reached a seventeen-degree starboard list. Faces of the crew began to look worried, apprehensive—but there was no sign of panic. I noticed two sailors drawing greasy gloves across white bulkheads leaving dirty brown streaks on the white paint they had spent hours scrubbing to keep spotless in happier times. They laughed like children for once permitted to make mud pies while wearing Sunday clothes.

"A slippery film of fuel oil now covered the heaving decks and beaded the wheelhouse windows as waves thudded against the glass. Those windows were forty-five feet above the surface of the ocean.

"As plates in the hull gave way and stringers buckled, the ship began to break in several places. All along the starboard side, steel stanchions were bent out of shape and life lines torn loose; boats hanging in davits were smashed to driftwood. The seas were too heavy for the destroyer to get within any range to help us. One of our officers and two members of the crew tried to paddle a raft carrying a line across the relatively narrow but dangerously rough lane of water between the ship and the shore on the port side, but they were unable to make any headway against the outgoing tide. It was obvious by this time that *Pollux* was past salvaging. Could we save ourselves?

"The captain went into his cabin and came back with cartons of cigarettes which he tossed on the chart table for the men. Two supply officers, an ensign and a lieutenant, now conferred with the captain. Their plan was to have a raft lowered at the port side. If the raft could be pulled forward by a line on the bow of *Pollux*, they thought the rocky promontory could be reached. The captain agreed to let them try. A raft was made ready and lowered. The two officers stripped and put on life jackets over their greased bodies. The temperature of the water was thirty-three degrees—liquid ice! As they climbed down the cargo net, I wondered how one of them must be feeling. Three weeks before, he had brought his fiancée east. They were married a few days before we sailed.

"The men got on the tossing raft and a couple of sailors on the bow tried to pull the awkward craft forward, away from the ship and towards the shore. When about halfway between the tip of the rock and the side of the ship, one of the officers was washed off the raft. He was caught by the other—just barely—and after a struggle was pulled out of the water. The seas rushed through the narrow space like water in a mill race—with all the force created by a bottleneck. The men tried to paddle hard but to no advantage. Unable to reach the rock and probably unable to land on it even if the raft did succeed in gaining the land, the men were hauled back to the ship, frozen to the bone, but safe.

"The closer one looked at the sea going over that point of land, the difficulty of landing on it from a boat became all too clear.

"One boat remained undamaged—the portside motor-whaleboat. The captain decided to use it to carry a line through the surf to the rocky beach. If a stout line could be rigged, it might be possible to ferry rafts back and forth. Four men and an officer boarded the whaleboat as it was being lowered into the water. Twice the boat crashed against the ship's side, as if the sea was trying to spill the men into the freezing ocean. When the whaler hit the water, the engine was running and the boat roared away on a mad dash for the shore.

"The coxswain at the helm had served time in naval survey ships; his experience, gained from landing on exposed beaches, enabled him to steer the boat around foaming ledges to a jarring landing among the boulders. The officer was able to jump onto a rock; two of the crew followed but fell into the frigid water. A returning wave rolled them up on the shore and they scrambled to safety. The boat with coxswain and engineer was flung into a narrow cleft in the rocky face of the cliff. The sides of the ravine were so steep they could not get out to join their companions. The three on the beach eventually signaled: 'No place to make line secure. We are going to look for help!' They started to walk eastward along the beach, hoping to climb the steep snow-covered hill a half mile further on. They soon looked like three black ants against the bleak landscape. We all wished them luck.

"I went back to the chartroom to inspect the chart of Placentia Bay. There was no sign of habitation for miles around in the area where we now knew *Pollux* had gone ashore—nothing but an endless expanse of desolate terrain. Rockwell Kent's stark black and white wood block prints of Greenland came to my mind. As I stood looking at the chart and wondering about our chances for survival, something warm and greasy was thrust into my hands. I looked down to find a ham steak, just as it had come from the frying pan. What a moment to eat anything! The danger of our position and the erratic motion of the ship had everyone feeling rather brackish. In one corner of the bridge a seaman was heaving into a bucket, his face a pale yellow. But I realized that if, by some miracle, I did reach shore, every ounce of food inside of me would be important. I forced down the ham in spite of a large lump in my gut.

"Later, *Wilkes* flashed us a message, 'Help on the way.' The captain told me to send back: 'We are trying to land crew. Any help must come from the beach.'

"All four quartermasters were busy with the stream of messages that flashed from the starboard searchlight platform which was now dangerously close to the encroaching seas. Airplanes from Argentia were searching for us. We felt like a bent needle in a frozen haystack. Who could save us from the bitter cold and the constant pounding? A cheer went up from the men, crowded together on the boat deck, as two navy amphibians streaked a few hundred feet overhead. The engines could barely be heard above the thunder of the breaking seas. We tried frantically to signal to them with our small searchlight —the power line to the big light was now dead—but no contact was established. The planes circled and headed northward. Except for the crippled destroyer *Wilkes*, still on station a mile or so off the coast, we were alone again.

"Several attempts to get a line ashore finally succeeded. A grapple with a line attached caught on the rocky promontory. But it was difficult for any of the men now ashore to reach the place. We were glad to see that the two men caught in the ravine where the whaleboat dumped them were able to start a fire using the remains of the battered craft. At least they would not freeze to death for a while.

"Suddenly, the attention of every soul on *Pollux* was riveted on the engine-room area. There was a new sound rising above the roar of the sea—a violent hissing from within the ship. Ruddy faces blanched. Had water finally broken into the engine room and reached the boilers? Was the ship about to explode? We waited—

wondering whether we'd all be dead in a scalding flash. When the chief engineer informed the captain that he had let off all steam by the hand valves and was securing the engine room to avoid an explosion, the collective relief was solid enough to touch.

"I kept looking at the line from the ship to the grapple on the rock. How to make that line into a life line for all of us was the problem. As the ship jerked from side to side, the line alternately slacked and then became bar tight. When it slacked, a wave, boiling through the chute, would hit the line playfully and set it swinging. The swinging line gave me an idea. I asked the captain for permission to try to get to the rocks by going down the line hand over hand. Tying a bowline around my waist, I prepared for the attempt. Several of the men took one end of the line; others stood by to pay it out carefully to avoid any kinking. They would be quick to haul me back to the ship if I washed off. I removed my heavy overshoes and tightened a life jacket firmly around my body. As I secured the jacket, I remembered an ensign's constant reminder from back in my Naval Reserve days: 'Never fail to tie the top lacing!' I stepped up on a small portion of the ship's rail that was still standing and closed my hands around the line. Strange memories crowded into my mind, disconnected fragments of the past—skiing at Lake Placid—kissing my wife good-bye on my last leave—Central Park in the spring—the time I shot a sparrow with my first BB gun—standing on the diving board at the Intercollegiates for my last dive—.

"I started down the line hand over hand. As I left the side of the ship, worming towards the freezing seas, I was engulfed in a thunderous barrage—the tumult of breakers below—and behind me the booming and crunching of the ship slowly but surely disintegrating.

"As I progressed my hands began to slip. Fuel oil from the leaking bunkers covered the ocean. When the line slacked into the water it picked up this cruddy stuff. I concentrated on the idea that my wife was standing on the rock waiting for me. My feet reached forward trying to search for a foothold somewhere. An icy wave swept over me squeezing the breath out of my lungs like air from a collapsing balloon. Gasping with a convulsive shudder I tried to hang on. Another wave hit me. I suddenly weighed a hundred tons; the weight dragged me down, down into the oily sea. I bounced off rocks beneath the surface. I tried to swim, thrashing about with all my strength. I came to the surface and then went under again. I cursed the guys on the line—were they going to let me drown in the icy sea? I struggled desperately as my mind and body went numb. I vaguely felt the life jacket, like a hand under my chin, forcing my head to the surface. 'Pull me in, for God's sake,' I yelled. Although almost unconscious with the cold, I heard voices crying, 'Heave and ho! Heave and ho!' My throat choked with emotion. The line around my waist tightened. The guys wouldn't let me drown. Suddenly I was out of the water, scraping the rough flanks of the old *Pollux* . . . on the deck a limp soggy sack. Another attempt had failed.

"In the sick bay, still above water, praise be, and still warm, kind hands rubbed me down, gave me a stimulant that burned all the way down to my heels. Somebody found me dry clothes which didn't fit, but who cared. The lurching of the ship knocked me off the bunk so often, I said to hell with resting and struggled back to the bridge.

"There was still heat in the wheelhouse radiator. A few men clustered around the warm spot. Although faces showed anxiety there was some kidding about how many points against them their last liberty was going to count when each met St. Peter at the pearly gates.

"I was directed by the captain to send a message to *Wilkes:* 'We are unable to get to the beach.'

"The roaring gale continued to moan through the rigging and the king posts—the vertical structures on the cargo deck which serve as support for the large cargo booms. Seas had increased to an appalling ferocity. I looked forward from the wing of the bridge, saw a crack beginning to open across the deck forward of the bridge. A mountainous wave crashed over the starboard side and foamed across the splitting deck. Fascinated, I watched the rupture widen. There was a deafening ripping sound and a stunning report as if a sixteen-inch gun had exploded. The entire forward section of *Pollux*, as far back as close to the bridge, as if cut by a giant can opener, bent and toppled towards the vertical cliffs. What was left of the ship immediately took a steep list to starboard. Seas poured into the wardroom. There was a general sucking in of breath as people on the bridge waited to see whether the entire superstructure was going to slide into the ocean. The bridge careened and shook under the onslaught of the waves that seemed to be moving in for the kill, but the hull settled and held fast.

"Grimly the captain faced the men on the boat deck and slowly said, 'All hands who feel that they can make the beach may abandon ship.'

"I had a leaden stomach when we sent a message to *Wilkes:* 'Ship is breaking up. Am abandoning ship.'

"The port side of *Pollux* was black with men, as about one hundred of the crew prepared to slide down lines or scramble over cargo nets placed on the side of the ship. The sea was soon dotted with heads struggling in the water—a horrible paralyzing suspension of thick bunker oil and wreckage. Men tried to pull themselves along by means of the slack line still attached to the broken whaleboat and the upturned bow section of *Pollux,* but the greasy manila offered a precarious handhold. Wreckage scattered everywhere on the surface was a hindrance to shoreward progress; most of the pieces were too small to float a man and exertion in the frigid sea was agony. I saw a large wooden raft surfing on a wave near the beach, spilling men into the water as it caromed off sunken ledges. The tarry oil soon made anyone in the water unrecognizable. Some men went down as soon as they hit the surface, others almost reached the rubble beach but were swept off, again and again, by the battering waves. In the flotsam, a torpedo-shaped whirling paravane, fins spinning dangerously, crushed swimmers who tried to reach for it. Helplessly struggling men who could hardly lift arms out of the glue of oil and wreckage tried to assist shipmates in greater distress. Lines were thrown to shouting men still alongside the ship to try to pull them back on board, but their strength was so depleted by the cold that they could not hold on. A gunner's mate thrashing about in the water, seeing a shipmate descending on the boat falls, shouted before he sank, 'For God's sake, go back. Don't come in!'

"The rapid listing of the remains of the superstructure still brought crew to the rail. A storekeeper, with many years of naval service to his credit, whom I knew well, paused with one foot on the rail and called out before he jumped, 'What an undramatic way to die!' As the oily water covered his face he slowly sank out of sight. Two deck hands turned to a third and yelled, 'Come on, Yardbird, we'll get you over. Just stick with us!' The three of them jumped—one never came up; one drifted on the surface until a wave dashed his body against the nearest rocks; the third tried to swim until he, too, sank out of sight.

"Undaunted by these harrowing sights, a bosun's mate, after a last puff of his cigar, leaped off the fantail, looked up with a terrified expression as the numbing shock of cold struck, and then slowly drifted out to sea.

"An active deck hand, who earlier had arduously worked his way out the length of the cargo boom nearest the point of land on the port side, hoping to be able to get a line ashore—only to find the boom was just not long enough—was now battling the wreckage in the water. After a few minutes, he waves to us, shouted something, and with a knife cuts the lashings of his life jacket. A sea swept over his head and he was gone.

"All this action took place in a very short space of time. As the group on the bridge, hesitating to jump, clung to the lee railing and watched our shipmates in distress, many wept, horrified at the sight. The roar of the sea failed to smother many of the cries that floated up to us on the wind. The captain's face was twisted in grief.

"As soon as the rapid listing of the wracked hull appeared to slow down the captain ordered, 'No more men over the side.'

"About fifteen men had managed to reach shore. They appeared as dark shapes stumbling among the boulders on the beach. It was now about midday. *Pollux* had gone ashore seven hours ago. Looking seaward, we saw another destroyer appear. She rounded the distant headland battling heavy seas. We knew under present conditions she could not help us in any way except to lie off and wait. Our rescue had to come from land—there was no other way. And help from land would take the form of a miracle.

"A gasp of hope passed through those of us left on the wrecked ship as we saw one of our oil-covered shipmates leave the beach and slowly find a way over the sharp rocks and slippery snow patches down to the ledge of the nearest promontory. The captain directed two experienced sailors to crawl forward to the ragged portion of the remaining foredeck. Each carried a coil of heaving line. Swinging arms back and forth, they cast the lines weighted with knotted monkey fists towards the rock. Again and again the lines were thrown, but despite the strength of the southeast wind blowing in the right direction, the lines always fell short, out of reach of the shivering figure waiting on the rock. Our hopes sank again.

"The captain decided, however, that there was no sense in leaving *Pollux* as long as the wreckage held together. We would wait until the very last minute before casting ourselves into the sea.

"I kept looking for some part of the shore where waves would carry me on to rocks that would offer some kind of handhold. There was no obvious place. I began to think that we were all certainly going to perish. I visualized the telegram to my wife—'The Navy Department regrets to announce the loss, etc., etc.' That was the low point of the day.

"Signalmen were now told to gather together all confidential and secret material and prepare to cast it over the side in weighted containers. The navigator had looked up the tidal range for Placentia Bay. At this time of the month the difference between high and low tide would amount to twelve feet or more. Low tide was due at 6:30. We hoped at low tide some ledges might be exposed that would enable us to clamber ashore. But as the tide ebbed, waves increased in size and fury. Hope again turned into despair.

"I suddenly noticed flakes of snow in the air; whether snow had been falling for a long time, I could not remember. One of the destroyers was signaling again. I tried to get out the door from the bridge to the starboard searchlight platform but the door was jammed; it was impossible to open it. The half-inch metal around the wheelhouse had rippled and bent like warped veneer. The searchlight was useless now; no power there, and seas swept over the platform every now and then, although the area gave a clear view of the ocean. Sliding along the slippery, heaving deck, I ventured behind the radio shack. I could at least see the destroyer from there. Evidently the signalman on the tin can realized that something was wrong because he had waited and then slowly sent: 'We are floating life rafts with a messenger.' We soon could distinguish the rafts wallowing in the seas, but in spite of the gale blowing straight in our direction, outgoing tide prevented the unwieldy rafts from getting close to *Pollux*. Once again assistance came close but not close enough. By this time the officers had ransacked their cabins still above water to collect whatever clothing was available to pass out to the men who had need of a covering.

"Another oil-soaked shivering figure had joined the one on the point. Helplessly they watched the broken halves of the ship pound to pieces against the reef. Decks were swept clean of wreckage and another crack was spreading across the remaining deck close to the bridge. The power of the savage seas was unbelievable. By this time, most of the people on board had given up any real hope of survival. A few were lightheaded enough to feel that if they were told to climb the nearest king post and fly to the top of the cliff they might be able to do it.

"Finally, the navigator devised a useful plan. He had found a large spool of Belfast cord—a lightweight strong line. He crawled up to the machine-gun platform with the cord and, using a mouthpiece from one of the telephones at the gun station, made a kind of free-swinging pendulum. Whirling the contrivance around and around over his head, he let the weight sail gracefully through the air. Aided by the wind, the mouthpiece and cord dropped at the feet of the men on the rock. Quickly, a heavier line was tied to the Belfast cord and the two men, hauling carefully, pulled it across the boiling chasm to the rock ledge. Joined by a couple of other survivors, the group secured the heavier line to an outcrop of rock while we tied our end to the gun platform.

"Blood again flowed through all of us as the fire of hope rekindled.

"A bosun's chair was rigged to the line and an ensign was assigned to test the maneuver of being pulled to shore. As the bosun's chair slowly swung down the line, swinging to and fro, with the ensign holding on to the canvas seat with both hands, no one dared breathe.

Deliberately, the men pulled on the hauling line. As the ensign's feet landed on the rock, a roaring cheer went up from everyone.

"The chair was pulled back and another man got across, followed in quick succession by another and another. Clothing, food, alcohol, and instruments were wrapped in blankets that each man held in his arms as he traveled from the ship to the rock. There was no time for reactions as individuals landed ashore. To get everybody off the ship before the hull disintegrated completely was now the pressing task. But soon, in typical navy fashion, the race became a game. Yells, cheers, wisecracks ricocheted from ship to shore as each man was pulled to safety. It was felt to be a race against death to get everyone off the ship before the tide rose again.

"For a couple of hours, man after man landed, dazed at the success of the operation. There was so little space on the shelf of rock that individuals had to find a way up to the craggy base of the cliff. Just before dusk only a solitary figure remained on the bridge. Seas were beginning to break over the smokestack. The figure climbed into the chair, cut the line that held it, and slid down towards the rock. A cheer went up from all hands and echoed against the cliff and out to sea. The captain was ashore.

"We now gathered as best we could in the narrow space under the overhanging vertical wall of rock forming the cliff. An icy wind drew us together like cattle in a snowstorm. Had we escaped drowning only to freeze to death in the snow? We could do nothing but wait, trapped by the precipitous head wall. But word passed around that someone had seen several people high on the edge of the mountain. Perhaps help of some sort was on the way.

"To keep a strong spirit, a good voice struck up an old war song —"Tipperary"—and we kept on singing a string of favorites until throats were sore. A new moon appeared among the clouds, cold and clear. The stars in Orion flickered overhead.

"As we waited and wondered, the night chill was bone-penetrating. We stamped feet in unison to keep blood circulation active. We pummeled each other weakly to keep individuals from lying down and freezing. When cold becomes intense the desire to give up and sleep to death is so alluring and so easy to satisfy. From somewhere, a huge hunk of canned meat appeared and was passed around. Each of us tore out a piece of it with oily hands leaving behind black smudges. The tide was rising now and with the higher water level seas began to sweep the ledge, threatening the position of some of the group. Spray from breaking seas blew over us and froze on our clothes like a coat of mail. There were over one hundred men on this narrow terrace.

"I gradually became aware that something was happening over against the side of the cliff. There was a shout, 'There he goes!' Looking forward as well as I could in the dark, over the mass of heads, towards the front of the line, I could just make out the figure of a man being pulled up the side of the snow-covered rugged precipice. The swinging body occasionally made a silhouette against the night sky. Rescuers had evidently arrived on the crest of the cliff and had lowered a line to us. Hope again warmed our stiff bodies. Men became animated who had fallen silent in despair. What strange power hope of survival brings to desperate men.

"But pulling one man up at a time was going to be a long, slow process. Some of us realized that danger from incoming tide still ominously threatened. Hours went by. The line moved slowly. Suddenly, out of the darkness, a massive wave hit waist-high, clutching at our legs as it drained off the rock platform. Men all around me were soaking wet all over again. I looked out at the ship. She was still in about the same position and seemed to be putting up a battle against the waves, providing us with a lee. Seas broke clear over her funnel now. I could make out the fluttering shape of a tattered ensign. A light glowed on the bridge, shining through the ventilating holes behind the closed shutter of a searchlight. In all that misery and wretchedness the light was comforting to me, like a lamp in the window of a solitary farmhouse on a vast lonely plain.

"Another wave sent a wall of water over us. Behind me there were cries and shouts. Five men had been swept off the ledge into the sea. Flowing tide would rise for several more hours. What would become of us? While thinking about this new predicament, I felt someone tying a bowline around my waist. There was a jerk and I was suspended in air being pulled up and over the face and crest of the cliff. At the top, the line was removed. I fell exhausted into a snowbank.

"Presently, a man raised me to my feet. I saw four or five Newfoundland fishermen pulling on the line again. These men, together with a few others, working like pack horses, lifted to safety up the seventy-five-foot height—the total weight of the entire crew that survived the landing on the rock shelf at the base of the cliff.

"One of the group now led me further up the hill. I stumbled over rocks and snow as if intoxicated. After about half a mile we came to a large fire of scrub spruce. I managed to make a way to the edge of the fire before I fell again. I lay in the snow until someone made room and pulled me towards the blazing circle of fire. The heat seemed the first warmth I had ever known.

"More and more men kept arriving at the fire, staggering towards it, wet and frozen. As some of the crew dried off, they made space for newcomers by moving to an outer circle. The glow of the burning wood embers, the whirling smoke and the shadows cast by the bent figures ringed around the flickering flames, must have presented a spectacle like a company of Druids assembled around a pagan burnt offering. The Newfoundland men scrounged the hillsides for anything that would burn; suitable wood was scarce; small fir and spruce trees were heaped on the fire, building up a bigger and bigger blaze as more and more men arrived. The life-giving fire was circled by a babble of incoherency as men who had hung on through twenty hours of horror could hang on no longer. Some fellows worked over weaker shipmates until they fell flat themselves. At the outskirts of the fire, where cold wind retained its sting, men pounded others to keep everyone awake. For bone-weary seamen the cold was still a trial even though we were now safe on land.

"Intermittently there was a sharp report, a Very pistol sent a ball of light flaring into the sky to guide survivors to the shelter. Nearly all food and equipment had been washed off the ledge by the encroaching waves. Very likely it could not have been hoisted up the cliff anyway. However, as gradually the effect of shock and numbness wore off, hunger and a maddening thirst took its place in the minds of the crew. In spite of the chill as it was swallowed, men ate handful after handful of snow. Dirty or clean made little difference. We craved anything wet, but relief was only temporary.

"A Newfoundlander approached the fire and said, 'There are fifteen men trapped in a cleft. We need some help to haul them up.' For over an hour men stumbled back to the edge of the escarpment to help hoist up the trapped survivors. These were the men who went ashore in the whaleboat, along with some of the swimmers who had made it to the beach. In that narrow cove the group had huddled around a small fire, circled by bodies of the drowned who had washed ashore. They were in worse shape than most of us. Too weak to walk, several were carried up on improvised stretchers, some with severe hallucinations. At the fire most of the group were eventually brought around but unfortunately, in spite of efforts to revive them, several died of exposure.

"I began to go blind from the snow, smoke, oil, and cold. Bursting pain in my eyes prevented my closing them, which reduced any fear I had of falling asleep and freezing to death. The hours seemed to drag on forever. Sometime during the night, a rescue party from a navy mine sweeper reached us. They had been guided by Newfoundlanders over long miles of trail bringing blankets, canned soups, and medical supplies. We didn't heat the soup but ate it frozen from the opened cans. I don't think I will ever enjoy anything as delicious as

Rough terrain across which Henry Strauss and many other survivors walked to reach the St. Lawrence mine shack, a white spot at right center. Air Photo Division, Canadian Government.

the can of frozen Pepper Pot soup I was given. To some degree the frozen soup quenched our thirst.

"Like many others, I occasionally felt lightheaded. At one point, I found myself wandering over a hill about half a mile from the camp with my vision hazy and enlarged. Turning quickly, I stumbled back towards the fire.

"All through that long night the tireless Newfoundlanders kept cheering us and tending the fire. We were told that the three men from the whaleboat who had set out for help had reached some houses about five miles away from the coast. One of the three that had started collapsed about a half mile from the village and had died. The other two had been lucky to meet with assistance.

"A short time before daylight, five of the Newfoundlanders from the village of Lawn, who had spent the night rescuing us, said that they would take five men with them to get help from St. Lawrence, the nearest town. Four others and myself joined them. For about a mile and a half we scrambled over mountains, slid down icy slopes and crossed ravines filled with alders. Sometimes we trudged waist-deep in snow. Halfway down one hill, a bursting pain went through my head, and now completely blind I staggered along until a hazy vision began to return. We finally walked onto a frozen lake, where, standing patiently, we found five little horses and sleds. The horses or ponies were small and shaggy, a bit larger than a Shetland. They could travel in waist-deep snow where horses would bog down or cut themselves floundering about. The sleds were crudely made from heavy wood with steel-shod wooden runners, a plank down the raised middle and two posts to hang on to at the back end.

"Each of us got on a sled and began a mad ride up and down hills that seemed perpendicular, now across patches of moss where there was no snow, now across half-frozen streams where sled and horse sloshed through water. The little animals never faltered. Newfoundland breeds giants of endurance not only in men but also in beasts. We survivors held on as best we could, but I, for one, grew weaker and weaker. The jolting pain of the ride seemed as if it would never end.

"By this time dawn was upon us. I saw objects through a whitish haze. Everything seemed a weird mirage. What I took to be a wrecked vessel turned into a scrub spruce about three feet high. Eventually we reached the fluorspar mine buildings that the men had talked about. Here people took us to the mine shack, fed us tea, and dried our clothes by a pot-bellied stove. The food they gave us came out of their own lunch boxes. They took gloves, sweaters, and scarves that belonged to them and insisted we accept the clothing. Then a truck carried us to the village of St. Lawrence where we were given medical treatment. We said good-bye to the grand little horses and the wonderful men. We were told that sleds had already been sent to pick up survivors; some of our crew had already begun to arrive at the mine shack we had left only an hour ago. Two of our little group were now sent to one of the local homes to make room for the people who would soon be arriving. The Newfoundland housewife in whose home I was lodged treated me with the kindness of an angel. No one could have been more gentle or thoughtful. To these people and others we owe our lives. The woman fed me hot soup and in spite of the pain in my eyes, I fell asleep. A few hours later my group was taken to a ship and headed for the base of Argentia. The remainder of the crew finally reached the mining camp on sled or on foot.

"I remember the last portion of my journey as a series of isolated incidents—being carried from the house to a motor launch—down a gangway—being put in a bunk—being led off a ship to a bus—following someone into a barrack's infirmary—a dark corner bed where cocaine was put into my eyes—then sleep—sleep that fortunately held no more dreams of dying."

15

*Coasting Tales— A Hard
Chance at Cape Race*

Having left St. Pierre before 5 A.M. we were abeam of Lawn Head by 9:30. There was no wind and under power we spent an hour as close to Lawn Head and Chambers Cove as safety of *Neptune* permitted. Even in the brilliant sunshine of early morning, with a calm sea lapping the rocks, the bold cliffs looked dangerous. Sedimentary strata with granite intrusions strongly folded and twisted, presented a cutting edge at the tidal zone. Had the U.S. ships grounded a mile farther north, they would have run up on a sand beach.

A mackerel sky warned that the fine weather we were enjoying would deteriorate, and accordingly a course was set for Cape St. Mary on the north side of Placentia Bay. I hoped to reach the harbor of Trepassey by nightfall, which would amount to a run of one hundred thirty five miles from St. Pierre. There was so little wind, sails were furled; the diesel pushed *Neptune* over a glassy surface heaving gently in response to a slight swell from the east. Such a calm day is rare for the outer reaches of Placentia Bay. Many ships have been lost here. The large three-masted former whaling ship *Southern Cross,* with a crew of two hundred men, had hunted seals in the Gulf of St. Lawrence. With a full load of pelts she was homebound in March, 1918, when heavy weather was encountered crossing Placentia Bay. The lighthouse-keeper at Cape St. Marys caught sight of her shortly before a snow squall obscured his view. No sign of *Southern Cross* was ever seen again. No wreckage—nothing. The capacity of the ocean to devour is ever-present. A month after our passage, a trawler

The lighthouse at Cape St. Mary's has guided mariners for a century.

Murres breed on tiny projections all over the face of the cliff.

disappeared in a sudden gale on route from a harbor near Ramea, our first port of call, to a boatyard at Marystown, a village north of St. Lawrence. Due to some misunderstanding about her time of arrival at the yard, the ship was not reported missing for several days. A massive search by surface ship and aeroplane produced an upturned lifeboat—sole evidence of another tragedy.

No sudden storm threatened *Neptune.* Soon after the high land of Cape Chapeau Rouge dropped astern, a blue line on the horizon ahead marked the eastern side of the bay. We finally closed with Cape St. Mary about 1700 (5 P.M.). I had hoped to arrive when light was still favorable for photography, because the cape is noted as a nesting place for sea birds, chiefly gannets. We sailed as close as we dared to the large masses of cliff that have broken away from the mainland, forming what geologists call "stacks." Although daylight waned, we photographed birds concentrated in large numbers among crevices in the perpendicular walls and on shelving rock platforms at the edge of the sea. The bird sanctuary is a spectacular sight from seaward, a view that few people have ever seen, since passing ships give the area a wide berth. Gulls appeared to congregate on the western cliffs, gannets on the precipitous stacks.

The lighthouse at the cape, situated somewhat to the west of the stacks, is perched on top of layer upon layer of horizontally stratified early Cambrian sedimentary beds. At intervals this material is eroded, so that huge pillars are left with shallow coves on each side. By using binoculars, we could distinguish green and yellow mosses, lichens, and low bushes partly covering upper sections of the eroded rock face. The high cliffs resemble the crumbling masonry of medieval castles.

We stayed at this interesting headland taking pictures as long as light allowed. In the meantime storm clouds gathered in the western sky. Darkness had fallen by the time *Neptune* had crossed St. Mary's Bay and rounded Cape Pine. We turned north toward the narrow opening of Trepassey Harbour accompanied by rain and fog. I was satisfied with our day's activities when the Danforth anchor took a firm grip on the bottom, in eighteen feet of water, behind a barrier beach in Trepassey. I was also somewhat relieved. The night was too foggy and dark to search for a better anchorage.

Next day an easterly gale and continued dense fog made a delay in harbor a pleasure. We shifted position to the shelter of the only wharf in the village, which proved to be the town dock. Across the harbor there was a frozen fish plant where we might have nestled up to one of the trawlers. To be on the safe side of the law, we reported our arrival to a detachment of Royal Canadian Mounted Police

A colony of gannets, gulls, kittiwakes, and murres breed on a huge section of the cliff at Cape St. Marys that has broken away from the mainland isolating the birds from intruders.

A section of Avalon Peninsula.

located not far away. Drug smuggling has made the police suspicious of strange crafts that enter out-of-the-way seaports.

For a short time in 1919 Trepassey was in newspaper headlines worldwide. Three United States Navy flying boats were trying to be the first aircraft to fly across the Atlantic, the first ambitious attempt at transoceanic flight anywhere. Two of the aircraft had reached Trepassey via Nova Scotia from Rockaway, Long Island. One, the NC4, had experienced mechanical difficulties and had been delayed, although it did finally reach Trepassey. Several U.S. naval vessels were in the harbor along with the three flying boats. Newspaper reporters and newsreel cameramen let the world know what was happening. Trepassey had never known such excitement. Finally, one evening the three flying boats started engines, taxied to the head of the harbor and then roared seaward, heading east over Cape Race. They took departure from Cape Race. The NC4 made a successful flight to Horta in the Azores but the other planes had to ditch in the ocean and were so badly damaged by rough seas that they could not continue. On May 31 the NC4 arrived at Plymouth, England.

On a morning in 1928 Trepassey was also the take-off point for a flight memorable in the life of a young American girl who aspired to be an aviator. Bill Stultz and Slim Gordon left for Ireland with Amelia Earhart as a passenger.

An interesting local story emphasizes the deceptive nature of the low barrier beach behind which we anchored the night we reached Trepassey. It seems a young lad from the village joined the crew of a Lunenburg fishing schooner that had called at the harbor in search of bait for longline trawl. At the end of the season, in November, he came to the wharves in Halifax, hoping to find a berth in a Newfoundland-bound vessel. He was lucky enough to happen upon a Nova Scotian coaster loading freight for Placentia Bay. The captain agreed to land him home, if he would work his passage. Within a couple of weeks, the vessel was abeam of Cape Pine inbound for Trepassey. The captain, unfamiliar with the coast, shaped a course for what he thought was the wide harbor mouth of the village because he could see houses there quite plainly. But the boy knew that the ship was heading in the direction of the low-lying beach—the land was scarcely visible at high tide. Somewhat in awe of the captain, the boy began to walk up and down in front of the poop, repeating in a singsong voice a bit of doggerel: "You're safe on Cape Mutton but not on Powles Head—You're safe on Cape Mutton but not on Powles Head!" Back and forth he walked repeating the refrain. Finally the captain took notice. "What the hell is the matter with you, boy?" he cried. "Well, sir, you're safe on Cape Mutton but not on Powles Head," repeated the lad. "What do you mean?" said the captain, exasperated. "Well, sir," said the boy, pointing, "I was afraid to tell you, sir, but the way the ship is going now, she's heading for the ledges off Powles Head in there. And if she escapes them she's going ashore on that beach. The land ahead is no island. There is solid ground between it and the main—the long beach is so low you can hardly make it out. The harbor entrance is in that way—to port."

"Glory be to God," exclaimed the captain. "Hard a-port. Trim the sheets."

While we waited in Trepassey for the fog and gale to clear, I told my crew a yarn I remembered from the time I worked in Newfoundland. When traveling on one of the coastal steamers, I spent an entire day exchanging experiences with John Murphy, a retired mariner. St. Mary's Bay was the locale of one of his stories.

Bark-rigged ships have three masts with yards on fore and main and a Bermudian mainsail on the mizzenmast. Or, as on some barks, a regular mainsail and topsail.

He was mate in the *Albatross,* a bark sailing home to St. John's with a cargo of salt picked up at Cádiz, on the Spanish coast northwest of Gibraltar Strait. Cádiz salt was preferred in the preparation of salt and codfish. The ship was reaching to the westward, with Cape Race over the horizon to the north, when the wind died. No wind blew for several days, and the vessel just lay in the water. A northeast breeze eventually developed, but that was of no use being a head wind for St. John's, so they stood on toward Cabot Strait until about eighty miles south of St. Pierre. The wind dropped again. About midnight, a fresh breeze started for southwest; with trimmed sheets they headed toward Cape Race. The captain's plan was to round the cape, keeping about six miles off; then, with a fair wind, they would have a fine sail down the southern shore.

Albatross made good progress for most of the morning. Later on, the wind began to veer, first to the south and then to the south-southeast. When the wind began to head them, the ship was braced and the sails trimmed; on the eastward course, heading as high as possible, they still hoped to clear Cape Race, but it was going to be a close nip. At sunset all the light sails were furled; wind and sea had increased. Laying out on the yards was cold and dangerous work. The captain thought they might weather Cape Race on the present course; but if wind increased, the topsails would have to come off and the main reefed; then she would be making leeway like a barndoor. They might be sighting land by midnight. Keep a sharp lookout, he told the mate.

The wind did increase to a miserable gale. In the darkness, the rolling and plunging hull made reducing sail difficult. Under small canvas, *Albatross* was not going the course; with a full load of salt she was deep in the water and taking lots of that over her bow. When the captain checked the barometer, he said the glass was still falling. They would probably get a hard breeze from the north before long and would not reach the cape until daylight under those conditions.

By midnight, the crew was forced to take in all remaining sail on the foremast and put a third reef in the main. Stiff halliards and braces, and rock-hard canvas tore hands to bits. Snugging down took hours. *Albatross* was still headreaching eastward. About two o'clock, an enormous cresting sea slammed aboard; the side of the galley house was stove-in and a wave of water swept the length of her, tearing the bucket-rack off the poop, smashing glass in the cabin skylight, and pulling the helmsman from the wheel. Luckily, he caught hold of a line as he was going over the side; he managed to hold on and another sea lifted him on board again. The mate was washed from amidships back to the break of the poop, where the iron hoops of the harness casks scraped and cut his face. Not long after that, they had to heave-to. The sea was raging mad and the ship was in danger—rigging and superstructure coated with ice. By daylight, wind moderated and sea lost some of its savagery. All hands, with poles, began to pound ice from lines and gear. By noon, wind had died completely.

The captain decided to set no sails until the elements gave some indication of what was going to happen next. Dead reckoning put the ship about forty miles to the west of Cape Race. Later, when a light air from east-southeast ruffled the ocean, *Albatross*, close hauled, began to move eastward; more sails were added and as wind increased in strength she was soon making a good eight knots. When the old man came up to the mate on the poop, he said that the glass was going down again. They might be heading for a second edition of the previous night. The mate said he had little stomach for that. Sure, they couldn't expect to escape everything, the captain allowed.

When the watch changed, at four o'clock, a thin drizzle wrapped the ship in a wet blanket. Before long, wind increased to gale force. The process of taking off sail began again. Finally, the foresail was clawed off her. When the foresail comes in, the ship more or less stops. Working aloft, as the sun went down, with the ship rearing like a wild creature, the mate could see that leeway was increasing. He told this to the captain. That worried man said to let the ship go on. They just might pick up the glare of Cape Race light. If the ship could not clear, they would have to put her head the other way.

During the night, torrents of rain beat down the seas, although,

The treacherous coast near Cape Race, a landmark familiar to the earliest transatlantic mariners, wrecked so many ships the British government finally installed a lighthouse in 1833. Equipped with giant hyper-radial lenses, 12 feet high, of which only a few exist, Cape Race light, 180 feet above sea level, can be seen at a distance of 20 miles.

from time to time, a hard squall pressed the ship to leeward. The captain tried to decide whether it was wiser to turn the ship about immediately, or to wait and chance picking up the cape. To be balked after all their efforts was disappointing. He asked the mate his opinion. Together they agreed to keep on course and maintain a vigilant lookout. They must be sure to glimpse the land before the ship was in great danger. So the *Albatross* staggered on in the darkness.

An hour after daylight, the mate stood under the mizzen boom, on the lee side, taking a careful look around. He saw a streak of white, glittering on the port bow. Visibility ahead extended about two hundred yards. Mist sometimes hangs on the face of the land like a curtain. There was no sign of land yet. He called to the man at the wheel to be alert, and ran forward for a better look. The forward lookout shouted that there were breakers on the lee bow. The mate ran to call the captain who scanned the face of the cliff, now visible. Too high for Cape Race. Must be Shingle Head. Call all hands. Wear ship. Run up the foretopmast staysail. The crew tumbled on deck and

Shingle Head, west of Cape Race, is a perilous place in a southeast gale. Air Photo Division Canadian Government.

set to work with the mate to loose the topsails and hoist the jibs. With the wheel hard over, *Albatross* began swinging to port straight for the breaking seas at the base of the cliff. The wind came over the stern as the ship turned. All the time, she was getting closer to the rocks, but she was answering the helm and continued to turn to port. The ship was wearing around and the bow gradually turned away from the surf. Fortunately, deep water extended close to the rocks. As wind caught square sails high above the deck, forward motion began to reduce leeway. All on board, including the cook, lined the lee rail and with straining bodies tried to push the ship along.

The kites—the jibs and topsails—caught more and more wind. *Albatross* had her stern to Shingle Head at last and the crew cheered their good luck.

The ship was now heading westward toward Trepassey. More sail was added but the wind blew hard from a direction that was producing leeway. They were really driving along by the land, gaining sea-room very slowly. The mate was concerned about the ship holding her own if they were to avoid Powles Head, and to the westward of that, Cape Pine.

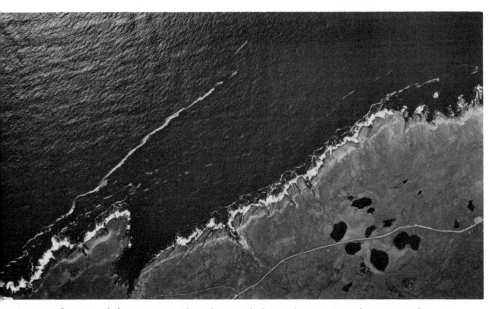

An aerial view of the coast at Shingle Head shows how it trends in a southwest direction. Air Photo Division. Canadian Government.

After a cup of coffee and a few doughnuts, my friend continued his yarn:

"That was a close one, said the captain. 'Too close,' I said. We are not doing much better now. She's going sideways as much as ahead. I just took a bearing on the wake. We are no more than holding our own.' 'Well now,' said the captain. 'We're edging off little by little and in the evening should be up to Cape Pine. We're not making half the leeway you think. The ship is deep.' 'I don't know about that,' said I. 'The wake is there and that's the course she's been coming through.' 'Ah,' he says, joking. 'You're mad . . . you're mad . . .'"

When the watch changed at eight bells, the sea was still ugly. An hour later, an unlucky wave broke over the ship's port bulwark, splintered stanchions and tore away ten feet of the poopdeck's rail. The mate was below in bunk, dozing. Captain called him to come on deck. The captain looked worried.

"He said to me, 'Better reduce the upper topsails. She's drawing off a bit now.' I didn't agree with that at all. 'The ship is reaching out a bit from land, captain,' I said. 'But look at the heave of the sea . . . tidal current is probably running in here like a river.' He said: 'Nonsense. I think she'll fetch Cape Pine. We have until dark to get over there.' The captain began to walk up and down the deck with

Powles Head extends southward for several miles with extensive ledges in Mutton Bay east of the point. Air Photo Division. Canadian Government.

his head down as if in thought. I said, 'I don't think the ship is doing that well, sir.' The captain made no reply and I said no more. I would have added sail instead of reducing it, even if there was a risk of losing canvas. Evidently the old man did not want to take that risk."

The western side of Trepassey Bay extends boldly seaward in a southwest direction. The tip of this land is Cape Pine. The constricted entrance to Trepassey Harbour is guarded by Powles Head, the end of a long, curving, low-lying, narrow peninsula. Bowl-shaped Mutton Bay lies east of Powles Head with Cape Mutton at its farthest point. From Powles Head, shoals and ledges extend south and eastward forming an arc of shoal water, an effective booby trap in wait for a ship a mile or more from land. This is not a restful place to be with an onshore wind. The mate suspected *Albatross* was heading in that direction.

"Close to eight bells in the afternoon, captain and I were having coffee in his cabin. He said: When it gets dark, we ought to see Cape Pine light. I shook my head: 'I'm dubious about that.' He squinted at me: 'What do you mean?' 'To tell the truth, captain, I believe we are somewhere off Trepassey—not far from land.' 'That's nonsense,' says he; 'anyway, we can't do any better with this wind.' I went on watch. In foul foggy weather I would rather be on deck than below. Jack Kielly was at the wheel. I said: 'Jack, my boy, we aren't out of trouble yet. Keep your eyes wandering. The watch on the bow only look straight ahead.' Some minutes later, I was looking aft watching our wake. A wild shriek from Kielly jerked me around. 'Merciful God, look there ahead—a string of breakers.—breaking mad.' I made a run to the cabin door. 'Come up, captain. There's white water all around ahead.' One look was enough for him. 'We're in Mutton Bay,' he said. 'No chance of getting out with this wind.' He took a quick glance aloft at the sails we had set. 'We have one chance only,' he said. 'Jibe the ship. Get all hands on deck. Then I'll tell you.' "

With all the crew working quickly, the ship was jibed around before she grounded in shoal water. Sheets and braces were trimmed. The captain said to let her run off about a mile. Presently, the captain beckoned to the mate. With this wind, *Albatross* would not clear Cape Mutton, where they were now leading. He told the astonished mate that his plan was to run into Mutton Bay a distance and then anchor. He said he had fished out of this place and knew the waters as well as the road to his house. First, the crew was to reduce sail. When that was accomplished, the captain took the wheel. They were now halfway across the bay. He put the helm down and headed straight for the land.

Calling to the mate, he told him to take the hand lead and keep sounding as the ship ran into shoaler water. They were going to anchor when the lead line gave ten fathoms. The mate was to give a signal. Meanwhile, the crew must pull chain from the chain locker and lay it on deck so that it would run out freely.

"Sounding was difficult due to wind and sea but eventually the lead-line mark showed less than fifteen fathoms. I waved to the captain. He put the helm over and the ship began to come into the wind. Man the braces; muzzle the sails; let go the port anchor. . . . Wind and sea began to drive the ship astern. When thirty fathoms of chain had rattled out, the starboard anchor was dropped. The captain shouted: 'Don't try to check the port chain yet!' We paid out both chains together until we had seventy-five fathoms on the port bower. The captain called: 'Brake the windlass; snub the chain.'

Anchors seemed to be well set and holding. Again the captain called: 'Haul all chain from the lockers, flake it on deck, then let most of it out. . . . The more scope, the easier she'll lie. . . .' "

But there was no way *Albatross* could lie easy. Wind and sea continued with vigor. The mate and bosun worked their way to the bow, dodging waves coming over the side. They were anxious about the chains. Every time the ship's head lifted to meet an oncoming sea, the links were wrenched bar-tight with a shuddering jerk. Some were stretching under the strain. When the mate reported these conditions to the captain, he said that he was more concerned about the condition of the windlass; if that gave way the ship would be a wreck in no time. The windlass must be blocked and strengthened. Fortunately, the bosun was an experienced ship's carpenter. In spite of the motion of the vessel, with all hands helping to place a few stout timbers, the job was carried out. Then luff tackles were put on the chains and three-sheeve blocks attached to strong eyebolts in the deck. When set up the tackles relieved some of the awful strain.

Before dark, the captain called the mate to him. Said he remembered there was a narrow channel through the breakers astern of them. Years ago, he had taken a small boat in that way. If a ship was driving for the beach, adrift, she might avoid getting hung up by keeping in the channel. The crew would have a better chance for survival. He couldn't see the narrow lane from the deck, but if the mate could reach the main crosstrees and notice the position of dark water when the rollers broke, that would be the channel. The captain would stay by the compass and mate would extend his arm in the direction, in that way the captain would get a bearing.

Hanging on for dear life, the mate slowly climbed the rigging. The motion almost made him sick. On the swaying mast, it was like being suspended from the pendulum of a tall-case clock. He watched the surf. There was a darker patch. He held his arm in that direction. On deck, the captain took a compass bearing.

After dark, there were bonfires on the shore astern of the vessel. People were encouraging them. If the ship drove ashore somebody would be there to help. The captain said that if the chains parted or anything else gave way, they were to run up the jib and topmast stay sail to turn the vessel quickly, then steer for the channel.

All night long, wind and sea tormented the bark, there was little comfort for anyone, but everyone aboard had great confidence in the captain. Off watch, the mate lay down on his bunk fully dressed in oilclothes and rubber boots. He lay there thinking for a while and must have fallen asleep. The second mate woke him to go on watch at 2 A.M.

"I went on deck feeling much better for having slept . . . not as nervous as I had been all day. Six hours before dawn, I said to myself, Come, blessed daylight, come. . . . Fires on shore were still burning. Along about four o'clock the wind began to slacken and fog wrapped us in a wet blanket. But spite had gone out of the storm. Seas slowed to a rolling lop. I went below to tell the captain. He was sitting at the table where I had left him hours before. I could see his lips moving. I believe he was praying. I said: The weather is moderating, captain.' 'I thought so,' he murmured. 'Yes, sir, it is moderating a lot.' 'Thank

God,' said he. I went for'ard to inspect the windlass and check on any damage to the forepart of the ship battered by the weight of those heavy seas; I wasn't worried about the chains any more, so I set the watch to removing the luff-tackles. The sea was going down fast. The men could get around the deck without any trouble now. As I walked aft, I felt a puff of wind off the land. I turned to face it. A light breeze was coming directly out of the bay. After a while the wind blew steadily. I ran to the companionway. 'Captain, I called, 'the wind is off the land!' Up he came, pulling on his jacket. 'Call the men; loose the foresa'l and two topsa'ls. Mate, get a maul ready; we may have to slip chains in a hurry—as soon as the sea drops a bit more and the wind freshens. I think the ship will work out against this lop. We'll have an ebbing tide in half an hour. The barometer is rising. I hope to move her at the first of the ebb.' "

In less than thirty minutes, a brisk northerly blew away the morning fog. The captain told the mate to set all sail, square the yards, and let go the chains. With a heavy maul and cold chisel, bosun and helper cut the ship free. The mate hated to lose the chain and the two anchors but there was no way to recover the gear. With wind from astern and square sails drawing, *Albatross* made good progress against the lop that still rolled in from the east and south. Crew felt cheerful again. All hoped that the northerly wind would hold. The ship had gone quite a distance into Mutton Bay before anchoring. To reach sea-room was going to take some time.

Presently, the captain allowed that the water close to Cape Mutton was rather deep close to shore. They had better change course toward Mutton so that the fore and aft sails could be set to drive the ship seaward quicker. Soon, with every stitch of canvas flying, the vessel forged ahead and reached a safe twenty miles offshore before the wind died. Later, in the afternoon, the normal prevailing southwester set in. *Albatross* had enough offing to clear Cape Race and set a course for St. John's.

Aboard *Neptune*, we were grateful that our faithful diesel often spared us the frustrating experiences of the hardy crews in the windships.

16

Neptune *Heads Northward*

Cape Race is the easternmost point of land in North America. On the earliest maps of the New World, drawn by cartographers whose knowledge of the area was obtained from the rough logs of mariners or from their own lively imaginations, one of the few easily recognized configurations is Cape Raz, as it was called. The cape was a dependable landmark for European fishermen approaching an unfamiliar coast. Centuries later it was the turning point for aircraft flying the Great Circle course from North America to Europe, before the introduction of high altitude flight and inertial guidance systems.

On *Neptune*, we were glad to see Cape Race in bright sunshine because the tall white lighthouse with an onion-shaped red-painted lantern is usually hidden by thick fog so prevalent hereabouts.

A few miles northward along the coast, I directed my crew's attention to Horn Head, where a splendid passenger steamer, S.S. *Florizel*, was wrecked during a southeast gale and snowstorm a few hours before dawn on February 24, 1918. The ship had sailed from St. John's for Halifax and New York on the previous evening with 138 passengers and crew. Apparently, the captain thought *Florizel* had passed Cape Race and changed course for Halifax. Ninety-four lives were lost. Many friends of our family perished.

One survivor owed his life to the amount of spirits he had taken at a bon voyage party. He slept soundly throughout the turmoil during which people who had sought safety on deck were swept overboard by wind and sea. By chance, the intoxicated man's cabin was not completely underwater by morning. He finally came to, secure in an upperberth, horrified to find bodies of drowned passengers floating into his stateroom through the open door. In a state of

Lord Baltimore settled a small colony of forty families at Ferryland in 1621. Discouraged by poor crops and the raids of pirates, after two years of struggle the group asked to be relocated in the Chesapeake.

shock, hoarse from frantic shouting for help, he was finally located and rescued.

The harbors of Newfoundland's Avalon Peninsula are rich in historical interest. European fishing vessels frequented these places of refuge for centuries, as did privateers and pirates. When opposite Ferryland Harbour we decided to enter hoping to buy some cod or salmon from the fishermen. This village was set up in 1623 by Sir George Calvert and his son, Lord Baltimore, who had received a large grant of land there from Charles I of England. The undertaking was not a success. Rocky soil was unsuitable for extensive agriculture. Discouraged by a series of cold winters, their fishing operation harrassed by pirates, the colonists were happy to be relocated to the Chesapeake Bay.

The entire coastline of Newfoundland is, with a few exceptions, a precipitous escarpment often reaching twelve hundred feet or more directly out of the water. The barren hills on each side of the en-

Photographs of the entrance to St. John's made fifty years apart show little change, but within the harbor dramatic alteration of the north-side shoreline has taken place since 1950.

G. M. Marconi with his two assistants and the Cabot Tower signalman the morning after the Italian physicist received the first transatlantic wireless signals from his station at Poldhu, Cornwall.

trance to St. John's harbor, however, are not more than eight hundred feet high, but they appear impressively massive as one approaches from seaward. I have often climbed the flanks of these red sandstone piles of rock which guard this ancient harbor, the oldest anchorage in the Northern Hemisphere. On the afternoon of May 20, 1927, I happened to be on the western side of the eminence called Signal Hill. I looked westward down the length of the banana-shaped harbor. My ears caught the humming sound of an aeroplane's engine. I finally caught sight of a high-wing monoplane, swooping low, coming toward me from the west. The plane passed through the Narrows, the harbor's entrance between the hills, and continued out to sea. I could look down on the plane as it passed me. Next day, the whole world knew that Charles Lindbergh had made the first solo flight across the Atlantic.

Stoutly built to honor the island's discoverer, Cabot Tower crowns a high hill overlooking St. John's harbor. Using a kite, Marconi hoisted his newly invented aerial to catch the ocean-spanning long wave signals.

Old Fort William overlooks St. John's. The visiting warship is a British light cruiser. Fort William, built to guard harbor against French invasion, was repeatedly captured, destroyed, and rebuilt from 1696 to 1784. France was determined to seize Newfoundland, key to the grand design to subdue English Canada.

Petty Harbor children at play.

Petty Harbor, a fishing village south of St. John's, was settled in early 1600s. The people were often harassed by French forces advancing on the capital.

A cove north of the capital.

Pouch Cove, a fishing settlement with some land suitable for small farming.

Logy Bay, north of St. John's, where fishermen have to contend with a rugged coastline to secure boats and gear.

Ancient pre-Cambrian rocks constituting the coast north of St. John's show sedimentary strata upended ninety degrees from horizontal yet with minimal deformation or folding. This condition is of great geological interest considering the formation has "floated" westward from its former connection with Europe.

In 1950, the finger piers on the north side of St. John's harbor were filled with sailing schooners.

A solid concrete quay has replaced the harbor's former finger piers. Prospecting for oil offshore by use of ships like Elf Aquitaine's drillship is expected to bring increased prosperity to the province. A large Soviet vessel occupies the right foreground.

Neptune sailed into St. John's in the wake of Sir Humphrey Gilbert's ship *Delight*. Gilbert was sent to Newfoundland with a squadron of three ships in August, 1585 to reaffirm the English claim to the island in the name of Queen Elizabeth.

When the ships approached the Narrows, they were stopped by a sloop sent out by the local "fishing admiral." By a Newfoundland custom that began early in the 1500s, the captain of the first ship of the fishing season to enter a harbor set himself up as the "admiral" of the harbor. He supervised the locations where fishing was allowed; allotted space where the salted cod would be dried; dispensed such rough justice as was necessary to keep the peace; and was not above accepting bribes. The iniquitous custom lasted for nearly a century. Captain Edward Hayes of the *Golden Hind*, largest ship in Gilbert's squadron, wrote in his log, as reported by Hakluyt, the naval historian: "being denied permission to enter harbor, we made ready our fights and prepared to enter notwithstanding." However, Gilbert, always the diplomat, first dispatched a pinnace to give the local authority knowledge that their coming was by order of Queen Elizabeth. "We followed the pinnace," Hayes continued, "and in the very entrance, which is narrow, *Delight* fell upon a rock on the starboard side by great oversight—in that weather was fair and the rock much above water. But English merchant fishermen sent out a number of boats which towed the ship clear."

Neptune's transit of the Narrows was unnoticed. I made arrangements to refuel at an oil dock. Our crew caught their plane to Boston. There was time to visit some old friends. With Will Hamann, who had signed on for the entire cruise, I climbed Signal Hill to show him where, in 1901, Marconi and his assistants flew a box-kite aerial and by means of receiving instruments located in the stone tower, heard the first transatlantic wireless signals transmitted from his station in Cornwall, England. The single letter "S" was repeatedly received at Signal Hill. Earphones picked up the faint but distinctive *dit-dit-dit* coming two thousand miles across the Western Ocean. If changes of such magnitude in communication have taken place within eighty years, imagine what research will achieve during the next century.

17

*Across Northern
Bays to Funk Island*

After the short stopover in St. John's and a visit to the only marina in the island, the Yacht Club at Long Pond, Conception Bay, Will Hamann and I fired up the diesel and set our sails for the northern leg of the cruise.

A fair wind carried *Neptune* across Conception Bay toward the village of Bay de Verde (one of many French names given to harbors along the coast) and a distinctive-looking bold island called Baccalieu. There is another island further north called Bacalhao. Both words mean codfish. Baccalieu is probably a corruption of a Basque term; Bacalhao is Spanish. French, Spanish, and Portuguese fishermen, along with the English, settled in harbors and coves on the winding coastline of the northern bays. To hide away, to be as inconspicuous as possible, was necessary to avoid restriction on year-round settlement in the country; a condition that persisted for several centuries, and which promoted widely scattered settlement.

As we passed through Baccalieu Tickle, the strait between the island and the mainland, the surface of the ocean was churned by a shoal of cod chasing a school of small bait-fish called capeline, from the Portuguese word, *capelina*. We were preparing to rig a line to catch something when, with an unexpected roar, a propeller-driven plane flew low over *Neptune* and banked sharply. Although I had never seen her before, I recognized the plane as a Cessna Baron. The plane must be one owned and piloted by my friend Jim Nields, of Hardwick, Massachusetts. We had tried to set up a rendezvous, as I

Fishing grounds around Baccalieu Island have attracted fishermen from many countries for centuries. The Portuguese word for codfish is *baccalaos*. The lighthouse on Baccalieu is so inaccessible that all supplies must be hauled up the cliff by derrick.

Veteran fishermen discuss the day's events.

The cleaned and washed cod are placed in layers and salted with coarse sea-salt for varying lengths of time. The purpose of the salt is primarily to dehydrate the fish protein and thus help to preserve it. The sun-drying process further reduces water content.

Codfish drying on racks called flakes at the town of Bay de Verde in Conception Bay.

was eager to make aerial photographs of the coast, but schedules and the weather had not worked together. Nevertheless, Jim had obviously flown up hoping for a change in the overcast. A capable pilot, with many Atlantic crossings on his log, Jim had taken the late S. E. Morison, the sea-going historian, over parts of Newfoundland and Labrador in order to make firsthand observations and photograph of landfalls supposedly made by John Cabot in 1497. Admiral Morison needed this information for his book *The Northern Voyages.* On one of the flights over Labrador, where barren terrain showed numerous lakes and ponds gouged out of the granite by glacial activity, they suddenly came to a stretch of coast, north of Cartwright, that looked more like Cape Cod than southern Labrador—a thirty-mile sweep of wide and sand beach with a stand of dark spruce behind it. There is little wonder the Norse called this unmistakable landmark "furdustrandir"—marvelstrand—so different from northern Labrador and their Greenland coast. Mention of an extensive sand beach in the sagas has confused historians who try to interpret the path of the Vikings from the printed page. These scholars could not imagine such a coastline in Labrador, and therefore insisted that the Vikings had reached Cape Cod or had landed even further south.

Weighing dried codfish. For export the unit of weight is one quintal or 224 pounds.

Upon entering Trinity Bay, we found wind shifting into the northeast, increasing in strength, and bringing with it a curtain of fog. *Neptune*, soaking along, made slow progress as a heavy sea began to build. My original cruise plan included spending a week in each of the bays—Trinity and Bonavista, but for various reasons, available time was now running out. To reach Notre Dame Bay and a harbor conveniently close to Gander Airport was the present objective. I regretted having to move along because there are numerous picturesque harbors tucked away along the shores of these two bays; places with delightful names: Ireland's Eye, Heart's Content (where Cyrus Field finally landed the first transatlantic telegraph cable, after years of discouragement), Happy Adventure, Fair and False Bay, Turk's Cove, and others by the dozen. Many of the enterprising fishermen who had worked for my father and grandfather came from this region. Although most of the men whom I dearly remembered have departed this world, I had hoped to find some of the younger generation still alive.

By the time our depth-finder indicated *Neptune* was drawing close to the north side of Trinity Bay, a combination of heavy sea and thick fog made the prospect of an all-night vigil dodging shoals on a lee

Along the shore of Conception Bay. In Newfoundland the ocean is never far away.

Men from Hibb's Hole may venture as far as twenty miles to fish at Baccalieu Island.

Bell Island lighthouse sits on top of layers of sedimentary rock of pre-Cambrian Proterozoic era. The iron deposits of Bell Island are a characteristic of this formation.

On narrow, rough roads long carts still carry heavy- or awkward-size freight.

Newfoundland children are at home on the water. Speaking of Newfoundland naval ratings in H. M. Navy, Prime Minister Winston Churchill was of the opinion that they were the best small boatmen in the world.

shore far from attractive. A decision to try for the harbor of Catalina was considered prudent. Seas were breaking on the Haypooks, a three-fathom spot, when course was changed toward a foghorn on Green Island, close to land near the harbor, according to the chart. By 1800 our anchor was down in twenty-feet of water. Catalina did not seem an alluring village at this hour. We cooked a delicious meal of codfish tongues presented to us by a friendly fisherman, and hoping for better weather in the morning, grateful for a quiet night in harbor, snuggled into sleeping bags as torrents of rain beat on the deck.

During the night, one of my oldest dreams was rekindled by our nearness to Bonavista. As a boy, I had read the story of Jacques Cartier of St. Malo, Brittany, who sailed for Francis I in 1543. Cartier's landfall, twenty eight days out of St. Malo, was Cape Bonavista (Buona Vista), a place well known to transatlantic fishermen. The promontory had been identified in 1501 by Gaspar Coret-Real, the Portuguese explorer, who gave it the name of Boa Vista, after one of the Cape Verde Islands. At the cape, Cartier's ships met extensive drift ice (not surprising for early May), suffered damage, and re-

A matter of some importance!

The names of villages like Portugal Cove suggest an ancient lineage.

Outer harbor of Brigus in Conception Bay. House in the background was built by American artist Rockwell Kent.

turned to Catalina to refit and to assemble a longboat in which to make careful exploration of coastlines where depths were too shoal to risk larger ships. Later, having sailed further north and meeting an icefield, he sent the longboat to visit a small island lying in the midst of the ice. The island was "so exceedingly full of birds that one would think they had been stowed there." These were great auks, flightless birds, eventually decimated to extinction by mariners in search of food. There were also other birds on the island—"ugly to attack—for they bite like dogs." Happily, these birds—gannets—still breed on the island, which is now called Funk Island, or, by New-foundland seamen, the Funks.

For a long time I had dreamed about landing on Funk Island. Although I am not an ornithologist, I am interested in photographing sea birds and Funk Island is unique for this activity. Moreover, as my father had mentioned the place so often, it had many dramatic associations for me. I had passed by several times and looked at the barren spot from a distance. On the 1951 cruise in *Seal*, a gale of wind made a landing quite impossible, and in fact, only a few persons had succeeded in getting on the rock in the last century. So I was deter-

Cape Bonavista on the east side of the bay was a frequent landfall of European seamen, such as Cartier in 1534. The lighthouse, in service for a century, now replaced by an automatic on a steel tower, is a museum displaying beautiful eighteenth reflector-lamps.

Fishermen from Bonavista Bay harbors built fine schooners in which to sail to Labrador following the migration of codfish.

mined to make a serious effort to land from *Neptune*. Her shoal draft would enable us to get close enough to use the small rubber boat brought along for the landing attempt. Cartier's men were probably able to pull up their longboat on the small area of the north endof the island which slopes gradually into the sea because the icefield smoothed the breaking waves, but normally there are only two places where even under ideal conditions one can hope to secure a foothold. Will Hamann and I could not do the job alone, so a former shipmate, W. R. Maclay, was flying to Gander from Philadelphia to help with the adventure. We had to be in Lewisporte within a few days to meet him.

Early next morning, *Neptune* left Catalina. Rain had cleared the atmosphere, promising an excellent day's sail. Scaffolding around the old lighthouse at Cape Bonavista indicated repairs were being made. No sooner had we dropped the famous landmark astern, however, when ahead of us a thick white mass of fog filled Bonavista Bay. Fog continued for twenty-four hours but at convenient intervals the curtain lifted enabling us to check dead reckoning. In spite of fog and a clearing gale of wind, we entered Notre Dame Bay. A course was charted among the numerous islands, until at some distance inland, we reached the busy town of Lewisport located on the Trans-Canada Highway. My sister, Mary, kindly drove out from St. John's, picked up Maclay at Gander, and brought him to *Neptune*. Having filled water and fuel tanks and added to our store of food, we were ready to leave. It was good to have Bill Maclay on board. With three of us on the ketch, I felt there was a sporting chance to make a landing on Funk Island. Years ago, at different times, Maclay and Hamann had been students in my biology class at The Hill School. We now made a good team.

I once took a boat through a passage called Dildo Run, saving forty miles between Notre Dame Bay and the harbor of Seldom-come-by on the island of Fogo. We tried to find our way in this unmarked channel but my memory was not reliable enough to guide *Neptune* among the confusing groups of small islands and shoals. We turned back before a wrong turn put the boat high and dry on a shoal. Later, we learned that a bridge too low for masted vessels now spans Dildo Run. Our path would have been effectively blocked had we persisted. By taking the long way around, against an easterly wind, we at length reached the harbor of Seldom-come-by where we were within striking distance of the Funks. Although our plan was to wait for suitable weather, there was a time limit, because Bill had to return home in a fortnight, and we wanted to be on the west coast of Newfoundland by that time.

The evening weather report for Funk Island was not encouraging: "southwest twenty to thirty knots; shifting into west twenty knots; showers, poor visibility tonight."

At 0400 in the morning, barometer was 29.75 rising. We decided to try our luck. Sunrise looked clear; not too crimson—the western sky was overcast. Southwest wind just a light breeze. As Funk Island is now a bird sanctuary under the protection of the Canadian Wildlife Service we had obtained permission to land. The larger of the two conspicuous islands is only a half-mile long and less than a quarter-mile wide. A Seldom-come-by fisherman, Morley Rowe, who fishes for turbot in deep water east of the island, said that in an autumn storm, the island and shoals surrounding it look like one frightful mass of breaking sea—"dangerous to get within six miles of it." Even in April, he said, the island is covered with ice "not much different from an iceberg but for a black line at the edge of the sea."

The Funks are probably the remains of a batholith—a dome of volcanic rock—associated with the great Appalachian Mountain system. For millions of years the granite has slowly been eroded by ice and now represents the smallest scrap of land above the ocean's surface between Newfoundland and Greenland. At the present time, an estimated two hundred thousand black-backed, white-breasted, common murres breed on the island. Murres occupy the ecological niche in the Northern Hemisphere that penguins fill in the Southern Hemisphere. There is also a thriving colony of gannets, fewer puffins, and a declining population of kittiwakes.

By 0900, we were close enough to the island to see an umbrella of birds circling over it, weaving a continuous pattern in the sky. The ocean was relatively calm, at least the twenty-knot southwestern in the forecast had not yet arrived. On board our little craft, a feeling of excitement and tension began to mount as probability for a successful landing increased. Morely Rowe had mentioned "two island rocks—one about ten feet above the surface, the other just awash." We spotted these hazards and began to circle the island at a distance of about forty feet. The fathometer indicated deep water all around. Although the wind was light and, after a while, died out altogether, huge swells, which seemed to erupt from the depths of the ocean, gushed foaming over the island's obsidian-black flanks, worn slipper-smooth by the grinding action of winter ice floes. At a narrow gulch and cove on the south end of the island—one of the two possible landing sites—the up-welling crests rushed violently in and out of the restricted space with a booming sound. In the past, several ornithologists used that cove to land, but obviously any attempt to beach a boat there now would invite disaster.

The crew make a safe landing on Funk Island. Notice that a swell has lifted the rubber boat to the level of the narrow landing shelf.

As *Neptune* progressed, close to the shoreline, the noise of the birds grew so loud one had to shout to converse. Gannets clustered at the north and western end of the island. Some murres were located at the edge of the gannet colony and intermingled with the much larger birds at several places, but the tremendous concentration of murres occupied the flat central area and the rocky southern slopes. At any moment, there was a continuous procession of birds on the ridges—some taking to the air, others landing. Hundred of murres in the water swam around the boat or dived for food. Meanwhile, scores of gannets soared and glided high overhead, their broad, six-foot-long, black-tipped wings giving them the appearance of being avian sailplanes.

After circling three times, we launched the rubber raft, having used binoculars to observe carefully the rock structure of the island as well as the behaviour of the birds. I piloted *Neptune* reasonably close to the place where a safe landing appeared possible. At this location, on the northeast side of the island, a narrow sloping ledge ran at an angle of about thirty degrees up the perpendicular side of the cliff to an area where a climb to a level surface looked easy.

Maclay and Will Hamann climbed into the rubber raft, our ace in

Bill Maclay rows the shipper toward the rock face and waits for a swell to lift the rubber boat. Notice the level of the ocean—a good fifteen feet below the narrow landing shelf.

the hole for this attempt. I stayed with *Neptune*, ready for any emergency that might require assistance. While the ocean appeared fairly calm, when the lads approached the face of the cliff, the swell there rose and fell about fifteen feet from crest to trough. Our plan was to bring the rubber dinghy as close as possible to the cliff, while the man at the oars was to watch the swells as some were higher than others. By manipulating the oars, he was to guide the boat to the narrow shelf of rock, about two feet wide, but now appearing the hundredth part of that dimension. In front of this ledge, the restless ocean lifted the raft up and down like a yo-yo. Just before the crest of a powerful surge swept the boat upward to its highest point, the man in the bow was to jump with the hope of landing on the ledge and not in the

The skipper misses the narrow landing shelf but hangs onto the face of the rock.

water. To my great relief Bill Maclay succeeded in reaching it. Then Will joined him, but not without a near capsize. They had pulled the rubber boat after themselves onto the shelf, when a mighty swell curved upwards and tore the boat out of their grasp into the sea. Fortunately Maclay had a firm hold on the long painter and Hamann clutched the oars.

Later, Maclay landed me on the island. Lacking the agility of my younger shipmates, I carefully considered the entire matter before jumping—and almost failed to reach anything solid. Missing the ledge entirely, I hung onto the face of the cliff like a limpet for a few moments while the next wave swept over me, then with a heave using knees and fingernails, I clambered up to the narrow shelf.

The incredibly dense mass of birds on the ground and in the air above the island created a bizarre scene: the shrill dissonant cries, the smell of death and guano, the hundreds of thousands of murres whose black heads, backs, and white breasts suggested munchkins in evening dress, standing upright occupying every inch of space on the level, along the ridges, perched on boulders, row upon row climbing

The narrow landing shelf looking east.

Murres occupy the ridges at the east end of Funk Island.

the sides of gulches dug out of the island's solid granite by glacial erosion and weathering, thus providing countless tiny footholds for the murres so the birds seemed to be standing one on top of the next —the various elements combined to engender a sense of surrealistic chaos, an avian bedlam.

Murres must stand upright, like their southern counterparts, the penguins, because their legs are located so far back on their bodies. In size, they resemble a small fat duck or a common pigeon. They have short wings, as Cartier observed, "no bigger than half a man's hand," but the chief function of these appendages is to serve as propellers. In clear water I have watched murres swimming with the speed of a dolphin. The late Leslie Tuck, Newfoundland ornithologist and foremost authority on murres, reported that they provide a link in the ecology of the species which constitute their food. Their excrement, rich in potassium compounds, is important to the growth and so to the abundance of the plankton, the small marine organisms on which they feed. Murre colonies are thus the fertilizer factories of northern seas.

Ornithologists who have visited Funk invariably mention the noisy

Murres lay one large black-marked bluish green pear-shaped egg. On narrow ledges the egg rolls in a circle, does not fall off. Both parents take turns brooding egg. Murres are the only sea bird in North Hemisphere to lay eggs in exposed places.

clamor of the birds. As I walked along the highest ridge—about fifty feet above sea level—this eerie sound, like an old klaxon horn, rose and fell in volume. The tiny murrelings, black fuzzy balls of down and feathers huddling under projecting slabs of rock, in chinks and fissures, or pressing together in dozens of small groups in the open, gave forth piercing cries which added to the cataract of sound.

Murres lay one large greenish blue egg with dark markings on the shell. The long oval shape allows the egg to roll in a circle, so as not to topple off the narrow ledge where the female bird alternates with the male in process of hatching the chick. The individual stands with the egg between the feet tucked into plump abdomen. Most of the hatching had taken place by the time of our visit, but there were numerous deserted eggs lying around which had lost their color and were obviously addled. Tuck has noted one interesting tendency on the part of some female murres. Normally, the egg is laid, brooded, and hatched on a narrow bare rock space—a more hazardous place

After hatching murrelings seem to be on their own. When the young are about three weeks old the entire colony becomes restless as they all get ready to return to the sea.

Adult murre and young in water. From mid-July to the following May the ocean will be their home.

On the flatter central section of Funk Island the large murre colony meets the much smaller colony of gannets. Gannets have the lowest world population of any sea bird.

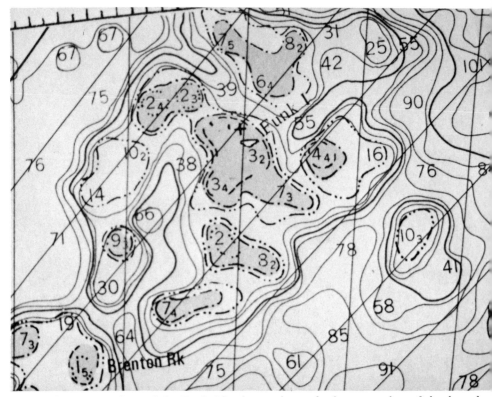

The marine chart of the Funk Island area shows the large number of shoals and ledges surrounding the small island, making the vicinity of the island a maelstrom in a gale from any quarter.

would be hard to find. Birds are massed so closely on the narrow ledge that if a flight of adults seeks to join the group, individuals are jostled, eggs are displaced, trodden upon, often destroyed, yet the colony continues to grow. But Tuck also observed during his study of murre behaviour on Funk that sometimes females gather small stones or pebbles and place them near the feet. He wonders: is this a vestigial nest-building characteristic or is it a nest-building habit in the process of being acquired by natural selection? Would not Charles Darwin be fascinated by this murre behaviour!

When *Neptune* was circling the island for the last time before leaving we noticed some of the young murres being led to sea. I had been afraid the entire colony would have left Funk by mid-July when we were due to arrive, but a phone call to Leslie Tuck had been reassuring. He described for me how the young take to the water and we were privileged to witness part of this momentous event. On the central part of the south side of the island, the exfoliated surface of the rock dips gradually toward the ocean. Down this slippery path, washed by ocean swells, scores of adults marched in stately fashion with young birds in tow. The wings of the adults beat a whirring tattoo, while murrelings struggle to walk erect and to move as fast as their elders. This display of instinctive behaviour was a marvelous sight.

At the edge of the drop-off, the parade did not stop. Without hesitation young and old plunged downward into the surf, one group followed another in rapid succession. Hundreds of black heads soon began popping up all over the surface of the ocean creating an animated scene as the murres, young and old, gathered into clusters and swam away from the island. Now the sea would be their home, offering protection and nourishment. Not for ten months would the urge to seek land reassert itself.

The isolated situation of Funk Island creates in ideal breeding place for the species that gather on the rock. According to observations made during the past four hundred years, the bird population changes in time as to dominant species and number of individuals. After the great auks had been exterminated which, considering the wholesale slaughter of the birds, took an extraordinarily long time, immense numbers of arctic tern took over the island as a breeding place, although none are at present found there. In the 1930s murre colonies were estimated at ten thousand. Tuck's present estimate runs to more than two hundred thousand nesting birds, making Funk one of the dramatic bird islands in any ocean. The present gannet colony is also increasing. Cartier mentioned gannets on the Funks, then for a century the large birds disappeared. Tuck now considers there are more than two thousand pairs nesting which agrees with the rough estimate we made.

Gannets, even resting on land, are majestic birds. Compared to murres in size, they are enormous, with white bodies and black-tipped white wings. The stout bluish gray wedge-shaped bill becomes a powerful weapon when the birds, having circled high above a school of fish, fold wings somewhat and plunge into the ocean sending up a geyser of spray. Fishermen have caught gannets in nets at a depth of thirty feet, which shows how far the birds can dive to seek food.

The most distinctive feature of a gannet is a large piercing eye surrounded by dark eye-shadow. A thick straight black line, which extends along the upper surface of the bill, curves around the eye enlarging into a black triangle of pigment. Then, sweeping backward toward the head and neck, it reverses direction, curving sharply forward under the bill, creating a villainous expression.

Gannets make a nest of sorts, utilizing small stones, fish bones, excrement, and some of the meager supply of plant material that grows in the crevices. On a more or less flat space near the center of the island, the eastern nesting murres mingle with the western nesting gannets, an extremely hazardous position for tiny murrelings, one would judge, especially when the voracious appetite of gannets is considered. I saw several nesting gannets reach over and casually seize in their powerful bills squealing murre chicks and swallow them in a gulp. Evidently, murres are willing to pay a price in the struggle to restrict the nesting territory of the gannets.

Although at noon there was still no sign of the twenty- to thirty-knot southwest wind that had been forecast, there had been a wind shift into the northeast and signs of a rapid change in weather increased. I found getting back into the rubber raft almost as hazardous as landing from it onto the island, but I successfully managed to fall into the boat at the right moment. We immediately got *Neptune* under way and headed west for Seldom. By 1330 the northeaster had increased to thirty knots and transfer to or from Funk would have been out of the question. The weather gods having given us a quiet morning were vigorously stoking their wind boiler.

18

Wandering Continents

On the morning following our successful visit to Funk Island we cleared Seldom-come-by at 0700. Easterly wind that had hastened our departure from Funk, having slackened somewhat during the night, now increased to thirty knots, dragging fog on its biting blast. *Neptune* rounded Twillingate Point in flying spray and heavy seas.

During the flight from Boston to Gander, Bill Maclay had met a group of English and American geologists who planned to spend August on New World Island studying the coastal geology of certain sections in Notre Dame Bay. The project sounded so interesting we decided to learn more about the program by visiting a harbor near their base. We were now heading in that direction, and by early afternoon, in a small bay called Virgin Arm, we set about anchoring in a narrow cove. Since the northeaster had become a full gale accompanied by torrents of rain, we took quite a while to set the Danforth anchor as well as the forty-pound CQR plough using on it sixty fathoms of chain, to restrain *Neptune* from dragging. A radio report of seventy-five-knot winds along the south coast of Newfoundland partly explained our local weather.

In spite of gale and rain, the geologists appeared on shore bundled in oilskins, sou'westers and long rubber boots. They were carefully ferried on board and *Neptune*'s cabin was soon filled with a distinguished group of men and women from Oxford, the British Museum, Amherst College, and the Universities of Illinois and Edinburgh, a most unlikely group to find on a rainy day in a Newfoundland outport. Over tea and crumpets we yachtsmen were brought up-to-date about geological theories recently developed to explain certain features of Newfoundland's rock structure.

Newfoundland is situated at the northeastern-most tip of the Appalachian Mountain system—an ancient system dating from the Paleozoic era—the very dawn of life on earth.

Because the island has an exposed precipitous shoreline, the coast is a geologist's delight offering indisputable evidence of past changes. And since thin soil, which overlies most of the island away from the coast, has been severely eroded by glacial action, the rocky skeleton here is also readily revealed. There is no better place in the world than Newfoundland, many geologists feel, to study the anatomy of an old mountain system.

The geology of the island represents a cross-section of the Appalachian system formed during the mountain building period of five hundred million years ago. To simplify a complex subject: there is a west coast section where the early Paleozoic rocks are only mildly deformed by heat and pressure; a central section—the Notre Dame Bay area of central Newfoundland—where Paleozoic rocks appear to have been pushed into folds, the strata broken by faulting (one layer rising about the other) and intruded by granite—volcanic rock; and thirdly, an eastern section called the Avalon Platform, where Paleozoic formations are also mildly deformed, as in the west coast region, although in other ways the geology of the west coast is quite different from the Avalon Platform. Thus there are three regions in Newfoundland defined by geological structure and by faunas preserved as fossils within the rocks. Dr. Stuart McKerrow of the geology department at Oxford University, one of our visitors, was interested in gathering data which might help to explain how such different geological structures now exist side by side in an area as small as Newfoundland. The key to such an explanation lies in the concept of continental drift, or, more correctly, plate techtonics.

About 1912 a German meteorologist, Alfred Wegener, impressed by the apparent physiographical "fit" between various land masses —such as east coast South America and west coast Africa—envisioned a single great land mass which supposedly began to separate into the various continents during the Mesozoic era. The widely distributed seed fern, lossopteris, and other flora, supported this view of the world, but Wegener's theory of continental movement gained little support and languished until the 1960s when evidence of seafloor spreading from oceanic centers indicated that ocean basins were not permanent global features.

Following World War II, introduction of atomic submarines capable of extended cruising in every part of the world's oceans increased the need for accurate charts of the sea bottom. Oceanographic research supplied many of these needs and, in addition, has increased our knowledge about ocean basins in hitherto undreamed of ways.

We know, now, that under the surface of the north Atlantic stands the greatest mountain range on the planet—a system greater than the Andes, Rockies, and Himalayas combined together. This is the mammoth range of the Mid-Atlantic Ridge—the most rugged section of the recently discovered forty thousand-mile mid-ocean ridge that snakes its way around the globe on the bottom of the seas. Along the crest of the Mid-Atlantic Ridge a large central rift valley extends, averaging twenty miles in width and about five thousand feet in depth; the inner flanks of this huge crack are rough and block-faulted. Seismic refraction studies indicate that heat flow along the trough is higher than normal. Photographs taken at the valley floor show hot matter from the deep mantle up-welling toward the surface of the floor along the axis of the ridge. The "toothpaste" hot lava looks as if it had been squeezed out of the cracks like toothpaste from a tube. Pillow lava—as this material is called—molten at twenty-two hundred degrees Fahrenheit—cooled and solidified under pressures of two tons per square inch. Thus new ocean floor is continually being formed in the Mid-Atlantic Ridge valley and the floor slowly moved away from the axis with the drifting continents.

Using this new knowledge and a great deal of other related information, a novel theory called Plate Tectonics was proposed to explain and correlate the data. This proposes that the outer thirty miles or so of the earth is a brittle shell or lithosphere that is broken into six large and many smaller pieces or plates. Convection currents or up-wellings from the deep molten interior of the earth cause these plates to move about slowly relative to one another and to the interior. The motion of the plates generates the great undersea ridges. Continents and oceans ride on the plates. For example, virtually all of North America and the western Atlantic ride on the American plate; all African and most of the eastern Atlantic ride on the African plate; Europe rides on another plate; and so on. The eastern and western plates meet at the Mid-Atlantic Ridge. Modern geology is concerned with acquiring greater understanding of the forces that continually create, alter, and move the massive plates that make up the floor of oceans and the face of the planet on which we live.

To explain origin of geological formations characteristic of central Newfoundland, Canadian earth scientists, especially Dr. Tuzo Wilson of Toronto University, proposed the existence of an ancient ocean, a pre-Atlantic which closed at some period in the past, just as the Pacific Ocean is closing at present due to plates overlapping and the absorption of one plate by another.

According to the pre-Atlantic theory, the limestones of western

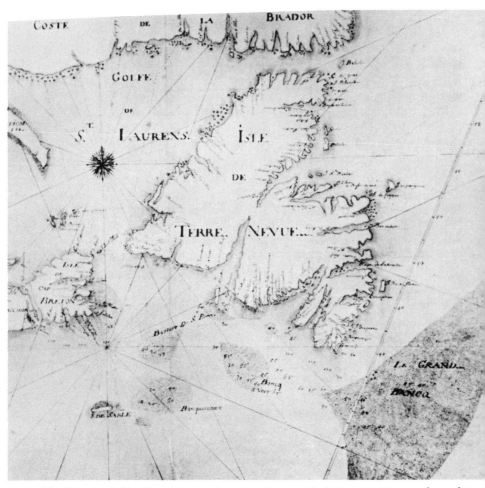

Draftsman of this 1650 map has incorrectly extended Fortune Bay northward to meet Notre Dame Bay. The irony of this misconception is that it unwittingly illustrates the plate techtonic hypothesis which produced the present shape of Newfoundland by fusing a European mass with Appalachian rock of the west coast.

Newfoundland were continental deposits at the eastern edge of the North American continent in Ordovician times. The Avalon platform was part of another continent, a part of Europe, such as Wales. The plate bearing this land moved across the ocean toward North America. Pillow lavas and crystalling rocks of central Newfoundland are the remains of an ocean floor that was folded, crumpled, and squeezed into contact with continental rock and sediment when the two different thrusting masses rafted together, just as one might create folds in a carpet by pushing both ends toward the middle. When the ancient ocean was reduced or eliminated by the colliding continental masses, land areas were formed on which material could collect. The sandstones and conglomerates of central Newfoundland indicate that these deposits were laid down in lakes or rivers. Molten volcanic rock at the collision zone explains the granite intrusions that also are characteristic of rocks in the central region of the island.

Many millions of years later, when changing convection currents deep inside the earth caused the plates to move slowly apart to form the present Atlantic Ocean, the Avalon platform remained attached to the eastern edge of the Appalachian platform, giving Newfoundland its present shape.

Professor McKerrow and his associates are interested in examining evidence of the faulting and the suturing process. They also look carefully for invertebrate fossils, chiefly Brachiopods, marine bivalve animals superficially resembling clams. This investigation has discovered that Brachiopods occurring in Paleozoic rocks along the fjords of Notre Dame Bay are similar to those commonly found in Wales and the Bristol Channel coast of England, whereas in the Cambrian strata of the Newfoundland Northern Peninsula and Port au Port such fossils are absent. A good deal of additional fossil evidence has been collected to support the concept that the geology of western Newfoundland is quite different from the Notre Dame and central region.

Look at a map of the island. The western Long Range Peninsula represents the remains of an ancient New World mountain system, while the eastern Avalon section was at one time part of Europe. A suture running from New World Island toward Cape Breton diagonally across the central area where rocks show complex folding indicates the result of collision by the two masses. Newfoundland's present shape is thus due to a remarkable phenomenon—the relocation of huge land masses by our earth's crustal movements.

19

In the Wake
of Earlier Voyagers

Leaving to port the numerous attractive bays, islands, harbors, and tickles of Notre Dame Bay, some of which we had explored in 1951 and now regretfully passed by due to lack of time, *Neptune* was sailed along the high, massive-looking extremely steep cliffs of Cape St. John. The wide bands of horizontal strata, layer upon layer of undisturbed sedimentary rock, signify river deposits layed down on the old western platform described by the McKerrow group.

As I focused binoculars on the exposed paleozoic rock, evidence of crustal events spanning six hundred million years of our earth's development, glancing rays of the afternoon sun brought into relief the strikingly beautiful formation. The coast of Newfoundland has been cruised by Europeans for a longer time than any other part of the New World. I thought of all the seamen who had sighted this cape or other impressive geological phenomena we had seen. Did any individual ever speculate about the odd appearance of such cliffs, or notice rock which displayed wavy layers like the waves of the ocean, rising and falling, or which sometimes had twisted and folded layers, as if contorted by violent forces. More than likely the reaction of mariners was to regard the rugged coast as a potential threat to life and property. And with good reason. There scarcely is any stretch of Newfoundland's coastline that has not witnessed a wreck. In the days of sail tragedies were frequent.

I look away from Cape St. John and turn seaward. We were passing a small steep-sided island called by schoonermen Gull Island Cape

Stratified Paleozoic rock similar to the formation at Cape St. John.

John, to distinguish it from other islands bearing the same name. This desolate crag appeared bare of vegetation except for a thin layer of moss which partially covered the granite slopes in a few places on the east side.

In 1867 Gull Island laid a trap for the brigantine, *Queen* of *Swansea*. This event must have made an indelible impression on the seafaring community of the northeast coast for, even today, old fishermen from Green Bay will ask: Do you know about the wreck of the Queen on Gull Island?

In mid December, 1867, the *Queen* of *Swansea,* a 200 ton barbentine, commanded by a Welchman named Owens, left St. John's for Tilt Cove, a harbour on the west side of Notre Dame Bay, intending to load copper ore for Swansea, a seaport of Wales. Captain Owens was not familiar with the northern bays, and since December can be a stormy month a pilot, William Duggan, was engaged as navigator's assistant. The ship also carried two lady passengers, the mine manager's daughter returning home for Christmas, and a friend of hers, also Dr. Downley, the medical doctor at Tilt Cove who had been visiting colleagues in St John's.

The expected ship never arrived at Tilt Cove. For a long time the families hoped that if the Queen had been wrecked there would have been survivors. In those days the only means of communication during winter was by overland mail; for the northern bays this was a slow and uncertain mode. The fate of the Queen became an unsolved mystery. The ship had left St John's only to disappear without a trace.

Sometime during May of the following year, a group of men from Tilt Cove ventured as far as Cape St John hunting seabirds as a source of fresh food after the long winter. As their boat circled Gull Island where they considered searching for gull's eggs, one of the men caught sight of a stout line hanging over the side of a cliff. They rowed toward the eastside landing place and got ashore. On scattering to investigate, two of the men soon found part of a ship's sail stretched out and frozen to the ground. When the rumpled canvas was lifted they were horrified to find on the ground beneath the sail the bodies of nine men and two women. Further search located two more bodies huddled in the shelter of a boulder.

A diary found on the body of Dr. Downley told the sad story: Not long after the *Queen* had cleared Baccalieu Island, she was struck by a southwest gale that blew the ship far to sea and nearly overwhelmed her. Efforts of captain and crew kept the damaged craft afloat, although part of the bulwarks had been torn away by pounding waves, and several heavy sails were blown to shreds. Since the *Queen* was now far off course; the main effort was directed to getting back to Notre Dame Bay. Fortunately a wind shift from south westerly, which was dead ahead, to north west helped the captain lay a course to Cape St John and the shelter of Green Bay. Present position could only be established by dead reckoning, and its accuracy was a great source of worry to the captain. Continued bad weather prevented a sun sight to establish a better line of position.

The northerly wind increased to a freezing gale. Seas smothered the ship as she labored heavily. On the morning of December 18, without warning, the *Queen* struck. To the anguish of all they found themselves wrecked on desolate Gull Island. If only the compass course had been a few degrees closer to south the ship would have reached safety. Tilt Cove was only fifteen miles away.

With great difficulty all the company landed, and a hawser was run out to secure the ship to the shore. Four of the crew, including the pilot and the bosun, returned on board to transfer provisions, but the plunging vessel parted the hawser. The battered hull slipped sternfirst into the breakers, and before their eyes sank out of sight in deep water with their companions trapped below deck.

On the fifth day, Dr. Downley wrote that the group was in desperate straits, totally without food or water. The island had not yielded any sustenance, not even a few boughs for a rough bed. In wet freezing clothes, desperate with thirst, they lay on the cold bare rock and covered themselves with what was left of a sail.

About three days later, Downley had lost account of time, but he thought it was Christmas Day. He was still alive as were some of the others. Snow had fallen and they had gathered some to help the awful thirst. To write was difficult for him. There was no hope of rescue. Death would be a blessing. They had tried to gather drift-wood for a fire but the flotsam was so wet the flame soon snuffed itself out.

Ironically, a fisherman from Shoe Cove, south of Cape St John and a few miles closer to Gull than Tilt Cove, was hunting rabbits on the high land behind the village just before Christmas. He is said to have seen a light or a fire on Gull but the light soon disappeared and he did not report the sighting. Fishermen sometimes landed on the island to boil the kettle for a mugup.

Neptune was now heading northward toward the town of St. Anthony where, years ago, Dr. Wilfred Grenfell established the base hospital of the Medical Association he had founded. "The Doctor," as he was usually called by those who knew him, had been a friend of my family since his arrival from England on the coast of Labrador in the 1890s. Grenfell was the same age as my father and the two men had somewhat similar characteristics. Both were extremely active physically and somewhat impetuous in their desire to get on with the job at hand. Sir Wilfred Grenfell's great gift was his ability to interest men and women in the work he was doing or in the projects that his fertile mind envisioned. The colleagues he gathered around him were truly remarkable people who carried on the humanitarian work he began and who inspired others to continue to do so, even down to the present day.

St. Anthony is no longer an isolated village of a few weather-beaten houses and a noisy pack of Eskimo dogs. A motor road now extends along the coast of the Long Range Peninsula from the Trans-Canada Highway, itself a twisting black-topped ribbon which follows, more or less, the old, now partly abandoned railway line. When we called at St. Anthony in 1951, there was as yet no connection with any kind of highway for the rough track that traversed the town. Besides the Grenfell Mission truck there was one other car owned by the telegraph operator. On the day we arrived the local constable had to handle his first traffic accident: the automobile had backed out of a lane into the oncoming truck.

Neptune rounded Fishing Head at the wide entrance to St. Anthony harbor as storm clouds scudded across the sky threatening rain and fog. We had sailed offshore all day passing near a spot where, in

On Fishing Head overlooking entrance to the harbor of St. Anthony.

Encountered in fog, icebergs are cold, gray menacing monsters; in sunshine, brillant, beautiful, fascinating jewels. This picture was taken in July.

Brad Middlebrook surveying the town of St. Anthony. Grenfell Hospital and other buildings at left in distance. A road now connects both sides of the harbor. Notice exfoliation of rock by water freezing and thawing.

1942, a Canadian Air Force patrol plane sank a Nazi U-boat, the war's first kill in North American waters. The squadron leader, a Newfoundlander, lived to see the end of hostilities but none of his flight crew on that occasion survived European battle action.

In 1951 we encountered no icebergs south of St. Anthony, but in the following year, during the same week of July, on a night run from Notre Dame Bay, we were surprised to find drift ice along our course and at daybreak counted twenty-five large bergs we had to avoid. *Neptune* sighted a few widely scattered large icebergs in the same area. A mariner can thus expect a high degre of variation in the northeast sector berg count.

An easterly gale, with rain and fog, offered little inducement to leave harbor next day. We inspected the large new Grenfell hospital constructed with funds supplied in large part by the Provincial government. Thanks to the hospital's business office, we were able to use mechanical laundry equipment in the basement to do a big wash. Dr. Gordon Thomas, the medical director of the Grenfell Association gave us a review of the many changes that have taken place in the delivery of medical care in the north, proving that the various hospitals and nursing stations of the Grenfell organization will continue to provide an essential link in the chain of community service.

Grenfell floating hospital-ship *Maraval* on the haul-up slip. During summer, *Maraval* covered a thousand miles of northern Labrador coast.

One pleasant result of our layover was the opportunity to visit the St. Anthony fish freezing plant. We were able to buy all the codfish tongues on hand—ten pounds. The tongue muscles resemble bay scallops and are a delicacy.

Sea conditions had improved slightly by the following morning when we put to sea at dawn. Thick stratus clouds to the south looked like bags of wind, but a weak sun was making an attempt to penetrate the overcast. By 0800 *Neptune* was approaching the towering headland of Cape Dégrat. In historian Admiral Samuel Eliot Morison's opinion this promontory was John Cabot's landfall. The massive cliffs are on the latitude in which Cabot is said to have made his westering. In those days and long after, navigators used latitude sailing as a convenient method by which to maintain an accurate great circle course. A ship set out with the noon sun at a known altitude; the navigator would endeavor to maintain that noon angle throughout the voyage by the use of his astrolabe, and in later centuries by cross-staff, a crude forerunner of the sextant. Cape Dégrat is not far from the low craggy ridge forming the east face of Cape Bauld, the extreme north tip of Newfoundland. We rounded Cape Bauld at

Cape Degrat, on latitude 51° 37' N, is considered by marine historian S. E. Morison to be John Cabot's landfall. There is a high island to the north which Cabot called St. John's, since it was John the Baptist Day. French fishermen later called the island Belle Isle, after an island off their Brittany coast, and Belle Isle it still is.

0818. A freshening southwester hit us smack on the bow as we left the cape behind and under power pushed against wind and sea into Sacred Bay. Whence came such a name for this rough-looking shore? For many years, French fisherman claimed as their own this stretch of coast and Jacques Cartier spent part of a week wind-bound in a nearby harbor on his first voyage; hence the origin of the name is probably French.

We were now following the track of much earlier voyages. The lowland ahead of *Neptune* welcomed Norsemen over one thousand years ago. The coastline of the bay may have changed in appearance from what it was in earlier times (raised beaches on the Labrador side of the Strait of Belle Isle show that considerable uplift has taken place) but the present approach to L'Anse-aux-Meadow, where the site of a Viking camp is located, looks anything but alluring from seaward. The head wind had propagated a steep sea in the shallow water and spray was flying over islets and ledges. Lowland and shallow water may have been welcomed by the tired Norsemen, as a distinct change from the lofty rugged Labrador coast where finding

Cape Bauld is the extreme northern tip of the island of Newfoundland. Norsemen from Greenland passed close to it heading west about A.D. 1000

a convenient place to disembark is often perplexing. In the Vinland Saga, the landing is described in a translation from the Old Icelandic thus: "there were extensive shallows there and at low tide the ship went aground, high and dry. But they were so impatient to land that they could not bear to wait for the rising tide to float the ship; they ran ashore to a place where a river flowed out of a lake. As soon as the tide had refloated the ship, they took a boat and rowed out to it and brought it up the river into the lake where they anchored it. Then they decided to winter there and built some large houses."

In 1961 a Norwegian husband and wife team, both trained scientists, had uncovered the remains of what looked like a Norse settlement at L'Anse-aux-Meadow, (Meadow is obviously a corruption of some French term—I suggest *mégère*, meaning fox—Bay of Foxes is not an unlikely name for this part of Newfoundland.) The discovery of the Norse remains was not quite the result of a single happy accident. Helge Ingstad had made the study of primitive people his career. He had lived with Stone Age Indians in northern Canada and with the Apache in the hills of Arizona. Eventually he became interested in, and made a study of, the remains of Norse settlements which had flourished for more than four hundred years in Greenland.

Danish archeologists discovered evidence of Norse habitations at L'Anse-aux-Meadow on Épaves Bay. After the area was carefully explored, outlines of the houses were grassed over. Notice the flat stones which mark fireplace sites.

Certain events, such as the devasting Black Plague, diverted the attention of Europeans from the Greenland colonies for a century or more. When communication was resumed only ruins of the settlements remained. The Norse had vanished.

Ingstad believes the Icelandic Sagas tell a factual story of adventure and discovery of new land in the west, although descriptions of the voyages—originally oral and transcribed at a much later date—are often vague, repetitive, disparate, and befuddling to a translator who is trying to render an intelligible narrative. Deciding to look for signs of the Norsemen along the Atlantic coast, starting from Rhode Island, Ingstad reached north Newfoundland without a solid clue. As a guest on board a Grenfell hospital ship, he was visiting a remote harbor north of St. Anthony, near Cape Bauld, when as was his custom, he asked the village people the whereabouts of any unusual mounds or signs of old building sites in the vicinity. A knowledgeable fisherman, George Decker, said that over by Black Duck Brook (that runs out of a lake into the sea) at Lancy Meadow (L'Anse-aux-Meadow) there were outlines on the grassy plain that might be the remains of some habitation. When the sod at this place was carefully stripped, and some excavations carried out under the direction of

Sagas describe the islands and the bay where the Norse landed.

Mrs. Ingstad, a trained archeologist, several significant observations were possible: there was no evidence of flint chips to indicate an old encampment of Eskimo people; no European artifacts, such as sixteenth-century fisherman might have scattered; however, a fire hearth and an ember pit characteristic of the Greenland Norse were uncovered. This was an exciting find and plans were made for a detailed examination of the site.

During the following three summers a team of Icelandic, Swedish, and Norwegian archeologists under the direction of Mrs. Ingstad worked over the area. The foundations of structures excavated by these experts conformed to the pattern of Norse culture well known in Greenland, Iceland, and Scandinavia. The grassy plain yielded the remains of nine ancient houses, fire hearths, and ember pits—where live coals were banked at night to be still glowing by next morning for another day's cooking. A crude forge yielded a stone anvil, bog-iron slag, and charcoal. Eventually, Carbon 14 dating placed the age of these materials to be about A.D. 1000. One of the most interesting objects that the careful sifting of the remains disclosed was a small soapstone-spindle whorl indicating the presence of women—since the whorl was used as a flywheel spinning a wooden shaft to twist raw wool into yarn for knitting clothes. Such whorls have also been found frequently at Norse sites in Greenland.

While the dig was in progress, Helge Ingstad cruised the coast northward along Labrador in his powerboat. He noted the long sand beach at Cape Porcupine—the Marvelstrands—as well as other landmarks mentioned in the Sagas. As he entered the Strait of Belle Isle on the return, Ingstad considered that the appearance of the bay between Cape Bauld and Cape Onion had a striking similarity to the approach to L'Anse-aux-Meadow described by the land-seeking Norsemen.

In any event, the Meadow's site is definitely Norse, whether or not it was Leif and his men who actually landed and lived there, or some other expedition from Greenland who followed after Leif. The western colony did not survive, according to the Sagas, because the Greenlanders were repeatedly attacked by a fierce people the Norse called Skraelings, whose black sealskin kayaks "were so many the bay appeared sown with coals."

We visited the site and the nearby museum set up by the Provincial government. Replicas of many artifacts are displayed. The originals are in Oslo. From the top of a hill overlooking the bay and the grassy plain, standing by a high stone cairn whose stones may have been laid up by Norse hands nine hundred years ago, it was not difficult to imagine the square sail of Viking ship making for the rocky shore.

20

~~~~~~~~~~~~~~~

Strait of Belle Isle

During the evening of our second day at L'Anse-aux-Meadows, the whistling wind showed signs of easing as the barometer began a slow rise. All day the northeaster had churned the open shallow bay into masses of whitecaps, like acres of waving arctic cotton. When the ship's clock struck 0200, the four sharp notes woke me and I went on deck to look around. The wind had moderated enough for us to continue the voyage, but instead of calling the boys I pulled on a heavy jacket and looked overhead. The sky was alive with lights flickering all over the cold black dome; the exquisite beauty of the night was spellbinding. I could sense the thrill that astronomers—professional or amateur—must feel when they peer through telescopes or probe deep within the universe by means of specialized cameras. I imagined that I was back with Galileo, sharing his surprise and satisfaction when he saw three satellites, the moons of Jupiter, encircling that planet; a discovery that became one of the great turning points in the history of science.

As I looked across the sky at groups of stars, it did not surprise me that the early Greeks and Romans recognized constellations and named them after mythological heroes. Below Cassiopeia, at this hour, in its sprawling "W" shape, the Great Nebula of Andromeda was clearly visible as a hazy patch of light. This nebula, a giant spiral galaxy somewhat like our own, contains one hundred billion stars and enormous volumes of dust and gasses. Its diameter is about sixty thousand light years, which means the light I was seeing had been traveling through space for two million years. And within the Great Nebula, stars are dying, astronomers say, as a result of cataclysmic explosions millions of times more powerful than any nuclear blast

At Eddies Cove a family was cleaning the day's catch of codfish.

man can set off on earth. In my favorite constellation, brillant, beautiful Orion, Betelguese was conspicuous. This important navigation star is a super-giant red body whose diameter is so wide our sun with most of the planets could be placed within its boundry. Somewhat dazed by the immensity of space, I called the crew to admire the spectacle. I was reminded, as I got into warmer clothes, of another night, years ago, when I was fishing on the Grand Banks in the schooner *Democracy:* on watch with a venerable old fisherman who, as he gazed in admiration at the maze of planets and stars overhead, turned to me and said, cryptically, with a tone of wonder in his voice, "And one man do'in the guiding of it all!"

Faintly luminous streaks of an aurora tinged the northern quadrant of the sky as we began to get under way by recovering the Danforth anchor that had been securely wedged among rocks on shore. Then we tackled the stout chain of our main kedge, the forty-pound CQR plough.

Leaving behind shadowy outlines of fishermen's boats on moorings in the narrow cove that had sheltered us, we headed *Neptune* for the group-flashing light on Cape Norman, and having rounded this point of land set a course for Pointe Amour on the Labrador side of Belle

Northern Newfoundland children.

Isle Strait. As we headed westward in darkness, under sail and power, several pin points of light on the port side indicated the location of small fishing villages scattered along the harborless south side of the strait. Evidently a powerline had finally brought electricity to this remote coast, replacing the candle and oil lamp that had served for centuries.

The shortest route across the north Atlantic lies from Montreal to Liverpool, via Strait of Belle Isle. For centuries, large numbers of ships, both freighters and ocean liners, used this route during those months when the St. Lawrence was open, usually from May to November, in spite of recognized hazards—ice in early spring and fog at any time of the year. Just before dawn, a twenty-thousand-ton-class Canadian Pacific liner swept eastward through the strait like a stately dowager. Even at that hour the ship was ablaze with twinkling lights. We wished the passengers a safe crossing as we plunged across her wake heading now toward the Labrador side.

Ebbing and flowing tidal currents in this relatively narrow strait, pumping water from the Atlantic into the Gulf and then out again every six hours, are influenced by the earth's rotation and produce strong and unpredictable water movements that have caused ships to get off course into dangerous situations. Years ago a lighthouse, a foghorn, and eventually a wireless station were set up at Pointe Amour, at the western end of the strait. In May and June, heavy field ice and large icebergs often drift into the strait from the Atlantic. Rotation of the earth forces this ice to the north side. In 1925 a new Royal Navy light cruiser went ashore in thick fog at Pointe Amour while trying to avoid a grounded berg. I remember a long forty-mile journey in an open motorboat to see this wreck . . . in fact, I still have a bugle that came out of her.

When a ship is declared a total loss by captain or insurance underwriters, what usually happens is that coastal people feel free to remove whatever can be pried loose or recovered by dredging or diving. This activity increases in proportion to the distance from legal jurisdiction. While threat of casualty, which always accompanies any wreck, is a shocking event for watermen, there is also something elemental and exciting about the unnatural happenings. Realization that a stout ship, mortally wounded, is being pounded to pieces by furious seas inflames the imagination of a spectator. Prospect of finding unexpected treasure has suddenly appeared. Strange-looking equipment, a whole array of interesting desirable objects dangle, as it were, in tantalizing fashion often just out of reach. Furnishings and cargo of the broken ship arouse the latent cupidity of all within gunshot.

The earliest childhood memory of my father involved a wreck. He was five years old, and with a younger brother was playing with toy boats along the shore in front of the seaside homestead. Suddenly, out of the fog, a large red ship's lifeboat, crowded with men, swung around the nearby point. Some of the seamen manning the oars had white and red bandages tied around their heads, others were only half clothed; the boatload of sailors looked like pictures of ravaging robbers. And in the bow of the boat holding the painter in his hand, ready to jump ashore, stood a huge black man. Never having seen such wild-looking individuals, least of all a black man, the terrified boys ran for their lives back to the house crying that fierce pirates were landing in the front cove.

The lifeboat's crew were survivors from a large bark that had wrecked on an outlying sunken reef a day's journey westward. The ship's back had broken, but a good deal of the cargo was prime lumber and large timbers which my grandfather was able to buy and salvage. The wild-looking crew remained a vivid image in my father's memory. I, myself, can recall a carved weatherbeaten quarter board, bearing the name *Edward Cardwell,* fastened to the wall of our carpenter shop. It was the only surviving structural souvenir of the lumber-carrying bark wrecked so long ago.

Two unusual pieces in my parent's home, a doublehanded silver sugar bowl bearing the crest of the Dominion Line and a beautiful green Wedgewood dish, with oak-leaf decoration in high relief, for serving or displaying fruit, were reminders of a wreck at Pointe Amour on September 25, 1895.

The ocean liner *Mariposa,* twelve thousand tons, the favorite passenger ship of the Dominion Steamship Line, en route from Montreal to Liverpool, ran ashore in dense fog, in the same locality, it was said, that a man-of-war, H.M.S. *Lily,* had come to grief in 1892. The *Mariposa*'s captain was an experienced mariner with a record of thirty-three years of transatlantic navigation without accident. The presumed cause for the grounding was the reduced speed of the ship. After two days of dense fog, she was proceeding at head slow speed at night but a strong current on the starboard bow must have set the liner off course. She ran up on a shoal to the north of the point, the lookouts having heard no sound of the lighthouse fog signal. Had *Mariposa* been three hundred feet to the right of her course, she would have escaped the reef on which she ran bow first. The plates of her hull were torn and buckled as far back as amidships, for the ship was heavy with a full cargo. With twenty feet of water in her engine room there was no prospect of hauling her clear, although the stern still floated free with twenty-five feet under her keel at this point. Sea had been calm during the night when the ship struck, but at daybreak wind increased to gale. The furious surf on the rocky coast made unacceptable a tentative plan to land the sixty-six passengers by boat.

By means of a line-throwing gun, a breeches buoy was finally rigged from ship to a station on the beach. The bow had been sharply elevated by the collision and the distance from it to the shore was six hundred feet. This forbidding chasm, filled with sound and sight of cresting breakers roaring landward in a welter of foam, presented an awesome spectacle to the apprehensive passengers assembled together on the damaged foredeck.

One by one the corseted Victorian ladies had to shed their stately reserve and allow themselves to be lashed into the fragile-looking, uncomfortable swinging seat of the breeches buoy, before being slowly pulled across the wide gap between ship and beach. As they swayed shoreward down the line, forty feet above the hissing surf, several, overcome by the frightening experience, became hysterical and were unconscious when the buoy reached safety. Eventually, the entire crew was removed from the wreck, since the hull lay in an

Neptune anchored in a Labrador tickle. Notice lack of trees and the moss-covered hills.

exposed position especially vulnerable to attack by the prevailing southwest wind.

Tents were hurriedly improvised and fortunately the fog cleared on the day following the stranding. The *Sardinian,* an Allen Line steamer from Liverpool, saw the wreck and stood in close to shore at Forteau Bay making possible the transfer of passengers by small boats. When all were safe on board, the ship continued on to Montreal. *Mariposa*'s officers stayed in the tents and supervised the landing of most of the valuable cargo, which included twenty bullocks, twenty-five hundred sheep, four thousand bushels of grain—the remainder washed out of the damaged main hold—tons of cheese, butter, tinned meat, eggs, and apples. Local schooners and boats of all sorts were employed to move the cargo, each receiving one-third of the portion salvaged. Fortunately calm weather prevailed for a week before another gale broke open the hull.

My own wreck experience involved a Norwegian freighter.

By mid-October, 1922, the seasonal marine products operation had almost ended; most of our fishermen had been taken back to their

Mainland Labrador landscape. Low spruce or fir trees may be found in valleys.

homes in Newfoundland. A small group remained to load a vessel going to Spain with a cargo of dried salt cod. For several days thick fog had filled the lower Gulf of St. Lawrence, and as long as a strong southwest wind held, a change in weather did not seem likely. To load the vessel properly a string of cold, dry, clear northwest wind days was needed.

Extending ten miles seaward from our home island lay another group of islands of various sizes, most of which had been bought from the Canadian government by my grandfather in the mid-1800s for commercial reasons. Beyond this archipelago were clusters of islets and breaking ledges. A sensation that had long fascinated me arose from a habit I had developed of standing quietly and gazing far to the south in the direction of these distant islands. From the crest of a low hill to the west of our home, I could look seaward, first to the nearest island separated only by a narrow channel, then over a wide bay to the islands on the horizon, from whence came the sound of a restless sea; a continuous sound, sometimes rising in tone, then falling, but continuous, persistent, a distant muted mysterious sound as if from a large conch shell pressed close to one's ear, or the hissing

sound of escaping low-pressure steam. I would often stand for minutes listening to this sound of the distant breakers. Even when the
view was concealed by fog it was thrilling to listen as the sea intoned
its ineffable song.

On this particular morning, I had walked up the long boardwalk
from the western wharves and stopped at the top of the hill. My
grandfather had placed a flagpole at the spot years ago. As I stood by
the pole to listen, there seemed to be an odd unusual note on the
wind, a deeper sound overlapping the noise of the sea. The southwester was blowing a stiff thirty-knot breeze. After listening for a
while, I found my father and asked him to come to the flagpole.
When I told him what I had noticed, he listened for a few minutes.
Then he said, "There seems to be something out there, all right. The
low noise might be just a quirk of the wind but then again it might
be the whistle of a steamer lost in the fog. Not the first one to be in
that predicament. But why is it continuous? A ship in fog would blow
an intermittent signal. This sound seems to be continuous; I'd say the
direction might be in the vicinity of Burnt Island. That's a rough spot
in a southwest gale. If we have a lull, we may be able to take a look
around."

Early next morning, the wind having decreased somewhat, although the sea was still rough, my father and several of the crew
started out in one of the big motorboats. I was allowed to join the
group.

We headed for Whale Island, a large elongated island about twelve
miles distant; a group of shoals extend south from it, hence its danger
zone stretches seaward further than any of the islands in the group.
There is a large triangular wooden tower on the highest point sixty
feet above sea level, a landmark used by ships passing in clear
weather, but there is no fog signal on the island. As we drew close
to Whale the seas were enormous and the sound of the horn, or
whatever it was we were looking for, did not get any louder or more
distinct. The pounding of the boat in the rough sea completely
drowned out any other noise, forcing us to stop the engine in order
to listen. After a moment the motorboat was turned westward toward Burnt Island, a location my father had originally considered
most likely.

As we drew closer to the rocky shore of this high rugged island,
more than twice the size of Whale Island, we again picked up the
hornlike sound, but it did not seem to come from any specific direction. Every once in a while the boat's engine was stopped and as we
rolled around in the trough of the seas, heads turned to left and right
to sample the rustle of the wind. The continuous sound seemed quite

diffuse, as if deflected from several surfaces. Perhaps the waterdrops in the dense fog influenced the direction of the sound.

We continued working our way around the island, trying to keep in touch with its shoreline. When the sea grew rough we knew we had reached the outer coast where the sound was louder coming through the fog bank. Gradually, out of the curtain of mist . . . the black outline of a large single-stack cargo carrier . . . perfectly upright and heading seaward . . . but she was not moving. The ship's whistle blew continuously, and by the feather of steam coming from the windward side of her funnel the lever was obviously tied down. Evidently the steamer had come close to Burnt Island in the fog, had reversed course when land and breakers were sighted, and while attempting to seek safety in deeper water by heading seaward, a covered ledge had stopped her dead. She was to all appearances firmly aground.

From the tossing motorboat the ship looked enormous, perhaps ten thousand tons, a big tramp steamer. Rounding her stern we noticed a long foreign name and the word *Bergen* which indicated Norwegian registry. Waves running along her sides rose and fell wildly and spray dashed high over the bulwarks on the weather side.

There was no sign of any living person on board. Two of her lifeboats were missing, the blocks of the falls, hit by seas, swung about wickedly and banged against the steel plates of the ship with mournful clangor. After we had circled the wreck twice, my father decided to try the risky prospect of boarding the ship. By anchoring to windward of the hull—which appeared to be as steady as a rock—our boat was allowed to drift down toward the steamer's side. A man holding the anchor line carefully paid out rode until the stern was as close as possible to the high wall of steel. The ship's superstructure towered above us. We rose and dropped as if on a rollercoaster as seas passed under our craft. "Be careful, skipper!" the men urged my father. I gripped the gunnel as if trying to steady the tossing motorboat. Like so many watermen in similar situations, neither my father nor any of the men wore a life jacket. Several seas were allowed to spend their fury against the massive bulk of the ship. The rode was slackened a foot or two bringing our stern frighteningly near the hull. Should the stern catch against the steel plates, the rudder would be smashed and the boat probably capsized. Everyone was tense and alert. After watching carefully for an opportune moment, my father finally made a leap for one of the lifeboat's falls and was soon able to swing on board the waist of the ship. Before doing anyting else, he ran to the bridge and cut the line to the steam whistle, stopping the noise abruptly. There was no point now in broadcasting the location of the wreck. Then he returned to the rail and helped another man get on board with him. We pulled away to a safer position and waited.

Location of the refrigerator and cold room on many steamers is located under the foredeck. The two raced there and were able to open the heavy doors, fortunately unlocked. What a sight for anyone who had not seen any fresh meat for nearly five months! Sides of beef and lamb, dozens of hams, slabs of bacon, cases of eggs, five gallon cans of milk—after making a quick selection of a few items that could be transferred to the waiting motorboat, my father hurried to the bridge and captain's cabin to see if any logbook, chart, or some records had been left behind that might give some clue to the disappearance of the crew.

For fear of rapid change in weather, the survey of the ship was finished promptly. Cargo hatches were too heavy and too securely blocked to allow investigation of holds, but from notes in the captain's cabin the heavily laden steamer was not carrying a mixed cargo, the bulk of her load being wheat or some such material.

The next task was to transfer safely the food taken from the cold room into the motorboat. By using a heaving line to lower them, a side of beef and a whole lamb carcass were eagerly seized and stowed. Two of the hams fell into the sea when the lashing slipped, but one fell into the boat; a case of eggs dashed against the side of the steamer with superficial (we hoped) damage. Milk and a case of lettuce completed the unusual cargo. We headed immediately for our island before the hazard of nightfall was added to the uncertainty of fog.

Next day, a freshening gale and persistent hazy weather forestalled further investigation of the steamer but the cooks were busy preparing a feast. Later, a northwest wind cleared skies and calmed the sea. When our boats finally arrived again at the scene of the wreck, the contrast between our original sighting and the seascape now spread before us was astounding. At least forty boats were tied up to the ship like piglets around a sow. A score of men swarmed like worker bees all over decks and superstructure trying to hacksaw or unscrew anything that looked removable whether useful or not.

Gradually, we learned that captain and crew had safely escaped from the wreck which they considered about to founder in the tremendous seas that swept the ship immediately after she grounded. They had rowed about in the fog, not knowing where they were with any accuracy and eventually, among the islands, had come upon a small fishing village called Old Fort. The captain summoned assistance from Halifax by means of land telegraph, hoping a powerful salvage tug would be able to install some sort of temporary patch over the damaged hull and with the aid of pumps free the steamer from the reef. Meanwhile, he could do little to prevent people from looting the ship.

A tug did arrive, but by that time the ship's hatches had been opened and cargo holds found to be completely flooded with cargo damaged beyond salvage. A temporary patch was useless if not impossible to apply as the bottom of the steamer had been torn open in a number of places.

After transferring to our boats some fittings and equipment, including the wireless apparatus, which the captain wished to save, we left the wreck, but not before I was able to notice the degree to which wreck-fever impels otherwise normal men to act irrationally.

From the ship's bridge, I noticed one man eyeing the huge foremast. He was evidently considering what a wonderful source of timber the tall mast would make—wood of any kind was extremely valuable on the treeless coast. Seizing a large fire-axe from a nearby bulkhead, he flew at the mast with joyful cries of glee, not realizing that the beautiful-looking spar was made of steel. Raising the axe over his head he dealt the stick a powerful blow because he was a skilled woodsman. Whamo! To his amazement the heavy axe flew out of his hands, nearly decapitating him and causing bystanders to scatter in terror. With shocked puzzlement, he carefully examined the strange mast, the like of which he had never seen.

On the forecastle deck, the anchor-winch attracted several mechanically inclined men. They bent over the massive winch trying to determine just how it operated. They poked at the controls, turned this lever, opened that valve. One of the men must have untwisted a restraining band because, with a great roar and rattle, the winch suddenly came alive, as it were; the catheads spun and ponderous links of chain ran out at a furious rate as one of the ship's huge anchors on the bow let go and plunged into the sea, sending up a column of spray. The anchor barely missed a boatload of men clustered around the bow, but smashed completely through a small punt in tow.

After the ship was stripped of everything that could possibly be removed the hull was left to rust. For nearly five years the plates held together and from a distance the old wreck gave the illusion of a fine ship heading out to sea. But the restless surf of the surrounding ledges finally claimed her remains. She became an integral note in the mysterious sound of the sea.

I thought about my father and the long-ago days as by mid-morning *Neptune* came abeam the lighthouse, foghorn, and wireless mast at Pointe Amour and began to cross the wide mouth of the bay at

The buildings Forteau Hospital where Sister Bailey and later nurse Greta Ferris ran the Grenfell medical service for a large scattered community.

Forteau. From swirls and eddies oiling the surface around *Neptune,* the bay was suitably named. As I wrote up the morning entry in the log, I noticed that the day was July 28, so I was surprised to see, a mile or so beyond us to port, the glistening peak of a medium-sized iceberg. Even this late in July, a navigator evidently should be alert for ice in the strait during times of reduced visibility by fog or darkness.

The town of Forteau, a cluster of white-, yellow-, and green-painted one-story houses, clung to the distant curving shoreline of the bay. A Grenfell Association cottage hospital located here has ministered to the needs of people in the surrounding region for over seventy years. Sister Bailey, a courageous English nurse and expert midwife who established the station, created an awesome reputation both as a skillful healer of the sick and a resourceful dog-sled driver. During winter months she patrolled her extensive territory by means of special kind of sled with whalebone runners called a komatik drawn by a team of Eskimo dogs.

Our Bonne Esperance Island home, the birthplace of my father and now our summer place, was about forty miles westward of Forteau. In the autumn, one of our cows was usually put in a boat and ferried east to Forteau for Sister Bailey's use. At that time, a cow was a rare animal on Labrador and in constant danger of attack by the village husky dogs. I recall the delicate business of arranging a suitable belly-band around a cow named Rosie, in order to hoist her with safety by block and tackle from the head of the wharf into a waiting open boat. Rosie was not sure she was going to enjoy this unusual procedure, so alarmingly different from her routine of quiet foraging. Not without considerable protest was she securely deposited in the small motorboat for the long journey eastward. Fortunately, most of the annual cow transfers were made by means of the fortnightly coastal mail steamer, which eliminated the uncomfortable boat journey, but even so, the trial of getting a large animal into a small boat to be ferried to the waiting steamer was not without moments of acute frustration. I can imagine how, at the destination in Forteau, difficulties multiplied, since the reverse of the loading procedure took place—from steamer's deck into small boat, then to dry land. Lacking a wharf and hoisting equipment such as we used, the cow must be persuaded to step over high gunnel of cranky boat on to a rocky beach; a maneuver that called for a large measure of patience from both cow and herdsman. But evidently Sister Bailey's ingenuity was equal to a variety of emergencies, bovine as well as human.

In July, 1952, while cruising the Labrador coast, I put into Forteau to provide my crew with some trout fishing in a nearby stream. During the previous December an enormous tidal wave had created great havoc in the village. Forteau is a south-facing bay and a submarine earthquake or extensive geological faulting on the bottom of the Gulf of St. Lawrence must have generated the wave which, oddly, seemed to have an extremely narrow front. No other locality experienced such destruction.

A fisherman told me his experience: "I never had a chance to save a thing out of my stage [fish house]; it come so quick. All my fishing gear—salt, dog food, barrels, my brother's house lumber—everything was swept. T'were a big stage and we stored all our gear there for the winter. My dear man, that wharf and building were over a hundred years old! My grandfather had fished there all his life and never a sea had ever come above the landwash. I tell you, I didn't feel so good next day. The sea just swept in taking everything as it came without warning. That sea swept away nine stages alongshore —that same sea! I tell you t'was a wonderful sight [meaning terrible], I had two trapboats and a dory hauled way up on the bank, fifty yards from salt water, and they was swept away and all our fish-drying flakes. It were a cruel thing to do to we poor fishermen!"

In 1534 Jacques Cartier sailed the course *Neptune* was now following. As we fought against a foul tide and nasty head sea that had quickly developed, I wondered about the mariner from St. Malo.

Raised beaches at L'Anse au Loupe in the Strait of Belle Isle show that considerable uplift has taken place in the fairly recent past.

Before leaving home port there was some difficulty finding crew, and in fact the Norman fishing fleet was constrained from departing before Cartier had picked suitable men. Evidently the returns from fishing must have been more profitable than the honor and reward of being an explorer.

Most certainly, the seascape spread before our eyes had not changed significantly in the intervening years since the time of Cartier, except for shoreline. The Labrador coast has probably risen twenty feet since the sixteenth century, as numerous raised beaches attest to this. But signs of mankind are still minimal in the area. Cartier saw in the distance, to the east, the low coast of Newfoundland gradually rising to a high plateau that fades into blue horizon. On the right hand, steep cliffs of sedimentary rock slope seaward from a flat-topped escarpment. Here and there huge pillars of rock, like massive flying butresses, project seaward from the cliffs. Even in late July there is snow in shallow valleys eroded out of the rock face. Cartier on June 10 probably saw similar piles of snow, an odd sight for a Norman sailor. He must have suspected that the waterway he was cruising was the long-sought Northwest Passage to Asia, because

Puffins, looking like sea parrots, are the clowns of northern oceans. When Cartier passed through the Strait of Belle Isle in 1534 he mentioned these perky birds with orange and yellow bills.

not until his second voyage did he make the discovery—by sailing around it—that Newfoundland was an island and that the Great Bay was a gulf which led to a large river. One of the harbors in which Cartier found shelter, he named St. Lawrence, since the day he took refuge there was the festival of St. Lawrence, the Archdeacon of Rome. Map makers later misunderstood his use of the name and thought he referred to the Great Bay. In this way the gulf and river were given their names.

We sailed *Neptune* inside or north of two islands Cartier described in his log. Ahead, a conspicuous promotory of old red sand-stone stretched southward. East of this the explorer noted an extensive beach of white sand forming the shore of the small harbor *Neptune* was passing. He described its poor shelter from the south-east, and called the harbor Blanc Sablon, a name it still bears. Cartier probably landed on the flatter of the two islands mentioned, because he accurately described small black-winged birds, "having red and yellow beaks and red feet, which nested in borrows like rabbits." These birds are now called puffins and a group of them circled *Neptune*, flying low on the water like a flight of torpedo planes coming in for a strike. These perky active birds with parrotlike beaks always seem to wear a serious expression as they hunt for capelin or lance, small fish on which they feed. Hunting for food is a serious business for any animal, but for some reason the general appearance of a puffin invariably amuses a human observer, as if the bird's philosophical mien could not mask the personality of a clown.

The low barren island on which Cartier landed and observed the borrows of the puffins is now called Greenly Island. This tiny place, less than a mile in length and a few hundred yards in width, attracted the attention of millions of people for several months in the spring of 1928.

After Lindbergh's successful nonstop solo crossing of the north Atlantic from west to east in May, 1927, a number of aviators aspired to the honor and fame of flying from east to west against the prevailing westerly winds, judged far more hazardous than the reverse direction. Actually, two French airmen, Nungesser and Coli, had tried to fly from Paris to New York less than two weeks before Lindbergh's attempt. These men were fighter pilots who had served with great distinction in the French air force during World War I. They were idolized by the people of France. Their airplane took off from Le Bourget, was lost to sight in mist, and was never seen again. The death of these heroes caused widespread grief in the homeland.

When Lindbergh's plane was reported from the Irish coast and his chance of a successful flight seemed highly probable, Edwin James, who was in charge of the Paris office of the *New York Times* and an experienced journalist who had lived in France for many years, became so apprehensive about the safety of the young American aviator that plans were formed to rescue Lindbergh, should he land safely at Le Bourget. James feared the huge crowd converging on the landing field might prove hostile and destroy the plane or injure the pilot, so deep was the resentment and grief that a national from another country was about to succeed in achieving that which had ended so tragically for Nungesser and Coli. But the wild acclaim given to Lindbergh proved him wrong and was a great relief to James and to U.S. Ambassador Herrick who had advised against the timing of the flight.

By May, 1928, the first anniversary of Lindbergh's solo adventure, eleven men had flown the Atlantic from west to east but no one had succeeded in the east to west direction, although a number had tried. On March 14, 1928, an American-made Stinson monoplane with a Wright Whirlwind engine, the type used by Lindbergh, took off in secret from an airport in England bound for Mitchel Field, Long Island. The pilot was a much-decorated English aviator, Walter

Hinchcliffe, and his co-pilot was a woman, the Hon. Elsie MacKay, daughter of Lord Inchcape. Elsie MacKay was a wealthy adventuress who had been one of the first women to secure a flying certificate from the Royal Aero Club—in other words, a pilot's license. The British and American press made a big splash over this attempt, because of the secrecy surrounding it and also because a man was supposed to have accompanied Hinchcliffe, but seconds before take off a muffled figure had climbed into the cockpit. This figure was Miss MacKay who had disclosed her intention to no one. The Stinson was reported passing across the Irish coast but after that—silence. Stormy weather over the Atlantic probably ended the flight. Another east to west attempt had failed.

For several weeks during March at an airfield in Ireland a German flier, Herman Koehl, a stocky, dour man but an experienced pilot and navigator, together with his financial sponsor Baron von Huenfeld, had been waiting for suitable weather for an Atlantic flight. They had planned to wait until June if necessary, but the sudden take-off of Hinchcliffe gave rise to the possibility that other secret attempts might be under way. On one occasion in late March, after a three-hour flight, they had turned back because of adverse weather. Koehl was not one to take foolhardy chances.

The evening forecast of April 11 had predicted favorable conditions for the first eight hundred miles. A go-decision for the next morning was made. To replace a German co-pilot who had been dismissed by the baron, an enthusiastic Irishman, commanding officer of the Irish Free State Air Force, Commandant James Fitzmaurice was invited to join the flight. The aircraft, named Bremen, was an all-metal Junkers monoplane, powered by a single engine of 310 H.P., producing a cruising speed of ninety-three miles per hour. Fuel provided for a forty-hour flight. Koehl, known as a meticulous aviator, was director of Lufthansa's commercial service night flights in Europe, and Fitzmaurice, a fighter pilot during the World War for the Royal Air Force, had over one thousand hours flying experience. Baron von Huenfeld, who delighted the press by always wearing a monocle, was publicity director of North German Lloyd Steamship Line. His job was to pump fuel from the supplementary supply into the main tanks. Although a flight to the west in April's uncertain weather was exceedingly hazardous, the attempt had been planned and prepared with characteristics German thoroughness, leaving to chance as little as possible.

The early morning April 12 take-off was dramatic as the president of the Irish Republic and scores of officials, Irish and German, were on hand to wish Godspeed from Baldonnel Airfield, near Dublin. The

Small narrow Greenly Island was an unlikely spot for an aeroplane to land.

plane, heavily loaded with fuel, trundled down the runway for a mile. It began to climb; it reached about one hundred feet of altitude, then it flopped back to earth as spectators gasped in fear. For three hundred yards Bremen bumped along, wobbling first on one wheel, then on the other. Pilot Koehl finally regained control of the plane and managed a second lift-off. The Bremen was the ninth aircraft to attempt the east to west distance. Seven pilots had perished.

Twenty-eight hours into the flight there was still no word of the Bremen. Disappointed crowds had gathered at Mitchel Field while the *New York Times* news desk recorded 11,663 telephone calls during the morning of April 13. U.S. and European papers were full of speculation concerning chance of success or failure of the flight and conjecture about what had happened to the plane. False reports of sightings were made. Ocean liners arriving in New York reported bad weather in the western Atlantic, fog and thick snow flurries. Forty hours went by and still no word.

Then, on the morning of April 14, early edition papers carried headlines in heavy type: Ocean fliers safely on island off Labrador coast. Landed in snowstorm. Thirty-six and a half hours. Four hundred miles off course.

Anyone who knew Greenly Island found the news that a plane had landed there extremely difficult to believe. Winter conditions still prevailed; the island was covered with snow or ice; there was no extensive area to provide a landing space. But land on Greenly was indeed what Bremen had done!

Baron von Huenfeld eventually described the flight: The plane had met strong adverse winds and fog. Attempts to rise above the fog had been unsuccessful. At higher altitudes heavy snow pelted the aircraft. Descending to a position just clear of the angry sea brought no relief. Driven off course and uncertain of their position the fliers considered themselves lost, but a break in the clouds brought into view a snow-covered terrain and a large river. Back in fog again they were uncertain about what course to follow next. The compass seemed to be erratic. Fortunately another break in the overcast allowed the plane to reduce altitude safely. They thought they saw masts of a ship. Finding that they were now on a course that seemed to be taking them out to sea again, Koehl circled and flew Bremen down close to the supposed ship which was then recognized as an island with a lighthouse. A desperate decision to land was made. The Bremen pancaked on to the only piece of flat surface visible. Landing gear was smashed on contact and a wing was damaged but they were down somewhere in the New World and were still alive.

The Bremen had been put down most skillfully by Koehl on a tiny frozen pond, the water supply for the lighthouse-keeper and his family. Since the only means of travel was by dog sled, and since the nearest wireless station was at Pointe Amour, thirty miles away, details of the Bremen flight leaked out slowly. Frustrated newsreel cameramen and reporters could not reach the flyers. Plans to repair Bremen had to be scrapped. For a month or longer the successful aviators were front-page news. Finally peace came again to the tiny island and the disgruntled puffins returned to nest just as they had done since Cartier's visit, hundreds of years ago.

A footnote on the Bremen flight: the first dog-team to arrive at Greenly Island following the crash landing brought Greta Ferris, the Grenfell nurse in charge of Forteau Hospital and a worthy successor to Sister Bailey. Nurse Ferris had picked up the news from the courier hastening by dog-team to the wireless station. She immediately set out with medical equipment and first-aid supplies, in the event of injury to the aviators resulting from the desperate attempt to land.

Using binoculars I surveyed the flat profile of the tiny low-lying island. I recalled Greta Ferris's description of her excitement on meeting the aviators and of the tea party the local hostess hurriedly arranged at the lighthouse-keeper's dwelling to celebrate the successful flight. One of the Labrador men produced a battered fiddle and urged the wireless operator, Jeff Wyatt, to play it. Wyatt, an accomplished violinist, considered the tea neither place nor time but

Arctic cotton, a Labrador wild flower.

van Huenfeld insisted on some celebration music and sang a German ballad to the delight of the group. Greenly was indeed an historic site. Unfortunately, our pleasant early-morning weather had turned into a brisk southwest gale. *Neptune* was turned away from the island as we prepared for a long wet beat upwind in a welter of foam, since a strong tide was now running against the direction of the wind.

I would like to have spent a week or longer visiting the islands and harbors of this section of southern Labrador which holds for me so many memories of a joyous boyhood, but we were running out of time. Bill Maclay had to catch a plane from Gander Airport to Philadelphia in a few days, so after brief calls here and there to see old haunts, we snugged *Neptune* down for a rough night at sea. As we cleared the outer islands at dusk, with the lighthouse on Greenly Island winking its eye, as my mother used to say, I looked back at the shadowy land falling astern. Considering my age, I wondered whether I would ever again set eye on the familiar islands or wet a fly in a stream no one had fished before me. Would I ever look over the moss-covered hills to the distant mainland, where miles of marsh and upland had never felt the tread of human feet? Labrador is still a large, lonely land, but it sets a bewitching lure.

Dawn found *Neptune* working southward toward the west coast of Newfoundland. Throughout the night, a thirty-knot southwester had

Insectivorous plants, such as the Pitcher Plant, grow in sheltered boggy places.

meant hard wet going to windward under staysail and main, although *Neptune*'s pilothouse provided blessed shelter from cold flying spray. The early-morning weather report for fishermen called for increasing southwesterly wind freshening to full gale force. Although the barometer was at 30.3, the pointer had fallen sharply during the past hour. When we had weathered Point Rich, the northwest tip of a peninsula beyond which the coast falls away for a long stretch of lee shore in a southwest gale, we decided to seek shelter in the harbor of Port Saunders.

I had great apprehension of this coast in such a gale. Years ago this straight shore claimed the life of a coastal steamer, the S.S. *Ethie* on which I had made many voyages. Stanley Levens of Port Saunders once described for me the *Ethie*'s tragic end:

The four-hundred-ton steamer had been built on the Clyde by Scottish workmen. She was strongly constructed and could safely handle field ice providing it was not too heavy. For years she was the only form of transportation along the west coast of Newfoundland and southern Labrador. Stanley told me he had heard about the chance of a job at Humbermouth, so he took passage on the *Ethie* when she left Port Saunders, at ten o'clock in the morning, December 10, 1919.

The *Ethie* normally made a round trip from Humbermouth, west coast Newfoundland, to Battle Harbour on the Labrador coast, picking up and landing freight and passengers along the route. All during November, the captain had planned to pick up inbound freight from the coastal settlements on the return trip from Battle Harbour, but it so happened that November had been usually boisterous. Rough seas had prevented the local people from shipping freight because it had to be taken out to the steamer in small boats, since there were no wharves large enough for the *Ethie* to dock, and no harbors where the sea was calm enough to handle freight. Complaints of neglect reached the steamship's owners. As a consequence, the company's ship's husband had joined *Ethie* to investigate the cause of the complaints. On this particular round trip, calm weather had prevailed from Humbermouth to Battle Harbour and back to Port Saunders. Captain English (my dear old friend) felt sure he would be able to pick up most of the freight that was causing the backlog.

Before leaving Port aux Choix, a settlement on the north side of Point Rich, Captain English had remarked to a shipper that the barometer was falling slowly but steadily and a bad storm was not many days away. The captain said that unfortunately he was too far ahead and too far behind, meaning he couldn't stay in port to await the storm because the ship's husband was urging him to hurry on and

Bartlett's Harbor, west Newfoundland. Sheep forage for edibles on the beach.

"not be an old woman." The next safe harbor beyond Port Saunders was Bonne Bay, about seventy miles along the coast. Could the steamer reach Bonne Bay before weather deteriorated? In between those two places the settlements of Daniels Harbour, Parsons Pond, and Cow Head were wide, open roadsteads.

Having spent all day picking up boatload after boatload of freight at Daniels Harbour and Parsons Pond, it was 9 P.M. before the ship was ready to leave Cow Head. Wind had been southerly all day. At sunset, thick clouds closed in blotting out the horizon. Wet snow began to fall. Quickly the wind veered from southerly to northwest and blew a living gale. Spray in heavy sheets, like a hail of bullets, pelted the superstructure. Seas grew so enormous an occasional one broke clear over the ship, across the waist of the foredeck, and clean over the ship's single yellow funnel. The *Ethie* rolled heavily in the quartering sea. When the open bridge went down in a trough, a breaking sea would rush into it, so that Captain English would be knee-deep in water.

The tons of freight that had been picked up all day long now proved valuable. A half-filled cargo hold would have allowed the steamer to roll her gunnels under, until cargo shifted and she capsized. As it was, the hull was periolously close to a "knockdown" several times as the crest of a sea passed under the bottom, but the cargo ballast brought *Ethie* upright again. All passengers were extremely uncomfortable and fearful but put their trust in Captain English.

Cow Head has an open harbor, a rough place in westerly wind.

As the wind increased, the force of the surge was obviously pushing the steamer toward land, the lee shore, although blinding snowstorm and the darkness prevented any accurate conjecture concerning position. When the taffrail log was examined for a reading, the log line was found cut off, obviously by the ship's propeller, which meant that *Ethie* was going backwards part of the time. But all night long the little steamer fought the storm as firemen and engineers struggled to keep the engine going.

At daylight the snow cleared but the sea was like mountains. A serious condition now confronted Captain English. The ship would certainly not survive the gale. She would be driven ashore. But where would the wrecking take place? There would be no redemption if the ship struck in a dangerous location.

Walter Young, the steamer's mailman, had fished for lobsters from Bonne Bay to Ferolle Point. He knew every foot of the coast from long experience. Captain English asked for Walter's advice. Would the ship survive if there was a cove where two anchors could be set to hold her in deep water; say, behind Martin Point? Not a soul would ever get ashore alive was Walter's opinion.

"What would you advise?" pressed Captain English. Walter said, "Well, sir, somewhere ahead and to leeward of us, between the Whaleback and the Bannisters (Brandies on the chart) there is a reef. We can't get to windward of that ledge now. The best plan is to drive her straight for the ledge. The ship will strike but there is deep water inside of it. The tide is flowing now and will be at high water inside of half an hour. We may get over the ledge."

Captain English decided to follow that plan. The *Ethie* struck three times but high water and the tremendous surge of the sea carried her over. With engines going full speed ahead the sturdy steamer pounded her way further and further ashore. Surf boiled around the ship. To land passengers before seas tore the hull to pieces became urgent. Fortunately two families lived in the cove where the steamer had grounded. A life jacket was floated ashore with a line attached to it. The plan was to pull a dory back and forth to ferry passengers to the beach, but on the first trial with an empty dory the surf caught the boat broadside and she was beaten to matchwood in a few minutes. A breeches buoy was then quickly rigged and eventually passengers and crew were safely pulled ashore.

Levens said he recalled the experience of an eighty-year-old woman from Daniels Harbour. She got into the narrow seat brave enough, but when the line slackened before she was halfway across, she disappeared into the breaking sea and all thought she had fallen out of the lashing. But when the line tightened up, she popped out of the water, hanging on for dear life—a wonderful old woman.

"You know," Levens confided, "that poet chap Ed Pratt wrote a piece about the wreck of the *Ethie*. Said a dog carried a line ashore. There was no dog on board or ashore. Even if there had been, I doubt anything could have lived in that terrible surf. We were lucky to survive that wreck—"

Great hardship resulted from the lost freight, half a summer's work for some people. As Stan Levens said, sometimes it is better to have patience, than to rush ahead, especially when the sea, the wind, and the weather are involved.

When *Neptune* reached Port Saunders we found five large draggers, rafted together that had also sought shelter from the whole gale. To profit from the enforced delay the three of us set out across country to visit some interesting archeological digs which indicate that the Point Rich Peninsula, the area between Port Saunders and Port au Choix, was the center of a seven-thousand-year-old Indian culture that had lasted for over one thousand years! Some years ago, Canadian workers began to uncover sites of maritime archaic people —meaning those who lived off the land and sea rather than by agriculture—and from 1967 to 1969 the graves of hundreds of individuals, together with tools, weapons, and other artifacts, were by chance located. The graves were covered with a bright red powdered ochre. Archeologists consider this to be the sign of an ancient tradition within the culture pattern of peoples found along the eastern seaboard from Maine to Labrador.

We were interested in deductions made by anatomists and osteologists who had studied the skeletons—for instance, individuals seemed to have only a fifty percent chance of reaching adult stage, and many adults showed evidence of arthritis in vertebral column, elbow, and finger joints. While dental cavities were rare, teeth were worn down heavily, exposing the pulp area to infection. Large numbers of animal bones, claws, teeth, beaks, and polished stone effigies were found with the human remains, suggesting relationships between art and a religious cult. A hunter might carry the image of a seal or a fox to acquire some of the cunning of those animals. One beautiful stone effigy represented a killer whale, a powerful totem for a family of hunters to possess.

The origin and fate of these maritime people has still to be unraveled. Like some of the Indians of the U.S. Southwest, they seem to have disappeared three-thousand years ago.

Another interesting group, Eskimo people of the Dorset culture, also flourished in the Port au Choix area from about A.D. 100 to A.D. 700. Although they also adapted to and exploited a coastal environ-

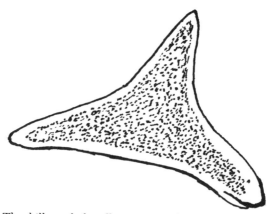

The killer whale effigy was used by people who lived 3000 years ago in western Newfoundland. By carrying animal carvings hunters probably believed they could acquire strength and cunning of the animal being hunted.

Gros Morne, north of Bonne Bay on the west coast, reaches about 2,500 feet in height and is one of the highest peaks in the Province.

ment, there is apparently no connection between their culture and the archaic Indian tradition.

Early in the morning of our third day at Port Saunders, only a few minutes past midnight, navigator Maclay roused Will and me with the word that wind had dropped, and better yet, seemed to have shifted into the east, a favorable offshore wind for us. We got under way promptly with main and genoa drawing nicely. By daybreak the wind had increased in strength and changed to southeast with rain. We replaced genoas with small jib. As we reeled off the miles down the coast, the land got higher and higher, up to two thousand feet close to shore. Downdrafts became severe. I was at the wheel at noon when a squall struck that threatened a real knockdown. *Neptune* is a very stable ship, but the pressure of wind was such that with rail under and deck awash I found it hard to relieve the main. Too much of a good thing, I suggested. Eventually we worked under the land to get more of a lee, took in the main and continued to make knots under jib and power in pouring rain and a curtain of mist. We noticed numerous waterspouts and williwaws to seaward where strong gusts struck the surface of the ocean.

By 1725, we were tied up at the government wharf at Corner Brook, Bay of Islands, after a wild seventeen-hour sail.

From the summit of Gros Morne the Long Range Mountains extend northward; there is evidence of glaciation in the valleys.

21

Homeward Bound

During my lifetime, Corner Brook was transformed from a hamlet of five houses and Mr. Fisher's sawmill into the business center of the west coast and the largest town in Newfoundland outside of St. John's. The impetus for this growth was the construction in the mid 1920s of a pulp and paper operation that has grown into one of the largest units of its kind in the world.

After we had picked up a supply of food, water, and diesel fuel and visited with friends, *Neptune* was again ready for sea. Bill Maclay found a plane which left nearby Deerlake Airfield for Halifax and thus was saved a long trip back to Gander. A new shipmate, Jim Diffenbeck, arrived from Pennsylvania. Jim had been a wartime fighter pilot but was looking forward to his first extended cruise at sea.

Bay of Islands, near the head of which Corner Brook is located, is geographically a drowned valley with a number of large branches called arms. The fjordlike bay extends twenty miles inland from the outer coast. High evergreen-covered hills and the lower meadows of this beautiful inlet have a softer look than the rugged terrain of the Long Range Mountains to the north, which we had so recently admired. As *Neptune* rounded massive fifteen-hundred-foot South Head and we were able to set a course to the southward, my heart sank a little to see curtains of mist descending the slopes. Our visibility was soon reduced to a small circle but at least the westerly wind was moderate. We streamed the log for the sixty-mile run down the coast to Red Island, lying off the western angle of the triangular Port au Port Peninsula, from which I hoped to take departure for Nova Scotia.

A supply of black spruce logs waiting to be made into paper at the Corner Brook mill, one of the world's largest.

After an hour, the wind changed directions until it blew from dead ahead. We took in all sail and started engines. I had recently noticed that for some reason the deviation of our compass on several headings seemed much larger than the amount our deviation card indicated. This uncertainty was disturbing since it meant we must keep a much more careful lookout for ledges or other hazards on our course. Fortunately the digital depth-finder was very reliable and provided a positive check on our dead reckoning track. During the afternoon, fog still thick as a polar bear's coat, the depth-finder suddenly indicated *Neptune* was entering shoaler water; nine fathoms, eight fathoms, seven fathoms registered in succession on the dial. A quick look at the chart showed no depths like that on our course. The engine was stopped while we listened intently for any unusual sounds, like the wash of surf. Three pairs of eyes minutely searched the restricted horizon ahead, as well as to port of the ship, to see what we might be running into. Happening to turn to the right, to seaward, I was shocked to see the unmistakable curl of waves breaking slowly over ledges just awash. Sunken rocks to seaward of us! That could only mean we were inside Long Ledge shoal at the northern tip of Port au Port. No place for us to be at all! *Neptune* must have been set toward the land by current or our compass was in error by

Fog rolling over the North Head at the entrance to Bay of Islands, west Newfoundland.

at least ten degrees. Quickly we changed course to escape the trap and regain our dead reckoning position. Fortunately we had sighted the shoals before becoming embayed and did not have to waste valuable daylight regaining a seaward station. The light shift of the fog and the moderate sea had alerted us to danger.

To compensate for adverse tides or for possible compass error, I set a course well offshore to avoid a reoccurrence of our experience, but, if possible, I wanted to see Red Island before dark in order to have an accurate departure before we entered the tidal currents of Cabot Strait. When the estimated distance on the log was reached, I changed course toward land, hoping to pick up Red Island, if we had not already overrun it. After several miles the engine was stopped. The blast of the foghorn in the distance was a welcome note and by homing in on it we caught sight of surf on the island's flank just as daylight faded. Red Island was quickly lost to view but we now had a point of departure. Checking time and distance on the log, we headed *Neptune* for the entrance to the Bras d'Or Lakes in Cape Breton, Nova Scotia.

Not long after midnight, the southwest wind shifted into the west and did not increase in strength, a small mercy for which we were grateful. With the staysail and mizzen set, the long hours of darkness went by slowly while the barometer fell a fraction in two hours. Fog at night is depressing, especially when there is a gnawing uncertainty about the accuracy of the ship's compass. Our radio direction finder, turned on every hour, picked up a sharp bearing on Channel Head. We had counted on St. Paul Island, a speck of land not far from us in the lower Gulf of St. Lawrence to provide a cross bearing, but no signal could be heard on its wavelength. We did record a bearing from Scatari Island, at the northeast tip of Cape Breton, and although the long distance to the station might have made accuracy doubtful, the fix agreed with our circle of dead reckoning.

Neptune was now in an area of Cabot Strait that had poignant memories for me. Near our present position on the night of October 14, 1942, the S.S. *Caribou*, a fine twenty-two-hundred ton ship carrying passengers and freight on a regular service between North Sydney, Nova Scotia, and Port aux Basques, Newfoundland, was torpedoed and sank in less than ten minutes. Many years before, I had made several voyages with the skipper of *Caribou*, Captain Tavernor, who was drowned in the sinking along with two of his sons.

Since 1900, the tri-weekly steamship ferry service across the Cabot Strait was one of the few links between the island of Newfoundland and the mainland of Canada. S.S. *Caribou*, built in Holland and especially strengthened to cope with winter ice floes in the straight had been on the ferry duty since 1925. She had left North Sydney late in the evening of October 13 with a full load of freight together with crew and passengers totaling 237 persons. Naval authorities had insisted on night crossings.

When the explosion and cascade of water signaled that *Caribou* had been stuck on the starboard side by a torpedo, the small minesweeper that had been acting as an escort sighted the outline of the U-boat on the surface and tried to ram her, but the U-boat dived too quickly. After the war, captured German naval records stated that the submarine U69, one of the three submarines in Newfoundland waters at the time, had spent three weeks in the Gulf of St. Lawrence hunting for targets. Only one other ship besides *Caribou* had been sighted and sunk. Less than a year later the U69 was caught and destroyed with all hands by H.M.S. *Viscount*.

For the passengers and crew on *Caribou*, there was so little time before the ship sank that many of the 134 individuals who lost their lives, including women and children, were probably caught below deck or were killed by the initial explosion, which also destroyed all but one of the lifeboats on the starboard side. This boat was launched successfully, but due to the rapid, heavy list to starboard, which put

S.S. *Caribou,* a steel icebreaker, was for many years the freight and passenger ferry operating from North Sydney, Nova Scotia, to Port aux Basques, Newfoundland, across Cabot Strait. She was torpedoed by a U-boat at night with considerable losses of lives.

the main deck there under water within one minute, only one of the portside lifeboats could be freed and launched. These two boats picked up some people, but the emergency life rafts, installed only three weeks previously, saved most of the survivors.

One young man, who took time to dress and put on a life jacket in his portside cabin after the explosion, reached the boat deck by crawling up the steeply angled companionway. With several others he tried to release the lashings of a life raft but as he stood on the deck the ship sank beneath him. Several families on the boat deck, parents and children, lost hold of one another when the sea broke over them. One man lost his wife and two children at this point. All members of some families vanished as the suction pulled debris into a swirling mass of wreckage.

The young man managed to swim to the surface and found many heads bobbing in the water around him. Darkness added to the confusion. The nearest life rafts were badly overloaded and unstable. Some of these soon capsized, throwing everyone back into the sea. After swimming around for a while in the cold water, he sighted a large raft into which all the women and children in the immediate vicinity were placed. Since too few rafts were available to hold all the survivors in their group, many of the men held on to ropes tied to the sides. One man, clad only in a suit of long woolen underwear, had his wallet clinched firmly in his teeth. Fortunately, all survivors were buoyed up by the expectation that the mine sweeper would eventually locate and rescue them. This feeling of hope kept many alive.

From four to six hours after the torpedoing 103 individuals were picked up alive, although nearly all required hospitalization. They had huddled together precariously on bobbing life rafts, exposed to a chilling wind or clung to flotsam in fifty-degree water, praying they would finally be spotted and saved.

On board *Neptune*, these were somber thoughts to contemplate as we stood our watches and waited for dawn. Since the wind was light, although fair, we were under power. A note in the log reads: "0700. Daylight at last; the circle of fog slowly expands. The unseen sunrise is a reminder that Earth's mother, the Sun, is patiently looking after one of her children. After all the years I have been at sea, night and low visibility have rarely failed to create tension and foreboding. Dawn is an exquisitely reanimating event."

We catch a radio-bearing from Low Point, Cape Breton, located a few miles east of the entrance to the Bras d'Or. We change course for Table Head. No land or any other ships in sight.

1135. Land-ho, dead ahead. *Neptune* entered the Great Bras d'Or Channel one hour later, 218 miles from South Head, Bay of Islands, Newfoundland.

In brilliant sunshine, we pick up a mooring off the Baddeck boat-yard. This pleasant village is the chief port of the Bras d'Or. Some cruising men, on the way north, have fallen under the spell of the lake and the surrounding gentle hills and have bought farm land, unwilling to leave this attractive place for the harsher climate of northern seas. We have enjoyed the Scottish atmosphere of Baddeck many times, but now we collected our mail and pushed on. The weather forecast predicts rain, fog, and headwinds. The lock at St. Peter's was closed by the time we had crossed the long arms of west bay. One side of the canal outside the lock seemed a good place to moor and enjoy a night's quiet sleep."

Next morning, first boat to transit the lock, we were not happy to find the Strait of Canso filled with a very heavy overcast. Our apprehension was warranted. We entered a bank of fog and did not emerge for several days.

The Nova Scotia coast lies more or less in a northeast-southwest direction. From Cape Canso to Cape Sable the length is about three-hundred miles. There are many harbors along the coast but also there are many outlying dangers, especially north of Halifax. A southwest wind means a long hard beat dead to windward. We started toward Cape Canso in thick fog and a fair wind, the moderate sea grew rougher by afternoon, but conditions changed several times during the next forty-eight hours. By late afternoon of the second day at sea

Bill Maclay, Brad Middlebrook, and David Phillips, members of *Seal*'s crew, enjoy the beauty of the Bras d'Or Lake.

we were somewhere east of Halifax. Fog had cleared briefly during the day; we picked up two offshore buoys which gave us a check on dead reckoning course, then fog shut in again. Will used the radio direction finder to pick up various stations, but our fixes were not reassuring. To prepare for another night at sea, I lay down for a couple of hours. When I again came on watch, Will said that we were off Halifax; he was able to hear the horn on Sambro Island. I walked forward to check the jib sheet, which had caught on a stay. We were under power. Our sails were not doing anything for us and hung limp, wet with dew. Circle of visibility in the fog was about fifty yards. There was just enough daylight left to look around the ocean. Suddenly from dead ahead—a tremendous blast of a foghorn. We seemed to be directly on top of it.

"Heavens," I called to Will, "we're too close to Sambro. This is a real danger zone!"

As I looked more closely over the almost calm sea I made out the ripple of a shoal to port; the sea just lapped over its smooth black back with a whooshing sound. Then I saw another one dead ahead and still

As both cook and foredeck man, Will Hamann was a valued members of *Neptune*'s company.

more broke water on the starboard side. There were ledges all around us!

Came another deafening blast from the horn. The vibrations shook sails and rigging.

In the midst of these ledges and halftide rocks around Sambro Island, I recalled an old fisherman's warning: Waves may have some mercy boy, but rocks have no mercy at all!

Very carefully we maneuvered *Neptune* until I could not see any more of the lethal shoals. I explained to Will that Sambro was one of the most dangerous places on the Nova Scotian coast, the graveyard of countless ships. Just to think of Sambro Island gave me shivers! Setting a course to take *Neptune* completely clear of all possible dangers we ran offshore for twenty minutes, then a new course was worked out in the direction of Cross Island, at the entrance to Lunenburg Harbour. Cross Island had a powerful foghorn and transmitted a radio direction finding signal. We estimated that we should be near the island by 0200 in the morning. At that hour the RDF signal came in loud and clear. By intently watching our depth-finder, we cautiously approached the shoreline until the depth of the water indicated *Neptune* was quite close; then, by using the sound of the foghorn as a reference, we slowly circled the island, checking our progress by use of the RDF and the depth-finder as well as the changing bearing of the horn. Eventually, we considered we had

Neptune under plain sail.

reached the opposite side of the island. In spite of dense fog and the black night our dead reckoning had avoided outlying hazards.

We now considered setting a course straight into Lunenburg Harbour. Unfortunately, there is a shoal in the outer bay and we were of no mind to hunt a warning buoy in the dense fog and darkness. So, somewhat reluctantly, I decided that we should poke our way into the bay for twenty minutes, then turn ninety degrees toward the western side of the outer bay, hoping to be able to anchor near the Ovens, a series of sea caves we had once visited. Groping ahead toward the shore, we depended more on our wonderful digital depth-finder than on the compass. *Neptune* was getting into shoal water when I turned on the spreader lights and went forward to see what lay directly ahead. After a short interval, large patches of floating seaweed appeared on the surface. I held up my hand and Will reversed the engine. Jim Diefenbeck and I dropped the heavy anchor. The sea was smooth and with all the fog around there was slim chance of a sudden change of wind, so we only payed out enough cable to provide minimum scope. By going astern again, we dug in the anchor. After the engine stopped, the unmistakable sound of waves surging over ledges caused some concern. The somber sound of surf seemed to come from our left side, at a short distance. Will rowed out the Danforth anchor from astern to keep *Neptune* from swinging about. Then he rowed at a right angle from a midships while I kept track of his position with the searchlight. There was no dangerous obstruction within fifty feet, about as far as he could go because of the fog. The ship's clock struck six bells, three o'clock in the morning. I stayed on deck as an anchor watch, while my crew got a much needed rest.

One hour or so after daylight, the shrill sound of children's voices was faintly audible. Lowering the dinghy in order to investigate, I rowed in the direction where my little compass indicated land should be, but I had not reached far enough to lose all sight of the ship when the fog cleared just sufficiently for me to recognize the location where we had anchored. I turned back to *Neptune*. On board, one could see, at a distance less than one hundred yards, a string of ledges on our right hand side. Surf breaking on these jagged pinnacles produced the sound we had heard last night. There was another but shorter ridge of rock on our starboard side. We had blundered into a convenient slot between two snares. Soon the sun's warmth burned away all fog. We entered picturesque Lunenburg in a cheerful state of mind. Three days later, *Neptune* had left Canadian waters, rounded Cape Sable, and crossed the foggy Gulf of Maine. We were glad to see Cadillac Mountain and enter Northeast Harbour, one of

Friendship greeted us with a lift in the fog.

the gems of the Maine coast. Having cleared customs and purchased supplies, we pushed on, but "patchy fog" would not gracefully let us be. Low visibility compelled eyes and ears to be alert while we crossed the entire width of Penobscot Bay, until, in a dying breeze, a clearing shower melted the fog. As *Neptune* entered her homeport, Friendship greeted us with the scent of pine trees and a lift in the fog.

Neptune proved to be a comfortable sturdy vessel under a variety of conditions. The fog and cold weather encountered was hardly typical of a Newfoundland summer. During the 1951 and 1952 cruises we recorded a combined total of five foggy days. Of course maritime weather rarely follows a discernible pattern except that present conditions will surely change before long. High and low pressure systems spreading over Newfoundland usually sow the seed of Maine and Nova Scotia weather to the eastbound clouds.

Local fishermen have a poor opinion of their island's climate to which they are exposed more than landsmen. As one veteran waterman said to me, "It's a job to get a good day."

But this tendency to disparage, and seemingly to relish adversity may be due to the Irish component in the Newfoundland character.

The tide had to rise before *Neptune* could get to our dock.

Just as Maine lobstermen have an inclination toward sly understatement. When I once asked a Swan's Island man about the cause of his obviously ailing back, he said, "I got that last spring shoveling fifteen inches of partly cloudy!"

Generally speaking, if one compares present cruising conditions in Newfoundland or Labrador with those prevailing a century ago, there are notable changes. Skippers are now fortunate to have many more navigational aids; although weather forecasting is still quite unsatisfactory. In the 1850s, when my grandparents sailed to the Labrador, the only transportation from New England, Nova Scotia or Newfoundland was by fishing schooner with accomodations none too comfortable. The passage north was often attended by dangerous episodes. The diary of Charles Carpenter, a contemporary and eventually a dear friend of my grandparents, vividly describes the feelings of a ship's company as these hazards are encountered.

Carpenter, son of a Haverhill, Massachusetts, physician, was engaged by a Montreal philanthropist to act as a medical missionary on the Labrador coast; he was to render whatever assistance was needed by the large floating population of Canadian and Yankee schooner fishermen. The young man secured a passage from Captain Tom

Chase of the schooner *Golder West,* eighty-five tons burden, on a fishing voyage for mackerel and codfish in northern seas.

Entry for June 11, 1856, begins: "Left Newburyport at high tide to float over the bar. Wind fair. Out of sight of land by sunset. Cape Ann last to disappear."

Next day, the noon sight put schooner 112 miles from departure. In the afternoon, thick clouds of fog lay on the horizon. At first, moisture-laden air floated over the ship like a veil of thin smoke; as the vessel proceeded, fog settled upon crew and rigging, dripping from every sail and line. The bosun sat on the box housing the bellows of the foghorn and kept pumping it throughout the night. The mournful groaning was some assurance against being run down in the murky darkness.

June 13: "Land-ho this morning. 'Where away?' 'On lee bow, sir,' There is a strip of black-looking land shrouded in fog, barely visible. We tack and run alongside of it but do not ascertain what land it is. Seal Island, the captain thinks, but we do not see any lighthouse; there are several shacks near the shore. Afterwards, we pass a brig close enough to shout a question; the land is Seal Island. We see two fishing boats hove-to on Seal Island ground. Thick fog lasts all day; rain and a smart breeze. Captain eventually considers we can change course to pass safely around Cape Sable."

June 14: "This morning I drank sea water and was soon able to throw up some bile. Felt much better. Lemons invaluable. Fog persists although less dense. We hail two fishermen; one says he is out of Cape Negro, the other hails from Ragged Islands. Later, fog lifts and we see land, a long blue line to the northeast. We now sail northeast along the Nova Scotia coast; not much wind, booms wing and wing, men are mending nets, rigging trawlines, oiling boots, making thole pins."

June 15: "Have talked to captain. He rejects Bible; reads Tom Paine. Still foggy. During the day fog lifted briefly, long enough for the captain to find Beaver Island light. In another lift, we sighted White Head, then the wet white blanket descended for the night."

June 17: "Fog, schooner becalmed; men jig for cod. Later a light breeze. Beautiful sunset, utterly defying description; western sky a censer with sacrificial flames fiercely burning. While reflecting on this splendid sight, I speak to an old fisherman. 'What a splendid sight!' 'Yes,' replies the old man, 'We'll have a fine day tomorrow.' Such is the impression on the practical sailor."

June 18: "Land in sight. No fog. We are running along the coast of Cape Breton Island, pass Louisbourg, the famous fort, and attempt to run inside of Scatarie Island to save miles, but wind is unfavorable;

On such a schooner, Mr. Carpenter sailed from Newburyport to Labrador.

we pass outside but close enough to the island to see the huge rocks that have claimed so many ships. Seaward is a prominant ledge, Shag Rock, where the surf's unceasing roar breeds terror in the sensibility of a ship's lookout approaching Scatarie in fog and heavy weather. Scatarie has a lighthouse at the eastern end. Keeper Jim Dodd is said to be a character. He keeps a brace of pistols under his pillow and is alleged to have made away with many a shipwrecked mariner carrying gold in his pocket. An old wrecker who also lives on the island is reputed to be rich from his beachcombing findings. Beyond Scatarie is Fling Island, a high fortification of solid rock except for one corner where shattering waves have cut through and isolated a precipitous chimney. A house for the benefit of wrecked mariners is located at one end of the island. We sight a vessel bound south; using spyglass I read her name, '*Buena Vista*, Harwich, Cape Cod.' Also, in the distance there is a steamer, probably bound for Quebec. On the starboard hand, some forty miles distant, we can see a smuge of

Cape North

Nova Scotia

North Sydney

Baddeck

Louisbourg

Scatarie Island

Bras d'Or Lake

Cape Breton

Strait of Canso

Cape Breton — Nova Scotia

high land, Cape North, a mountain at the tip of Cape Breton. Having turned north from Scatarie, we are now heading for the Gulf of St. Lawrence."

Contending with a head wind, *Golden West* was forced to make long tacks in the Cabot Strait between Cape North's one thousand foot cliffs and the southwest corner of Newfoundland at Cape Ray, which lies about ENE½E from Cape Breton. Eventually, the wind changed to southwest, so a NE½E course could be sailed. Wing and wing, the schooner raced along at eight knots leaving Port au Port on the starboard beam. The southwester freshened into a full gale. Captain decided to shorten sail. Out on the bowsprit the crew hung on as best they could as the schooner buried her bow in seas, then they wrestled with the flogging canvas, clawing folds into a layer that could be lashed down and properly secured. Next, the big mainsail had to be stowed. A sailor let go the peak halliard; down dropped the gaff swinging furiously out of control. A line on the gaff soon reined in the menacing pole, but not before the spar surged across the cabin-house roof several times, knocking some of the crew into the lee scuppers. Eventually the ship was snugged down and sailed all day under staysail and reefed foresail.

June 21: "Rough seas all night and fog. After breakfast, fog clears and gale slackens. We see Labrador. From the chart I try to identify the islands we are passing. Dog Islands, a small cluster; Old Fort Island, with a dozen houses stuck on rocks as if they are glued at odd angles to the bare granite. The wind freshens again, but the schooner forges ahead in the lee of the islands. Never did I see a prospect at once so wild and romantic and picturesque as the appearance of this coast. How thickly located are the islands and the smaller rocks, placed at every angle and position. In the distance, an iceberg, white as shining crystal. Around headlands and through channels we run with our sagacious captain at the helm. The crew are at their posts ready to haul away the jib sheet, or trim the mainsail, as our frequent tacks and turns demand. We sail grandly into port at Bonne Esperance with flag at masthead. I see many buildings and a wharf. There is a schooner in the harbor, the *Grand Island* from Newburyport. Also a ship flying the British flag. We let go anchor ten days, eight hours, twenty-eight minutes from old Massachusetts.

"I take my first wash in many days—warm salt water; brush teeth; unsnarl hair; feel better. Kneel and rejoice to Almighty God for his Goodness and Mercy in bringing us safely to this distant and desolate shore. Going on deck, find a Mr. Hayward, a short burly man from Southampton, England, who says he has been fourteen years in this wild country. He is a hunter and fisherman. I go ashore—first noticeable thing is the moss which, from the ship, appears a thin dry covering for the rocks, but which is a deep, soft, extensive cushion, elastic, springy in places. Light enough to read on deck at 10 P.M."

June 25: "Met a Mr. Chalker, who has lived here for fifty years; came from Weymouth, in Dorset, England. He is quite elderly, born in 1790. Appears very intelligent and talks readily on matters historical, personal, and political. He speaks grammatically but with a peculiar accent."

Carpenter spent a busy summer bringing first aid and social services to the crews of the fishing schooners. He tried to help souls as well as heal boils, toothache, and constipation. He removed a fish hook embedded in a man's cheek and saved the life of a fisherman whose dinghy had capsized. Carpenter could swim, a skill most fishermen lacked. In late August, he got a berth in the homebound schooner *Angelia,* Captain Morgan. The spell of fair weather that had brought them safely down the Nova Scotia coast was replaced by a nasty storm as they began to cross the Gulf of Maine.

August 21 entry begins: "Last night was a terrible night; all conditions conspired to make it full of discomfort, danger, and misery. The wind blew a howling gale, the seas were enormous and threatening. *Angelia* rolled both rails under, first one and then the other, violently and constantly. Through much of the night rain poured in torrents flung by the wind into the faces of the crew. Darkness added confusion to the midnight scene. A heavy sea burst over the ship and filled the aft companionway, flooding the cabin. The decks leaked, spilling water into the bunks below. Everything in the cabin seemed to be afloat. We are now hove-to under three-reefed foresail, drifting fast to leeward towards the Maine coast. Crew on watch very alert. Once, during the night, first mate gave a terrible alarm shouting, 'Light ho! Light ho!' A bright light plainly seen to windward. It could hardly have been on land; most likely a 'steamer running us down.' At all events, our brightest lantern must be hoisted instantly, a procedure which, in the confusion that usually attends excitement at night, took some time. We lose sight of the light and are at a loss to explain its presence. Crew say no light on the whole coast could have borne so far at sea, except, perhaps, Highland Light on Cape Cod or the light on Boon Island. So passed a long, miserable night."

August 22: "Rain ceased but wind still strong, fog thick. We must do something to save the vessel. Crew set reefed jib to help the reefed foresail. We drift SSW hoping that when the fog clears we may be able to run into Portsmouth. But, alas, fog remains mud-thick all day; we drift, still at the mercy of the wind. Twice a land alarm is raised but there is not distinct sighting. I sit aft near the helm. Seas rise like mountains all around; we sink down into a deep, deep valley; then gradually the mountain thrusts us upward, higher and higher, until we peer into the awful depths of chasms yawning before us. I envy the storm birds wheeling around the vessel or gathering in flocks astern. Soon another night of terror and tossing."

August 23: "Early this morning we were aroused by a loud shout, 'Land alongside'! All crew off watch tumble out of bunks double-quick and jump for the deck. I haul on my warmest coat and lay hold of oilclothes; tie sou'wester on tight. Land is not visible to my eye, however, perhaps old Uncle Ned, who shouted, did not really see the coast. Nevertheless, the wheel is unlashed and we steer off as fast as possible. The gale seems to be moderating although there is still a hatful of wind. Captain orders reefed mainstail hoisted and reef shaken out of the jib. There has been no cooking for three days. Everyone is starved. Captain orders last barrel of flour opened and we soon have some good doughnuts!

"A large Liverpool ship runs to leeward of us; a sight worth looking at to see her take the seas. But soon we make a better sighting. Land, land in old New England. A welcome sight at 0900. Our sighting looks like a round island, but proves to be the distant mountain, Agamenticus, located inland behind York, Maine. We eventually raise Boon Island with its tall lighthouse on the rocky shore. Presently Isle of Shoals is in sight ahead. We now know where we are. The mistake our navigator made in calculating our whereabouts in the gale was to over-estimate the ship's leeway, thinking we were drifting about three knots down wind, whereas the schooner probably held her own.

"About noon the gale died out. We were afraid lack of wind would give us another long night of drifting. But later, wind developed enough for the ship to move slowly along the course. My eye rejoiced to see dear old Cape Ann, as we drew near the land. The splendid sunset was lovely and fully appreciated by home-seeking, home-loving mariners. We sat on the windlass and bowsprit and talked of the future. I remain on deck all night. I can see the twin lights on Thacher Island, as well as the light at Rockport and the two lights at Ipswich."

August 24: "A pilot boat is hailed early this morning. The boat runs close to us and the pilot jumps aboard, *Angelia* adroitly. The pilot takes the helm and the command of the ship. After we sail inside Newburyport harbour, having crossed the bar, wind dies away and it is impossible to get to the wharves since the current is so strong. The ship will have to anchor and wait until tide changes or breeze develops. A few of the crew pack duffle in the whaleboat and row ashore. I join them, bidding farewell to the *Angelia.*"

The following June finds Carpenter again sailing north on another schooner. They round Cape Sable twenty six hours from Cape Ann and enter a bank of fog. Next morning at 3 a.m. captain calculates ship has Sambro Island abeam. The cry of "Breakers!" wakes Carpenter. He hurries on deck to find they are running past a string of drift nets indicating that land is close. Not being able to see anything except a waste of cold gray water, Carpenter sought the warmth of his bunk. Quick startling orders: Hard down helm, haul in the mainsheet, followed by hurried footsteps on the deck over head break the monotony of the long day. The cook does not please the crew and is replaced by a simple-minded boy from Saybrook, New Hampshire, who can, at least, make edible doughnuts.

The skipper is anxious to go through Gut of Canso but fog is so thick he dare not risk the passage. Next day, by dead reckoning, he thinks the ship has passed Scatarie and orders a course changed to NNE.

Early on the following morning, Carpenter is rudely awakened by the shrill cry: "Breakers ahead." The mate rushes down the companionway and after some moments rouses the captain, but the captain is so confident that the ship has plenty of searoom, he declares the warning is nonsense; there is no way for the ship to be near breakers! But the cry is repeated. Captain pulls on his foul weather gear and jumps on deck. Sure enough they are among breaking ledges, but on which coast could this possibly be? The ship is hove to. Captain says he worked out the dead reckoning five different ways and the result in each case was more or less the same, the ship should be miles at sea somewhere in the middle of Cabot Strait. Torrents of rain beat upon the crew clustered on the windward side keeping an eye on the hazards. The weather is so thick nothing can be seen except the breakers. The schooner is put on a safer tack, at least that is what the captain hopes. Soon after another ship is sighted. Her captain reports that he thinks Scatarie bears about northeast. If that reckoning is correct, they must be in Main-à-Dieu Passages between Cape Breton Island and Scatarie! Our captain is mystified by this report. The schooner is kept off the ledges and they wait for the fog to scale which it does about ten o'clock. Then comes the big surprise! The familiar promontory and sugar loaf of Cape Ray, Newfoundland, looms before their eyes and the schooner is to the southeast of it! The captain says his dead reckoning at least put them in Cabot Strait far from the Cape Breton Island coast!

From the tenor of Carpenter's diary, one can sense the nagging

The Whiteley house at Bonne Esperance Island. On the hill behind the house, W. H. Whiteley built a church for Mr. Carpenter.

uncertainties that plagued oldtime schoonermen. Coastal navigation was often a worrisome test of seamanship. Deepwater skippers, even in those days, had much less to be concerned about. Chronometer, sextant, and nautical almanac enabled them to practice the art of coming and going. Only when the ship reached soundings did concern increase. Today, there are almost miraculous navigational aid for big ships and for yachtsmen. On *Neptune*, I have tried to keep equipment as simple as possible, depending chiefly on depthmeter and on radio directionfinder. We do carry an old style harpoon log as a backup. Radar and Loran C would be a help in fog, although having these instruments on board might encourage a skipper to take undue risks. Actually, we have been in harbours with boats having these wonderful new instruments, yet they did not see t to go out in weather that we accepted as commonplace. Of course, the one indispensable item is an accurate compass. At any rate, we really have not missed the sophisticated gadets on our northern voyages.

As I review our experiences and ask myself questions about cruising in Newfoundland and Labrador, I feel that, for most sailors, the lure of this section of the north Atlantic littoral arises from the discovery that Newfoundland, and most certainly Labrador, are quite different from Maine or Nova Scotia. The precipitous coast or the tundra of the interior may not appeal to everyone. A towering escarpment faces the sea, and behind this barrier, as a result of glacial erosion of the Pre-Cambrian bedrock, one finds a thin layer of topsoil, a land of lakes, of clear-water streams with rapids and falls, or ill-drained swampy or marshy areas, and in a few places, mostly river valleys, forests of conifer. The land presents a barren arctic aspect until close observation reveals an embroidery of tiny flowering plants, brown and gray mosses and lichens, and acres of low bushes producing various kinds of edible berries.

The Royal Cruising Club's definition of cruising suggests it is the pastime of visiting places in one's own country or abroad in a well-prepared boat, of making new friends, and enjoying changes of harbor from time to time. Newfoundland and Labrador are excellent places to accomplish these admirable objectives.